FORGIVE ME

FORGIVE ME
BOOK 1

A. NASH

Forgive Me

Ariana Nash ~ *Dark Fantasy Author*

Subscribe to Ariana's mailing list & get the exclusive story 'Sealed with a Kiss' free.

Join the Ariana Nash Facebook group for all the news, as it happens.

Authors note on languages and content:

In this series, "Mafia" is used as a catch-all term for Italian organized crime. For legal reasons, the author has chosen to use the fictional name "Battaglia" in place of real crime syndicate names.

The opinions and beliefs of any characters within this series are those of fictional characters and are not indicative of the author's personal views.

www.ariananashbooks.com

CHAPTER ONE

Francis

Father Francis Scott locked the ancient office door at the side of St. Mary's Church, the heavy ring of old keys clanging with the movement. He stood a moment in the shadows behind a grand pillar along the church's south aisle, breathing in the silence as the day's trials tumbled at the back of his mind, like a TV playing to an empty room.

Father Hawker had told him it would get easier—to trust in himself and remember how he must carry the weight of his parishioners who came to him for guidance. In carrying that weight, Francis was serving the people, and serving God.

Nobody had told him how, once he fastened the stark white collar on, the floodgates would open. Not in all his training, all the years studying, had anyone prepared him for the baptism by fire that was *being a priest*. But an adjustment period was natural, he supposed, sighing. It would take time to step into the role, to find his feet. Three months was nothing when compared to the rest of his life.

He'd continue to take each day at a time and would find the strength to fulfil every duty expected of him. His stomach rumbled. And tomorrow, he'd try to make time to eat.

The staccato beat of shoes clipping up the nave punctured the quiet. The steps echoed through the church's ancient arches. Francis lifted his gaze, expecting to find a woman approaching the altar, but a man strode close. From the formal black trousers, deep purple shirt, and black silk waistcoat, he wasn't local. Francis blinked, unsure if his exhaustion had summoned a handsome hallucination. He might only have been in the parish of Kellerton for three months, but he knew the town did not produce men who looked like... well, looked as though they'd just stepped from the pages of a glossy magazine. He had the blackest hair Francis had ever seen—short on the sides, but tousled and gelled on top—and a slight warmth to his skin, as though he'd spent the summer abroad.

He knelt on one knee in front of the altar and bowed his head.

A brief flutter of *something* shortened Francis's breath. The stranger wasn't all that old, no older than Francis's midtwenties, but seemed to carry an air of sophistication beyond his years.

Francis should make him aware he wasn't alone, but as the stranger's lips moved in prayer, Francis remained motionless. What did he pray for? Of course, that was between him and God, and Francis had no right to wonder. He waited, listening to the blood rushing in his ears, and when the stranger's soft lips stilled, Francis cleared his throat.

The man's gaze slid sideways. "Do you often lurk in the shadows, watching your parishioners pray, Father?"

The question caught Francis off guard. That, and the fact his voice carried a dulcet, foreign cadence Francis wouldn't mind listening to for hours. Italian, perhaps? He cleared his throat again, smoothed down his black cassock, and stepped from the shadows. "Apologies. You looked to be in prayer, and I did not want to disturb you."

"I wasn't sure anyone would be here. Late, isn't it? Although, I assume God's work isn't nine-to-five." He scratched his nose and smiled, but it was the kind of flashy smile that didn't touch the eyes. Like the watch he wore, glinting under candlelight, his smile was for the assumptions of others, not for himself.

Francis had always been good at reading people, as a survival tactic, but he also knew first impressions were a long way from the truth. First impressions told him this visitor was passing through town, and that he was wealthy enough to purchase tailored clothes to fit his slim physique. If the watch was real, it was likely worth more than Francis's parishioners earned in a year. What had brought such an intriguing man to St. Mary's at near-midnight?

"How may I help you?" Francis asked.

"Don't you have a home to go to, Father?" he replied, glancing over his shoulder at the church doors.

Francis had a nearby house that came with the posting at St. Mary's, but it didn't yet feel like a home.

The stranger picked up on his hesitation. "Is this the part where you tell me this church is your home? I'm not sure I'd believe it."

There was that smile again. Francis sensed he was being mocked, but something had brought the stranger through St. Mary's doors and Francis was obliged to help any and all who needed it. "Perhaps you seek some guidance?" he offered.

The stranger gave a snorting, dismissive laugh and bowed his head again, probably contemplating leaving, but as he lifted his dark-eyed gaze and looked toward the confessional booth, his weak smile fell away.

No more needed to be said. Francis bowed his head and made his way to the booth. He stepped inside, closed the door, and placed the Rite of Penance book on his knees. He waited a while, expecting to hear the man's clipping walk, but the minutes ticked on for so long he began to wonder if the stranger had somehow left without making a noise. Then the shoes tapped on the marble floor, and the confessional door opened. Old wood creaked, and the rustle of fabric indicated the stranger was ready.

"Bless me, Father, for I have sinned."

That Mediterranean accent was thicker with the lattice screen between them, his voice deeper too, now they'd moved from the open nave to closer quarters.

"Please, go on. I am here to receive your confession."

He'd fallen silent, perhaps regretting his decision. A little prompting might help. "How long has it been since your last confession?"

"I don't know," he said. "I don't think I've ever been."

"Well, that's all right. If it helps, I'm new to this too," Francis offered, hoping to ease his nerves some.

"The youngest priest to be ordained in the diocese."

At twenty-four, Francis was indeed one of the youngest priests in England, due in a large part to Archbishop Montague's mentoring, and Francis's exemplary studies. But how would this stranger know all about Francis if he was just passing through? Perhaps it was nothing. His posting at St. Mary's had been in the local news after all, and much had been made of his age. "This is a confessional, not a conversational. Please, if you have something specific to confess, I'm here to assist with that."

A soft chuckle filtered through the lattice screen, and now Francis was being mocked again. Everyone had the right to confession. He couldn't refuse him, even if he was verging on being rude. He might treat confessing as a joke, but Francis did not. Still, he could have done without the late-night visit if this man was just here to waste both their time.

"How does this work? What do I say? If I confess everything, we'll be here all night." There was that chuckle again. Perhaps it wasn't disrespect, but nerves.

"Put into words what you have done wrong, what brought you here, to me. When you're finished, tell God you are sorry for those sins and the sins of your past life. I will give you a penance, you then make an Act of Contrition—"

"It's been a long time since I attended church." The humor had vanished and his tone had hardened, becoming colder. That admission had been true, and it hadn't been an easy one.

When he offered no further information, Francis asked, "Is that your confession?"

"No. Well, it could be. There's a real long list."

"You don't need to list everything. The minor sins, the venial, are forgiven through prayer and communion. What sin brought you here today? What made you seek God?"

A soft pause. "You did," he whispered.

"I..." Francis swallowed, trying to smooth the creak in his voice like he smoothed away the creases in his cassock. "What do you mean?"

"It's hard to explain."

"I'm listening."

"Yes," he said with a sigh. "You are."

Wood creaked and the confessional booth door opened on the other man's side. The sound of his shoes clicked a path back down the nave.

Francis set the book aside and stepped from the confessional.

If the stranger walked any faster, he'd be running. Francis almost called out to tell him that whatever had brought him here, he'd listen. That St. Mary's was a safe space, that *he* was safe, but the words lodged in his throat as he watched the man of many sins run from the church. What had he meant when he'd said Francis had brought him here? How was that possible when they'd never met before? Certainly, Francis would never forget someone as intriguing.

Francis's heart and head buzzed. He said a prayer to quiet himself, snuffed out all the candles, and left the church, walking down the cobbled pathway toward the main gate. There was no sign of his late-night visitor.

The air was still, the town quiet. Moths fluttered around nearby streetlights, and as Francis passed beneath them, the occasional bat dashed by in a blur. His cottage was the last in a row, with a little metal gate and tiny postage stamp of a front garden. Roses framed the crooked windows. Thankfully, he didn't need to tend the garden— the church's gardeners maintained it for him—or it would have been an overgrown mess.

He paused at the front door, key in the lock, and glanced up the road, back toward the church. Parked cars lined the narrow, winding street. A cat hurried out from under a battered and beaten old Land Rover and trotted across the road. One car stood out from all the rest: a sleek silver Jaguar. Perhaps the Rogers family had a visitor?

Inside the cottage, he flicked on the lights and the kettle but didn't bother with the heating. He had a mug of tea, a quick shower, and then he was between the sheets within half an hour of getting home. He stared at the cracks in the old ceiling, and the cobwebs he'd forgotten to sweep away. A slight draft disturbed them.

He closed his eyes, wiling sleep to take him, but the man of many sins was there, on his knee, head bowed, whispering a prayer. Francis's heart slowed and sleep crawled into the edges of his mind. He allowed himself a moment to admire such an intriguing figure in his dreamy state. The flashy watch, the polished black shoes, how—on his knees—his trousers had hugged his ass and clutched at firm thighs.

Francis snapped open his eyes, turned onto his side, and tried to reshuffle his thoughts far away from the man of many sins. He had a meeting with the town council tomorrow. Mrs. Roe would be there, with her stifling perfume and hands-on approach. She'd confessed to being an alcoholic and lately had been coming to confession more and more often. During his studies, he'd been warned about parishioners becoming too dependent on their priests. When secrets were spilled, and with priests knowing all of a parishioner's intimacies, it was common for emotional attachments to develop. He'd have to be careful with Mrs. Roe. Although, he wouldn't mind if the man of many sins returned. He'd listen to that voice for hours, listen to his sardonic tone with its note of derision. Did he have a problem with Francis personally, or was it priests in general?

It couldn't be personal. They'd never met before.

What sin brought you here?
You did.
How was Francis a sin?

An owl hooted and through the thin window glass, it sounded as though it was right outside. He glanced at the clock. 1:10 a.m. He had to be up at five. Tiredness rode him like a demon on his back, so why, when he closed his eyes, couldn't he sleep? Why did he see the man of many sins looking at him for the first time from the corner of his eye as he knelt at the altar? Remembering it now, he was sure the man had been smiling.

Francis had to stop this.

He knew where it was going.

Those dark eyes, with their long dark lashes... The soft lips, whispering a prayer...

Francis rolled onto his other side and steered his thoughts away from how his body reacted to his exhaustion-addled thoughts. Celibacy was a long road ahead, one he'd fallen along more times than he cared to admit.

Sleep finally wrapped him up and carried him away, but in his dreams, he wasn't alone. The man of many sins smirked, hand on his hip, gaze running over Francis, judging, disrobing, and then he went down to one knee, and those pretty, long-lashed dark eyes peered up at Francis, begging for forgiveness.

Two cups of coffee had barely touched the sides of his weariness. He'd make another once he arrived at the church. Hurrying out of the door, he said a quick good morning to the postman and marched up the street. The silver car was gone. It had rained overnight, but the space the Jaguar had occupied remained dry. He dismissed it. He had a busy day ahead. Morning prayer at nine, Communion at ten.

The large clockface on the church spire showed he was already fifteen minutes late. The gate creaked, and the cobbles were shiny underfoot. The weight of his predecessors pushed down whenever he walked the ancient path. The church had stood for hundreds of years and would likely stand for hundreds more. He could only hope to serve his parish as well as those who'd served before him.

Today was a new day. He'd do better.

He entered the church, apologized to Julia, the assistant, unlocked the office door, and stared at his desk. Nothing had changed; everything was in its place, just as he'd left it. Including the overflowing diary of daily duties and events. The sight of it deflated his eagerness to get started. More coffee was in order.

"Are you all right, Father? You look a little peaky this morning." Julia smiled kindly, touching her silver perm.

He blinked at her, and for a horrible few moments, he wanted to tell her how he was not all right at all, and how he wasn't sure he could do this. He couldn't be the priest they all needed him to be. He was failing. The weight of everyone else's sins buried him like quicksand, and he was about to go under. He wanted to tell her how he must not be doing any of this right, because if he was, then he couldn't stand another week of it, let alone the rest of his life.

He smiled. "I'm fine."

"Let me make you a nice cup of tea then?"

"Coffee, I think."

"Oh, the strong stuff. Must have been a rough night." She chuckled to herself and began making the coffee.

She had no idea how rough a night he'd had. He needed

to talk to Father Hawker, to confess last night's... thoughts. If he could find a moment in his schedule.

He sat behind his desk, opened his diary for the week, and there, tucked inside by Julia, was a letter from his solicitor marked *Private & Confidential*. He plucked the letter from between the diary pages and set it aside, leaving it there while he read the day's long list of commitments. It was endless; every single entry wanted a piece of him, and he was already running on empty. On top of that, the letter sat to his right, unopened. His heart fluttered, shrinking with every beat.

The lack of sleep, last night's events, the weight of the day. It all conspired to choke him.

He stood.

"Father?"

"I'm going to walk the grounds, get some air, I think." He hurried from the office, ignoring Julia's attempts to again ask if he was all right, strode between the empty pews, and raced at a near run, similar to the pace of the man of many sins. But that man would never come back. Francis didn't have such freedom.

He couldn't run. This was his life now. He'd chosen this. Devoted his heart and soul to it.

He could do this. He needed to do this.

Dashing out of the entrance vestibule, he spotted one of his parishioners making their way up the path to meet him.

"Father?"

Francis veered left so fast he almost slipped on the cobbles. "I'll be right there," he called. His chest hurt; something squeezed his heart. He needed to stop, to breathe, to center himself. He needed a moment, one small moment to himself, and after that, he'd be able to face the day.

The path wove around the east side of the church, following the natural curve of the land, passing between graves, old and new, some with raised earth, some sunken. The rain had passed, but grey clouds hung heavy in the sky.

He slowed as the old bench appeared ahead. He'd just sit and take a moment. That was all. He was allowed to stop, wasn't he? Sitting, he clasped his hands together in prayer and bent forward. "God come to my assistance, and Lord make haste to help me." Slowly, breath by breath, heartbeat by heartbeat, the pain in his chest eased and the panic shredding his thoughts fizzled away like mist in the morning sun.

With his heart no longer trying to beat free of his ribs, he straightened and stared out across the jutting headstones. A cool breeze whispered through the tall grass, and a shiver ran its icy finger down his spine, as though his body sensed what his mind could not yet see. Then he did see it. A woman's high-heeled shoe. Glossy black. Out of place among the graves and wilted flowers. He stood, and within a few strides, saw the foot the shoe belonged to, and the leg, and the woman, face down on the grass.

Francis rushed forward and instinctively reached for her, to see if he could help. Without thinking, without understanding, despite knowing in his heart she had already passed, he touched her shoulder and tried to roll her over. He'd seen the dead, performed funerals, comforted the grieving, but those dead were expected. The woman was just here, sprawled in the wet grass, the life long gone from her dull eyes. "God bless you... and watch over you..." He trailed off, unable to find the words as an icy numbness spread through him. The young woman's hands were bound behind her back, zip-tied there. He didn't recognize her as one of his congregation, but there was something about her that seemed familiar.

Her bright red lipstick had smeared across her wheat-brown cheek. Grit and dirt clung to that smear.

Why couldn't he look away?

Francis stumbled to his feet. The numbness spread further, all the way down his legs. He moved automatically and glided back down the path, into the church, and to the office, his mind and body present but also elsewhere. Julia handed him his coffee, he took it, and then calmly told her to call the police.

Hours of chaos followed, and he answered question after question. He kept the public away, fielded the local press, and remained untouched by it all. When the police asked him if he'd seen anyone suspicious or unusual in the last few days, he should have mentioned the man of many sins. But didn't.

When the furor died down, and the police had gone, the body too, leaving just a ring of fluttering police tape around the graves the girl had been discarded on, Francis stood in the same spot he'd stood that morning, only now it rained, and he shivered in his cassock.

He'd asked the stranger if he'd had anything to confess.

What sin brought you here?

You did.

Father Francis Scott was not a man of the world, and there was no doubt in his mind the man of many sins was from a whole other world to his, far beyond Francis's parish, but he'd come to St. Mary's, he'd come to Francis. And the next morning, a woman was dead.

That was an unlikely coincidence.

Part of him hoped he'd see the stranger again. And part

of Francis hoped the man never returned. But deep inside, he suspected the stranger would return, and when he did, Francis would ask if murder was one of his many sins.

He feared he already knew the answer.

CHAPTER TWO

Vitari

Vitari Angelini dialed the only number in the burner phone's contact's list and held the phone to his ear. Outside the rental car, people bustled to and from the roadside service station's main doors, like bees from a hive. Rest stops like these saw thousands of people pass through their doors every hour. Vitari was just another anonymous customer, exactly how he liked it.

A father and his two kids drifted toward their car parked near to Vitari's. The dad carried a McDonald's bag in one hand and tapped out a message on his phone in the other hand, while his pre-teen kids bickered. Vitari's gaze skipped to two teen girls giggling and bouncing from the service station doors, heading toward their old VW. His gaze skipped on, scanning brief snippets of normal lives he'd never touch: a woman in a pantsuit, traveling alone with a laptop case swinging at her side; the two pensioners who were in no rush to arrive wherever they were headed; some old guy cursing his electric car. The lives he touched ended in screaming and blood. These people had no idea they were being observed by the Battaglia's number one enforcer. They probably didn't even know who or what the Battaglia were. Just the way *the business* liked it.

Although what the fuck Vitari was doing in the ass-end of England, he had no idea.

He hated England, hated its too-green fields, its endless rain, and the CCTV cameras everywhere.

Don Giancarlo knew that, so he must have sent him here to punish him, or Luca had been whispering in the boss's ear again, trying to muscle Vitari out. As the only way out was in a casket, and Vitari was damn hard to kill, Luca was going to have to try a lot harder.

"Angel," a gravelly voice answered the call, using Vitari's alias.

"Ciao, Sal," Vitari greeted. "This is a fuckin' waste of time, man. The priest is nothing, just some good guy fresh out of priest school. Why am I here?"

"I'm going to ignore all you just said, stronzetto, and assume you haven't heard the news?"

"What news?" His heart sank. "I've been on the road." He'd been looking forward to hopping back on the yacht and being back home in Calabria by the weekend, but Sal's voice suggested that wasn't happening.

"Your knows-nothing-priest found a dead woman in his graveyard. You haven't left, have you?"

"No," Vitari lied. *Fuck.*

"You'd better get back there before the DeSica finish the job, or Giancarlo will nail-gun your balls to a wall."

Giancarlo would do exactly that. Vitari had performed a similar method of punishment for the don multiple times. Luca, the prick, would volunteer to hold the gun. "Fuck." He ended the call, hit the car's Start button, and revved the Jag's powerful engine. He was two hours away, and the fucking English roads were riddled with speed cameras. The fines would never catch up with him in the rental, but the British traffic *polizia* would—they did not fuck around.

Giancarlo had been very clear. If the DeSica caught up with the priest, then Vitari had better make damn sure he didn't talk. Or if he did, they all fucking died as a clear message to the DeSicas not to touch Battaglia property.

What the fuck some squeaky-clean priest was supposed to talk about was way above Vitari's paygrade, he just knew he had to get to St. Mary's before the DeSicas. He dropped a gear and launched the Jag away from the service station, onto the freeway. Hopefully he wasn't already too late. A body in a graveyard was sloppy, even for the DeSica idiots. They'd want that dealt with.

He roared the Jag past the father and the two pre-teens in their BMW and caught the middle-aged man's eye. Something predatory flashed in his gaze, jealousy too. Vitari flashed the old man a smile and rammed the accelerator to the floor, leaving the dad in his tire smoke.

Vitari would rather die in a hail of bullets than live behind a desk. He wasn't made to follow the rules. Society had given him nothing, and he owed it nothing in return. The only thing he cared about—the reason he breathed, his religion, his life—was family: the Battaglia, and Don Giancarlo.

Vitari wouldn't hesitate to kill a man of the cloth for the don. He'd done worse, earning the alias *Angelo della Morte*. What would Father Francis Scott, with his pristine cassock and haunted eyes, make of that?

A good guy like him? He'd probably vow to save Vitari's soul.

He could try, but Vitari's soul was beyond saving.

Perhaps Vitari would drag him down to Hell with him. Although, considering the depth of pain in Father Scott's eyes, he might already be there.

CHAPTER THREE

Francis

Evening communion was unusually busy, likely because word of the unfortunate young woman's death had reached all four corners of the town and everyone wanted a piece of the gossip.

Francis greeted his parishioners with his always-on smile and spent a great deal of time among them, making himself available, saying yes to far too many events, some of which he'd later have to cancel. As they all settled in the pews, two new faces peered back at him from among the crowd, which in itself wasn't unusual, but as had happened the night before, some people just didn't fit. And the two middle-aged men in the back pew didn't seem the sort to join in with Quiz Night down at the Carpenter's Inn. They hadn't arrived with anyone, weren't introduced, and nobody appeared to speak with them. Just a few polite nods and hellos.

Francis was accustomed to dealing with difficult people.

He visited hospitals, care homes, and prisons. He'd been sworn at, spat at, and exposed to various parts of the human anatomy, and he'd taken it all on board with understanding and grace. Much of those instances were not in the person's control, and so Francis had prayed for them, even as the burn of a slap or the heat of foul language had scorched his ears.

But there were difficult people, and then there were *dangerous* people. Those required a different approach, such as calling the police as soon as communion concluded.

Francis performed the communion, and as the congregation lined up to approach him to receive the blood and body of Christ, the two out-of-town men joined the line.

Francis's heart pounded. At least he'd get a good look at them. "The body of Christ."

"Amen."

One by one, the parishioners knelt and bowed their heads, and each one received the body and blood of Christ in the form of wafer paper and water from the chalice. The two men were next, and each fixed their gaze on Francis as though pinning him to a cross. He performed communion with them as he would anyone, but his fingers trembled as he placed the wafer paper on their tongues.

"Amen, Father."

They were here for nefarious reasons, he was sure of it.

"Amen, Father."

One of the men had a small cross tattoo on his neck, which suggested he took his prayers seriously.

Or perhaps finding a murdered woman had rattled Francis and these two men were here to legitimately worship, and like the man of many sins, they were just passing through. He'd undoubtedly never see any of them again. Although, these people weren't like the well-dressed stranger from the night before. Their clothes were scruffy casual, and their fingers flinted with so many rings that their knuckles gleamed in candlelight.

Francis fumbled his next quote and apologized, as his thoughts began to unravel. He reached for the lectern and shuffled the pages from the Book of the Gospel, searching for the correct line. If he could just get through this. Faces peered at him from the packed pews. The more time ticked on, the hotter he sweated beneath the cassock. The weight of his stole seemed to choke him, and the inside of the church glowed so brightly, it squeezed tears from his eyes.

What sin brought you here?

You did.

No, he couldn't think that now. "Lord, make haste..." He uttered the go-to prayer to steady his mind and heart, and by some miracle, managed to find his place in the book and completed the mass.

With communion concluded, he comforted those who needed it, spoke with others who merely wanted to chat, and somehow got through it, until there was nobody left in the church but him and Julia, collecting the hymn books.

He slumped onto the step beside the lectern and dragged his hands down his face.

"Father." Julia approached with a large stack of books in her arms. "I hope you don't mind me saying, but perhaps you should take a few days off? You've been working awfully hard, and I know you want to make a good impression on Father Hawker, but I think he'd agree with me if he saw you now." Her face was sympathetic. "Even men of God need rest, Father."

She was right. He'd almost collapsed during the ceremony. He could not continue like this.

"But there is much to do." None of it would go away. it

would all still be waiting for him when he returned to work in a day or two. In fact, it would be worse. Was every day like this for other priests? Did it ever slow down?

"Which will wait." Julia smiled.

"Yes, of course. Today was difficult. Why don't you go home, Julia. I'll lock up."

"Are you going to be all right on your own?"

He liked her; she was kind in the way not many people were, despite her own losses in the past. Or perhaps because of them. He knew she looked at him and saw her son, who had passed on. She'd found guidance and faith in the Church, and she had faith in *him*. He wasn't sure he deserved her kindness.

"Of course."

He waited on the step as she grabbed her bag, threw on her coat, said good night, and left him alone. Silence soothed his soul. He pulled his knees to his chest, making himself small among the enormity of the church. He should have found strength in his surroundings, as though he could absorb God from the stone, into his flesh, like a rechargeable battery absorbed power. But maybe he wasn't rechargeable. Maybe he was just one of those batteries that, once used, should be thrown away.

These thoughts were not constructive.

It was just the jitters, just the adjustment. Everything would soon fall into place. It had to, because there was no way out.

He stood, brushed down his robes, filled his lungs with air scented with holy oil and warm candle wax, and returned to the office.

The solicitor's letter still sat on his desk, waiting to be opened. He'd shuffled it around during the day, almost buried it, but he saw the corner poking out from the stack of other unopened letters. He couldn't handle opening it today. Tomorrow, just not today.

He took the ring of keys from the desk drawer, clanging the big chunks of metal together, and leaving the office, slotted the key in the lock.

A heavy hand clamped over his mouth from behind. He tasted salt, smelled rich cologne, and opened his mouth to cry out, but the hand tightened and yanked him backwards against a firm chest.

"You're not going to make a noise, are you, Father?"

A thousand memories tumbled behind his eyes. *Shh, don't make a noise, this will be our secret.* He wanted to be the kind of man who fought back, to be strong enough to stand up against evil, but as the heavy hand clamped his mouth shut and the smell of sweat and fabric softener and aftershave assaulted his nose and burned his throat, his empty gut heaved.

He hastily shook his head. He wouldn't fight.

Fear turned his blood to ice and spritzed his skin with perspiration, dampening his clothes and robes.

The man hauled him backwards, half carrying him. Francis's shoes squeaked on the smooth church floor. He trembled, hating it, hating himself.

"There's a good boy."

Francis's nostrils flared. He wasn't a boy. Not anymore. Rage, pure and clean, surged from the pit of his gut, thawing all the ice. Francis slammed his head back. The man grunted, his grip eased, and his thick fingers slipped between Francis's lips. Francis opened his mouth, let the finger slip inside, and slammed his teeth closed. The man screamed and Francis bolted, but whether his cassock snagged on a pew or his attacker tripped him, he didn't make it far. His feet went out from under him and he fell, the pew rushing up. His forehead smacked its edge, and he went down, sprawled in the nave, stunned.

Somewhere far off an inner voice screamed at him to get up, to run, and he knew he should, but he also couldn't because the pews were spinning, and he was falling while laying still.

"Son of a bitch bit me!"

The kick to his middle slapped him back into his heavy, lead-lined body.

"Rossi, leave him. Or he'll never talk."

Francis groaned and tried to get his hands under him. Maybe he could crawl away. "God, grant me strength." His vision blurred, turning pink. He got one hand in front of the other, even as they laughed at his efforts. He dug his fingernails into the floor and dragged his unwilling body forward. If everything would just stop spinning, he'd be able to get his knees under him, then stand.

This shouldn't be happening. What had he done to deserve this? Well, he knew what he'd done but these men couldn't know. Could they?

Nausea wet his mouth. His gut heaved again.

One of the men grabbed the back of his cassock and hauled him off his feet. His attacker shoved him against a pew. Francis clung to the hard wood; if he fell again, he might never get back up.

"Sit your backside down, Father, and let's play a game," the one with the cross tattoo said.

Francis slumped in the pew and wiped wetness from his face. Blood glistened on the back of his hand.

The two men—the same he'd performed communion for—stood over him. He didn't know them; he hadn't done anything to them. "I will pray for you."

The backhanded slap stole the air from his lungs.

Rough hands grabbed his jaw and forced him to look into the man's eyes.

"I don't need your prayers, I just need you to answer some questions, then maybe we'll see about letting you go."

Blood pooled in Francis's mouth and spilled over, running down his chin.

"Fucking hell, Rossi. Any more of that and he'll be useless. Let me do it." The other one tried to muscle in and pry Rossi off, but although bigger, Rossi was passionate and managed to shrug his companion off.

"Get your hands off me," Rossi yelled. "This is between me and God!"

Rossi thrust his left hand into his pocket, still holding Francis's chin with his right, and produced a pair of black zip ties—the same zip ties Francis had seen on the woman's wrists.

They were going to kill him.

He didn't know what they wanted, or what he'd done, but they were going to kill him like they'd killed the woman, and they'd leave his body for Julia to find in the morning. The horror of it rendered him useless. He couldn't move; terror had him in its clutches.

"Get his wrists."

Rossi's partner obeyed, grabbing Francis's wrists. He couldn't let them do this, but he didn't know how to stop them. They were both stronger than him, even when he wasn't bleeding and dizzy. If he tried to run, they'd catch him, killing him quicker.

Rossi backed off, freeing Francis's jaw, and curled his top lip in disgust. "A fucking priest touched me once. They're all the same."

Francis almost laughed—not because of his plight, but

because of the irony—but his laugh sounded like a sob. "I'm sorry for your pain."

"Jesus, Rossi, don't make this weird. Ask the questions."

"Right, so, here's the crux." Rossi knelt and laid a gentle hand on Francis's trembling knee. "You just gotta answer and we'll let you go."

Francis nodded so they thought he was beaten, but the second Rossi backed off again, he was going to make a run for it, and he prayed to God that he had enough strength left to keep his legs moving when that happened.

"When were you born?" Rossi asked.

Francis frowned. What kind of question was that? He blinked at the brute. "September, ninety-nine."

"Good, you're doing good. Now, where were you born?"

"'Where'?" Francis echoed.

Rossi snorted. "You're beginning to get on my tits. *Where?!*"

"I don't..." Francis swallowed. "Why?"

The slap left his ears ringing and his face ablaze. The pews around him spun some more, and the two men tilted sideways. Darkness throbbed closer, threatening to yank his consciousness away.

"'Why?' he asks. Fucking why? I'm the one asking the questions! Answer the fucking question or I'm going to beat it out of you."

"I don't, I don't know. I was... I was adopted."

Rossi glanced at his partner, who nodded for him to continue, or maybe to confirm the information was true.

A familiar creak filled the church—the sound of the front door opening. *Please, not Julia.* It couldn't be Julia, they'd kill her. The two brutes looked down the nave, but neither moved. Francis twisted to see, but a stab of pain tore down his side, making him gasp.

Rossi's partner nodded at him. "Check it out. I'll watch him."

Rossi stomped off, leaving the stockier, more reserved of the pair behind.

"Sorry about Rossi, he's a dick sometimes. Gets all out of hand. He has his uses though." Rossi's partner stared long and hard. "You don't know why we're here, do you?"

Francis shook his head. "Please... I don't know you, I won't tell anyone, please, don't kill me."

"Do you fear death, Father?" He removed a knife from his pocket. "Man like you, man of God, you probably can't wait to die, right?" He moved closer, filling all of Francis's vision. "Oh wait, you're Catholic. Don't all Catholics go to Hell?" He poked the tip of the knife against his own fingertip, drawing a bead of blood. "Unless you repent? Isn't that right? A guy like you, how old are you, twenty-something? What do you have to repent for, Father?"

Rossi had used fists, but this one was the more dangerous. Francis closed his eyes and begged God for help, prayed for guidance, promised he'd be better, do better, if he lived through this.

Fingers locked in Francis's hair, jerking his head back. He snapped open his eyes.

"A pretty boy like you, what did you do to Sasha, huh? Why does he want to know all about you?"

Francis had no idea who this Sasha was, or what he'd done. "N-nothing, I don't—I don't know—"

The man lifted his head, his face surprised. He freed Francis's hair and stepped into the aisle. "What do we have here? L'Angelo della Morte, in the flesh! Fucking hell, Angel." Rossi's partner grinned. "Didn't think I'd meet you here."

"Yeah, well, you know what they say..."

Francis knew that smooth voice. He blinked fast, clearing his vision, and twisted in the pew. Sparks of pain danced up his side, making his eyes water anew, but he saw the man of many sins walking down the nave, casually rolling up his sleeves. Fresh grazes bloodied his knuckles. His watch glinted. Dark eyes flicked over to Francis, then darted away.

"Angels find us in our darkest hours," the man of many sins said, or *Angel*, as the brute had just called him.

The brute brandished his knife and bared his teeth. "C'mon then, Angel."

Angel sprinted forward, *at* him, and they collided, grappling brutally. Angel landed the first punch, following it with a short, sharp second blow, then another, beating the brute toward the floor. Angel was fast, relentless, and vicious, and when the brute's cheek split open, Angel didn't stop. Blood splattered. The brute slashed the knife wildly. Angel danced back, then grabbed the brute's head and smacked it into his knee. The brute collapsed, but Angel wasn't done. He kicked him in the gut, once, twice. The brute spat blood onto the nave floor.

The violence was visceral, shocking, savage.

This was a nightmare. Francis was in a nightmare.

He couldn't be here; he couldn't watch this. He pushed from the pew, stumbled, and fell into a run. He had to get away—just get away. His tied wrists hampered his stride, but he burst from the church doors and stumbled through the vestibule, but a dark lump tripped him, and he went down hard on the cobbles, cracking his elbow. Lightning pain danced up his arm, into his shoulder. He cried out but managed to roll onto his front, then scrambled on his knees.

The lump sprawled on the path was Rossi. Cold, open

but unseeing blue eyes confirmed he wasn't threatening anyone ever again.

A prayer tumbled from Francis's lips. He slithered backward, trying to get away from the horror of it all.

Angel emerged from the vestibule. Blood splattered his forearms and delight danced in his eyes. He wiped the back of his hand across his cheek, smearing blood from his lips, and strode toward Francis.

He was no angel, despite the name.

He was a demon, come for Francis and his sins. "Stay back!"

He grabbed Francis by the zip-tied wrists and hauled him onto his feet. "Can you walk? Good. We need to leave before more DeSicas get here. Don't worry." He smiled. "You're safe with me. Mostly."

Safe? He wasn't safe.

This *Angel* had just killed two men. He was covered in their blood.

What kind of nightmare was this? "Is this real?" Francis muttered, led by his wrists toward the silver car with its door open and engine running.

"Yes, and it's about to get worse." Angel opened the rear door, and Francis slid into the back seat. The door slammed, jolting Francis's frayed nerves. He might cry, or scream, something, anything. But instead, he sat in silence, his tied wrists resting in his lap.

Angel pulled the car from the church gate.

Julia would find the two dead men in the morning. And there was nothing Francis could do to help her. He should have done more. Why hadn't he fought them? He'd frozen, too afraid to do anything. And now he was with a monster.

Sunset turned to darkness. Angel drove in silence, his

gaze occasionally flicking to the mirror, checking on Francis. Was he going to kill him like he had those other men?

Francis had to get away.

They traveled down back roads, taking twists and turns, passing through towns and villages, then joined a freeway, heading south.

Headlights from oncoming cars on the opposite side of the barrier swept over them. Francis shivered. He couldn't tell if he was wet from sweat or if he'd urinated on himself during the ordeal. His face throbbed, over his eye, and his lip had swollen. He poked at it with his tongue, tasting fresh blood. It felt wrong, he felt wrong, as though he'd been bruised on the inside, not just the outside. He'd only felt like this once before, as though he'd done something so terrible, he could never speak of it.

If he could get the attention of other drivers, would anyone help? But it was dark. Nobody would see him. "I need the bathroom," he said.

"Hold it," Angel replied. The first words he'd said in hours.

Francis could see Angel's hands on the wheel and the gear shift, and how his knuckles were all bloody and split. Francis had met adulterers; as part of his prison work, he'd met men who lusted after children, he'd had people confess heinous thoughts, but he'd never met a murderer before. And Francis had dreamed of Angel, had had improper thoughts about him, thoughts that had challenged his vow of celibacy. But all men were weak, and Francis was no exception. Celibacy was a journey, Father Donavon had told him during his studies, when he'd confessed to having sexual fantasies about men. A journey with no destination, a battle with no victor. The journey *was* the destination.

And now, he'd lusted after a murderer.

Why did Francis have to be so broken?

"I uh…" he croaked. "I really need the bathroom." He had to get away from this man. Nothing else mattered.

Angel's dark eyes flicked to him, unblinking. Francis stared back, even as his heart tried to pound its way through his ribs.

"The car's a rental, do what you have to. We're not stopping."

This man was an animal. Would he truly let Francis soil himself? Francis blinked and looked away. "Are you going to kill me?"

"No." Angel faced the road. His fingers tightened on the steering wheel.

He'd lied.

Would the rear door open if Francis tugged on the handle? He glanced down. These doors had child locks, didn't they? To stop children from falling out when the car traveled at speed. He dropped his head back and closed his eyes. Why was this happening? Tiredness pulled his body down, dragging him toward darkness. The car's engine hummed and the wheels rumbled, and perhaps if he fell asleep, when he woke up, it would all have been some terrible nightmare.

"Father?"

He pulled open heavy eyelids and blinked at the face now right in front of his. Dark eyes—beautiful eyes—a slim jaw, ending in an emotive mouth, too quick to smile. In the haze of exhaustion, he knew he shouldn't admire Angel's face, but Francis admired it anyway.

"There you are."

A cold, wet tissue touched Francis's face, wiping away the dregs of sleep. Thoughts tumbled. Angel was *touching* him. In the back of the car. They'd stopped… and Angel was leaning in through the back door and *dabbing at the cut* on Francis's forehead.

Francis jerked away, trying to vanish into the car seats.

"Don't move, I need to look at that cut."

They were in the car, in a parking lot somewhere. Drizzle fell like static under nearby lighting. Francis's thoughts spun, trying to make sense of it all. A service station. McDonald's arches glowed in the dark.

Angel poked again at the bruise over Francis's eye, reigniting its heated throb. Francis froze and stared at Angel's face, at how his chin had gained a whiskered shadow, how his lips pinched together, bleaching them of color. Rain drops sparkled in his black hair and on the tips of his lashes. How could someone so beautiful be capable of such terrible things? But beauty was nothing if it lacked godliness. Beauty in the soul mattered, and Angel's soul was in great jeopardy.

"All right." Angel produced a knife. Rossi's partner's knife. He brandished it and Francis's heart leaped into his throat, but with a quick flick of his wrist, Angel cut the zip ties holding Francis's wrists. "We're going into McDonald's over there so you can use the bathroom." His hand clamped down on Francis's shoulder and Angel peered up close, into his eyes. "You saw what happened to people who fuck with me. I'll keep you safe. Do you trust me?"

No, Francis didn't trust him. Why would he trust a cold-blooded murderer? He nodded.

"Good. We're going to get along just fine." Angel straightened out of the car and offered his hand for Francis to take. "In those clothes, there's no hiding the fact you're a priest, so let's get this done fast," he added.

Francis walked alongside Angel. The puddles he sloshed through soaked his robes, weighing them down.

Rain made Angel's shirt cling to his shoulders. He caught Francis looking, and his emotive eyes flashed an impatient warning. "Don't talk to anyone. Just the bathroom, that's it."

They entered the service station, passing into bright lights and noise. A few people loitered, talking on phones, children waiting with their parents. Half a dozen people dallied around the McDonald's self-service machines. If he yelled that he'd been kidnapped, would Angel let him go, or stab him here, in front of the children? They strode on, passed through the McDonald's seating area, and entered the bathroom.

Francis caught his ghastly reflection in the mirror and swayed on his feet. He was a bloody, beaten mess. How had nobody already raised the alarm? He gripped the basin.

"All right, Father, in you go, do what you've got to do." Angel took his arm, guided him into a stall, and closed the door.

Francis flicked the lock, stepped back, and slumped onto the closed toilet lid. Maybe he could stay here? Angel couldn't get to him. He'd locked the door. He buried his face in his hands and stifled a sob. This was it; he'd stay here. Hide. Wait him out. He breathed, maybe sobbed. Everything hurt. Men were dead.

"Francis?"

He bit into his finger to keep himself from shaking.

"If you think this flimsy toilet door is going to stop me from coming in there, you'd best think again. Finish up in there. You've got thirty seconds."

"Why are you doing this?" Francis blurted.

"Keeping you alive? I don't know. Maybe I won't. Maybe I'll walk away, but the DeSicas will find you, and that cut above your eye suggests it's pretty fuckin' clear what they had planned for you."

"I don't even know you people! Just let me go!"

Angel kicked the door, and it flew open, banged the side of the stall, and bounced back, but Angel was there, blocking its return.

He stared down at Francis, nostrils flaring. "I'm beginning to think you lied to me, Father. Get up."

Francis stood and wiped cold tears from his face.

Angel raked his glare over him, head to toe. "We're going to have to do something about that robe." He reached in, grabbed Francis by the collar, and yanked the strip of white free. Turning, he tossed it into the trash. "C'mon, I don't have time to play games."

"No! I'm not going."

Angel flew at him. His thin fingers encircled Francis's neck. He shoved Francis against the stall wall, rattling all the connected stalls. "Do not fuck with me, Father Scott. It would be easier for me to cut your throat and leave you here bleeding out. I'm doin' you a fuckin' favor."

He'd said a whole lot of words, but Francis only heard a few of them between the thumping panic in his head. He scrutinized Angel's eyes and saw death. His own, and Angel's. *God, grant me strength.*

Angel's grip loosened until he didn't so much as pin Francis to the wall as press him there, using his chest and thigh to hold him. His fingers skimmed down Francis's neck, spilling shivers down his spine. Francis gasped. He wasn't sure if this hurt, or if it was something else. But then Angel ran his tongue over his bottom lip, and his eyes narrowed, as though he were trying to puzzle something out. Then he backed away and turned toward the mirrors. He studied himself, straightened his shirt with its bloody splatters, and glanced at Francis's reflection as Francis emerged from the stall.

"Are you done playing games, Father?"

Francis nodded.

They left McDonald's and climbed back into the car. Francis had made sure to glare at as many CCTV cameras as he could find. The authorities wouldn't know he was missing yet, but once the bodies were discovered at the church, the police would begin searching. They'd see his face on the footage and know he was with *Angel*. Whoever Angel was.

He must have some kind of agenda, some reason for keeping Francis alive. He hadn't been passing through. He'd deliberately stopped at St. Mary's, perhaps even to kill that young woman. Three bodies in two days. It would be a scandal for the Church. But why Francis?

"What do you want?" Francis asked as they got underway.

"Right now, I want to get us both out of the UK."

"What do you want *with me*?"

Angel didn't reply.

Francis sensed this wasn't personal. They didn't know each other. So that meant someone else was pulling Angel's strings? Perhaps they wanted to ransom a priest? But if that were the case, why pick him, a priest of just three months from a small parish in South West England. There had to be targets of a higher value.

The car's headlights swept over a road sign for Plymouth, *Britain's Ocean City*. They passed over a brightly lit suspension bridge. Angel stopped at the tolls, waved a card, and the barriers lifted. Francis tried to catch the man in the booth's eye, but he stared dull-eyed through the plexiglass screen.

Did nobody care? Couldn't anyone see he was being kidnapped?

Angel appeared to know the roads well, and right after the booths, he turned into a residential area, weaving the car down old, winding city roads, heading for the waterfront.

A boat.

That was how he was going to smuggle Francis out of the country. As soon as they got anywhere near boarding a boat, Francis would raise the alarm. They had port control at the docks, checking for smuggled goods and people. They'd never let Francis board a ferry, all beaten up like he was.

But Angel pulled the car into a private marina surrounded by high-end waterfront apartments. This wasn't a port, and no ferries left from here. The boats bobbing in their berths were all privately owned.

"Out," Angel snapped.

Any good graces Francis had with him, he'd squandered back at the McDonald's toilets. He should have used the bathroom then too. He *did* need to relieve himself now but didn't dare ask.

They approached a marina office. A single light glowed from inside. Alongside, water sloshed around boats of all sizes, from little fishing vessels to superyachts three times the size of Francis's cottage.

"Stay out here," Angel ordered, and strode ahead, opening the office door. He greeted someone inside and the two of them struck up a conversation.

Francis stood at the side of the water. A hundred apartments lined the marina, some with their lights on. It was probably after midnight, but he was visible; anyone might look out of their windows and see him. How could he get attention without alerting Angel?

What if he just... ran?

He glanced again at Angel through the half-open door. He handed the man behind the desk a tight roll of cash.

Francis wasn't getting help here.

If Angel got him on a boat, Francis would never escape.

He bolted.

Ran hard, and ran fast. The slippery dockside cobbles undulated, almost tripping him, but he held his balance, and with his wrists free, he pumped his arms, head down. His robe whipped about his legs. Then he heard Angel's shoes tapping after him, gaining on him. He might stab him in the back and leave him gutted in an alleyway.

God, help me!

Faster, he had to run faster! But Angel was coming, and Francis's robes slowed him down.

Angel snagged his cassock and swung him around. Francis hit a wall, face-first. He spun and shoved, pushing Angel off. This was it, if he didn't fight now, he'd be dead by morning. He thrashed, but Angel was on him, all over him, pinning him still.

Cold steel touched Francis's throat, freezing him.

"Dammit, Father," Angel panted, chest heaving against Francis. "When are you going to learn you can't escape me? Do I need to cut you? Is that what you want?!" He snatched Francis by the robes at the neck and threw him back toward the bobbing boats. "Move!"

His legs wobbled, threatening to give out. He prayed so hard he forgot to breathe and stumbled on. Angel grabbed him, rough handling him onto the floating dock. The rigging from nearby sailboats clanged in the breeze and little flags fluttered, but otherwise the marina was quiet.

What if he jumped into the water? Would Angel follow?

The dark, sloshing waters appeared to be deep, and Francis couldn't swim.

Angel climbed aboard the back end of a large superyacht named *Dolce Vita* and left Francis alone on the pontoon, assuming he'd follow.

Francis lingered. He didn't have a choice, there was no way out. Just like the rest of his life.

He stepped on board.

CHAPTER FOUR

Vitari

Well, this was a shit show.

He should have killed the priest and left him with the DeSicas. Three murders in a church. Message sent. Job done. Don't fuck with the Battaglia.

Instead, Vitari had the priest on the yacht with him.

"What the fuck," he muttered to himself as he warmed the boat's engines. Kidnapping the priest was not part of the plan. He wasn't even sure why he'd done it. Just that, when he'd returned to St. Mary's and seen how those bastards had torn into Father Scott, he'd lost part of himself for a while. Those DeSica assholes were not killing Vitari's priest. It was bad enough they thought they could muscle in on the Battaglia operations back home and in Venezuela, bad enough their Russian prick of a leader thought his little operation was even half the size of the Battaglia.

But taking the priest was stupid. A dumb move. The boss was going to nail Angel's balls to a board.

Maybe he should shove Father Scott over the side of the boat? The wily priest would swim back to shore and ID him to the National Crime Agency. Vitari would be screwed if he ever needed to return to England. No, he couldn't let him go. There was only one way this ended—with Father Scott dead. So why the fuck was the priest sitting below deck, stewing in his holier-than-thou attitude, as though he knew every sin Vitari had ever committed, from jerking off to men's magazines to beating a guy to death on his sixteenth birthday.

"Stupido." He punched the yacht's wheel.

Vitari just needed space to think. There had to be a reason why Giancarlo had wanted him to check in on Father Scott in the first place. Probably to kill him... It was what Vitari did best, what he was known for. The attack dog on the end of Don Giancarlo's leash. L'Angelo della Morte.

Thoughts whirring, he piloted the yacht out of Plymouth's marina, and once past the breakwater, he set a course—not for Calabria, not yet—for Puerto Banús. Nobody would know he'd taken a detour to Spain, and it would give him time to figure out what to do with Father Francis Scott.

When the boss had sent him to England to watch a priest, he'd expected to find some grey-haired, middle-aged man nudging retirement, not a twenty-something brunet, sinfully handsome in his all-black robes, and with big brown eyes so full of emotion he must have seen the worst the world could throw at him and dared it to test him some more.

Fucking priests.

Fuck this mission.

Fuck Father Scott.

He'd rather be back in southern Italy, where he walked the streets like a goddamned king. Where everyone knew him, everyone respected him, where he had power. And where few would dare judge him like Father Scott did.

He flexed his bruised knuckles and gazed outside. The weather was clear, the starlit ocean calm. It was time to figure out what Father Scott knew that had the DeSica all over him and the Battaglia wanting him blown away. Vitari switched the controls to autopilot and descended below deck.

Discreet lighting haloed the dining area, lounge, and kitchen in cozy tones. Father Scott lay on his side on the couch, breathing softly. The slippery liar was faking it, like he'd faked needing the bathroom. Although, he hadn't faked those tears.

Vitari stood over him. Father Scott's chest rose and fell. The side of his face was marred by an angry bruise around a split in his forehead that should have stitches but appeared to have stopped bleeding. The split in his lip had scabbed over. He'd taken a beating elsewhere too, since he'd hugged his middle when he'd walked.

The DeSica would have killed him. He was lucky to be alive.

Vitari only had a few hours to figure out his next move, and to do that, he needed to know more about this circus he'd found himself performing in.

"Hey." He kicked Father Scott's dangling leg. "No rest for the wicked."

Father Scott opened his eyes. Yeah, he'd been faking it. Those brown eyes were too bright, too intense, too judgmental for a man who'd just woken up. Did he think Vitari was so easy to fool?

"Drink?" Vitari didn't wait for his reply and retrieved

two beers from the kitchen. He shoved the priest's across the table.

Father Scott sneered. "I don't drink alcohol."

Vitari smirked. "Of course not, you wouldn't want to dirty up your halo."

"Do you have water?" He sat up and hissed at the pain in his side.

Vitari almost told him to get his own water, but he needed him compliant, which meant keeping him amiable. Vitari poured him a glass of water and handed it over, then waited as Father Scott raised the glass to his lips, winced at the cut, but drank anyway.

What made a man devote his life to God? Did he wake up one day and have an epiphany, a vision, or was it a gradual process? It seemed a waste, for someone as attractive as Scott to be taken out of the gene pool. Humanity's loss. Vitari knew a few women who'd vigorously and enthusiastically enlighten the priest to all the carnal adventures he'd been missing.

Father Scott lifted his eyes and slowed his drinking, aware he was being watched. He set the glass down on the table and croaked, "Thank you."

Vitari swiped his beer and sat opposite. "All right, you're going to answer some questions, and no fucking with me."

"Yes." He swallowed and placed his hands cupped together beside his glass.

"Why are the DeSicas trying to kill you?"

"I don't know. I don't know who they are."

Was he lying? He spoke softly, calmly, in the same soothing voice he'd used in the confessional booth when Vitari had been tempted to spill his secrets. It was a dangerous gift, that ability to listen. People told priests everything, believing those priests had the power to cleanse their souls and take away their guilt, but a priest wasn't anything special. Just a man, like all the rest.

"The DeSica are Bratva, Russian mob," Vitari explained.

By the way Francis's eyes widened, he'd had no idea.

"Did they ask you anything?" Vitari asked. "Did they want anything from you?"

He wrung his cupped hands, then stopped when he saw Vitari watching. "They asked my birth date."

"Your birth date?"

Father Scott shrugged.

That didn't make any sense. "Anything else?"

His brown eyes lifted. "Are you going to kill me?"

"I told you, no." *Not yet.*

"DeSica doesn't sound Russian."

"It's not."

Father Scott glared back, and there was that fire again, that defiance, daring the world to take him on, to fight him. Daring Vitari to *defy* him. It had to be naivety, because not many people could look Vitari in the eye and challenge him. It would have been hot if it hadn't been so desperate.

"The DeSica are run by a vicious bastard called Sasha Zhukov," Vitari explained. "He's the Russian part, the rest of them are strays he's picked up. He'll recruit anyone ruthless enough. Albanians, Spaniards, fuckin' Iranians. Doesn't matter. Whatever psychos he can get his hands on."

"You know them?"

Vitari snorted. "The people I work for have history with the DeSica. But they're insects compared to my... to my people." DeSica were the enemy, that was the way it had always been for as long as Vitari could remember. He didn't even care to know why. Don Giancarlo had made it clear any DeSica operative was fair game. They were all savage animals and needed to be put down.

Father Scott's cheek twitched. "Your soul is not beyond saving. There is always redemption and forgiveness in God's heart."

Vitari had wondered how long it would take before he whipped out the Catholicism. "God gave up on me long ago, Father."

"He never gives up on his children."

He spoke with such conviction, Vitari almost believed him. "It must be nice, to have such faith. To be free of guilt, to hand off all your fuckups to some higher power."

He looked away, probably unhappy with Vitari's tone. "That's not how—"

"Don't preach to me. I don't need to be saved. Right now, you're the one who needs saving. And God isn't going to do that, I am. So, answer my questions."

Scott reached for his glass of water, leaned back, winced at the same unknown pain, and sipped. "This must all be a mistake." His hand shook, making the water in his glass ripple. "Look at me, I'm not... I'm not anyone."

"You're something to someone, or there wouldn't be two dead bodies in your churchyard."

"Three."

"Three?"

"The young woman."

Hm, Vitari had forgotten about her. "Tell me about her. You found her?"

"Yes." He sipped again, averting his gaze.

"You know her?"

"No."

"Still, it must have been difficult."

"What was?"

"Finding her, like that. You don't see much violence, do you, Father?"

He looked away again and it seemed as though he aged between one minute and the next. Vitari forgot sometimes, how most people lived sedate, uneventful lives. They followed the rules, stuck to their routines, had steady jobs, went shopping, had kids, attended council meetings, and lived their lives like sheep. Sheep weren't bad; they were happy being sheep. There was nothing wrong with that. Until the wolves came and slaughtered half the flock.

Father Francis Scott had just met the wolves.

"You have no idea why the Russian mob want you so bad?" Vitari asked.

"None. It's all a mistake. You should take me back."

"And you don't know the woman in your graveyard."

"No. Will you take me back?"

Was he lying? "Don't worry, after all this, you'll have a thrilling story to tell your flock and they'll love you even more for it." There would be no *after* but if he was going to keep the man compliant, he needed to give him hope.

He raised those big brown eyes. "I've answered your questions. Are you going to let me go?"

"Sure." He turned away, sensing Father Scott could see more on his face than he should. "Why don't you get cleaned up? There's some towels and spare clothes in the bedrooms."

Vitari returned to the upper deck and the yacht controls, kicked back in the pilot's chair, and watched the inky black ocean shimmer under the moon. He was going to have to report in soon, and when he did, Giancarlo would order him to kill the priest.

A bullet to the back of the head would do it. No more Father Francis Scott.

Shame to mess up that pretty face. He had the kind of next-door neighbor vibe that made him approachable, not intimidating. Traditionally handsome, in a... nice way. Like a Labrador that made friends with everyone.

A small pang of regret tripped his heart.

The family was everything, it was Vitari's life. The Battaglia was to Vitari what the church was to Father Scott. He didn't often question it. But Don Giancarlo wasn't always right.

What did the DeSica want with the priest?

Vitari needed more time...

Vitari finished off a third beer while chasing thoughts about Father Scott around his head. He had to get more information out of him, or the priest was dead. It was that simple. Whatever the DeSica believed he knew, it might be worth something to the Battaglia.

There was more to Father Francis Scott than sad eyes and silly lies, he was sure of it.

He ventured below deck again and followed the sounds of the shower running. The bedroom door was ajar, like an open invitation. Vitari eased it open a few more inches. The shower was at the front end of the yacht, behind another door leading off the bedroom.

The stained and bloody black robe lay crumpled on the floor. Vitari picked it up, intending to drape it over the arm of a nearby chair, but the priest's warmth lingered in the fabric. He scrunched it in his fingers, then brought it to his nose. The cloth smelled of warm wax and spiciness, like massage oils.

Water sloshed. He was naked back there, washing himself in the shower.

The door to the bathroom was open too. A small nudge would open it some more, maybe enough to see inside.

Jesus, those three beers must have gone to his head. He wasn't that desperate to see a man naked. Vitari draped the robe over the chair and left the bedroom. He'd fix them something to eat. The yacht was well-stocked with pasta, vegetables, spices...

He stopped in the kitchen, braced his hands on the counter, and laughed. What was he doing? Trying to make friends with the priest or wasting time so he didn't have to call it in? None of that was going to change a damn thing.

He should just go into the bathroom and strangle him in the shower, because the longer this took, the harder it was going to be.

He grabbed another beer and stared at the bottle, his thoughts far away.

"Erm, thanks for the clothes."

Vitari turned and saw a stranger standing in the same place as Father Francis Scott. Out of his robe and dressed in trousers and a simple blue and white V-neck sweater, he'd lost the godly aura and was just a man with damp brown hair that curled when wet and no socks. Maybe he hadn't found the sock drawer, and why it mattered, Vitari had no fucking idea. He leaned back against the kitchen counter and narrowed his eyes. The priest had no right to look so disarmingly *normal*.

"Sure," Vitari mumbled, then cracked open the beer and gulped down three mouthfuls without taking a breath.

"I want to help," he said, nervously rubbing one arm like a kid caught with his hand in the cookie jar.

He didn't want to help; he just didn't want to die.

Father Francis Scott stood there, all vulnerable and soft, but he was far from it. At the next opportunity, he'd try to run, and he was *fast*. Chasing him down had been an exercise in cardio and why Vitari had warned Sal to shed some of the fat he claimed to be muscle. Although, Vitari had enjoyed the sprint, and holding the knife to Scott's neck, feeling him panting against his chest, his heart thudding.

Yeah, he'd liked being that close to him, seeing the fear in his eyes, and something else too...

"Then you have to be honest with me."

"I have been."

"Father, you lie like I breathe."

"I'm not lying, I don't... I don't lie."

Vitari sauntered by him and sat on the large leather couch, arms spread along the back of the cushions. Was that *something* in Scott's eyes now, the way he skipped them down Vitari's body? Was there heat in that glance? Vitari had assumed his gaze had been full of disgust, but it was harder than that. Not disgust, but something... Defiance, again? Why did he have to be defiant around Vitari, even before he'd been kidnapped? What was he trying to prove?

"Sit." Vitari gestured with his bottle.

Francis sat on the opposite couch, upright, back straight, hands on his knees. Did he ever relax?

"I killed two men to keep you safe. You don't need to look at me like I'm the scum of the Earth."

"That's not..." He turned his face away. "That's not what I see."

"Oh?" Vitari leaned forward. "What do you see?"

Scott glanced over, but his gaze skipped away again. He was scared, and Vitari couldn't blame him. He'd been beaten, kidnapped, and had his life threatened multiple times.

Vitari smiled as he took a swig of beer and caught the priest's eye again. So judgmental. Had he ever had to steal to eat? Had he ever been shopped around like meat at the market? No. He could judge all he liked. Father Scott would never understand the world Vitari came from, the world he was now a king of. Sheep like him didn't survive among wolves.

"So if it's not you the DeSica want, it's the Church," Vitari said, airing one of many thoughts he'd dug up while Scott had shed his priestly skin. "Does anyone you work with or for have links to organized crime?"

Father Francis Scott became very, very still. "What?"

"The Mafia, Bratva, the mob?"

"Is that what you are? Mafia?"

Vitari tipped his bottle. "Guilty as sin. Although, technically mafia refers to Sicilian organized crime. But Hollywood has made it so every Italian-based syndicate is mafia."

Scott swallowed. "No, no links, to uh... that," he said, answering the earlier question.

Vitari couldn't be sure if he was lying, not when he sat so rigid, as though he had a rod up his ass. "You're going to have to be more helpful than this." Vitari rose to his feet and dangled the half-empty beer bottle in his fingers in front of the priest, swaying it gently. "Take it, relax, we've got a few hours. Let's figure this out."

He took the bottle, and as Vitari went to grab a few more, he caught Scott sniffing at the bottle top.

"You're Italian?" Father Scott asked.

Vitari laughed and popped the lids off two more bottles. "I'm complicated."

"The accent, I wasn't sure..."

He returned to the couches. "My father is Italian. I spent some time in England, when I was young." There was no harm in telling Scott a few home truths. He'd be too dead to repeat them anyway.

Scott took a few swigs of his first beer, chugging it back with intent. He'd clearly gotten over his *I don't drink* stance. Maybe it was like with the polizia—out of uniform, they drank, did drugs, hired girls and boys for sex, but once in uniform, they were upstanding citizens. As though the uniform turned them into new people. Did Father Scott's discarded robe mean he was a different person?

"Is your name really Angel?"

Vitari felt his smile bloom. "No." That name must have messed with his head. Had he prayed for an angel to save him, and Vitari—the Angel of Death—had appeared? Clearly, his God had a twisted sense of humor.

"So, what do I call you?"

"Angel," he replied, fucking with him, because he liked the way his eyes widened when he was surprised, or shocked, which happened to be almost every moment he'd spent with Vitari so far.

"You don't need to call me Father. Francis is fine." He leaned back too, mirroring Vitari's pose, and as he finished off the bottle of beer, he watched Vitari.

Francis appeared to be relaxing, but it wasn't real. In that clever head of his, he'd figured out that the only way to survive this was to befriend Vitari. They didn't teach that instinct in priest school. Where had he learned that survival technique, or was it just reflex? Some people were natural survivors. Some had no choice.

"You didn't kill that woman in my graveyard, did you?" Francis asked.

"No. I've no idea who she was."

"If you had nothing to do with her, then these DeSica people must have."

"If we can figure out what they wanted from you, I can use that to smooth things over with my people." *Keep you alive.*

"I wish I knew. I do." He grabbed a fresh beer from the table. "I'd help. I'd tell you everything. But I don't know anything. They were there during communion, and came back after, when I was alone. They asked about my birthday and where I was born—"

"What?" Vitari leaned forward again. "You didn't say that before."

"Didn't I? I... thought... I... It's a lot. I'm tired. I don't know what I said—"

"Francis," Vitari said, perhaps too harshly when he flinched. "Where *were* you born?"

"That's the thing, you see. I don't know. I was adopted."

"Adopted." Vitari squeezed the bottle in his grip. "Adopted from where?" A distant whooshing filled his ears, blood rushing to his head.

"Stanmore Boys' Home. It's a... uh... a children's home in Essex."

The whooshing grew louder, sweeping him along. "I know it."

"Oh, you do?" He raised those sad eyes.

Vitari stared at Francis, stared hard, and tried to remember if he'd seen his face before. He would have been younger back then, his face rounder, more boyish. Francis Scott. Francis was a year younger than Vitari, and he had that wholesome, golden boy look about him.

He'd have been in a different wing, where they kept the *good* boys.

Vitari stared at the bottle in his hand.

Stanmore was a large part of his past he tried to forget.

But scars couldn't be forgotten; they would always be a part of him, hidden under his skin.

Was Francis one of those boys he'd caught glimpses of? The smiling, laughing ones, trotted out as the best examples of how brilliant Stanmore was, while the rest of them shivered under thin blankets and waited for the sound of the deadbolt clanking in the back door.

Vitari got to his feet. What were the chances of him and Francis having survived the same boys' home? That wasn't a coincidence. Don Giancarlo had to know. That was why he'd sent Vitari to England, to St. Mary's to watch a priest. Both from Stanmore? The world wasn't that small. His meeting Francis wasn't by chance. Vitari didn't believe in fate.

But what did Giancarlo think Vitari would find in Father Scott?

"What's wrong?" Francis asked.

"Nothing." He couldn't look at him. He'd *know* the sin inside Vitari; he'd see all the horrors of his past.

Blood thumped through his ears, deafening and numbing at the same time. He'd left the boy he'd been behind in England, because Vitari wasn't weak, like that boy he'd once been. He didn't get picked out of a lineup and taken to the cold room across the yard. He wasn't told to face the wall while they...

That wasn't a thing that happened to him. It happened to the others, not him. That hadn't been his life.

"Angel?"

The glass bottle exploded in his grip. He saw blood but didn't feel the shards of glass digging into his skin. The thudding grew louder, joined by a high-pitched whistle, as though he might pass out.

Fuck, what had he done?

Francis was next to him, his big brown eyes offering peace and comfort, but Vitari didn't deserve those things.

"Your hand." Francis reached for Vitari's right hand. Blood dripped onto the work surface. Francis ran the tap and shoved Vitari's hand under the flow of water, washing away glitter-like pieces of glass. In his mind, he imagined screaming at Francis not to touch him, but the words were locked behind the pounding in his head.

Francis was talking. Vitari didn't hear the words, just the soft sounds of them. He liked that voice, liked the way it muffled the screams from his past.

Francis plucked large bits of glass from Vitari's palm, and now his tone turned chastising, something about keeping the wound clean. Strands of damp hair had fallen over Francis's forehead. He didn't seem to notice how those unruly bangs swung in front of his eyes.

Vitari had been eleven years old when the Battaglia had saved him from Stanmore—shipped him off to another country, another world, one where his fists gave him power, and his tongue and quick wit lashed others like a whip—and it had felt like freedom. As though he'd found the place he was supposed to be.

He'd killed the memory of the boy he'd been at Stanmore and buried him long ago.

But when he met Francis's gaze, he saw that boy reflected in his eyes. Because Vitari had so desperately wanted to be one of the good ones. He'd wanted someone to be proud of him, to show him off to the world, to know he could be good too, if they'd just give him a chance.

But they never had.

Francis stood back, having fallen quiet. "It looks worse than it is. Just a few cuts. Are you all right?" he asked.

Was Vitari all right?

Some days, he still wanted to be one of the good ones, but it was too late for that. So he'd *take* one of the good ones, instead. He flicked Francis's unruly bangs from his eyes, as a test, so he didn't have to commit to anything more if Francis recoiled. But he didn't recoil. He blinked, his lips parted, and a brief muddle of expressions crossed his face.

A taste of those perfect lips, that was all Vitari wanted. He dropped his hand, touched Francis's chin, tipped his head up, and the priest's soft lips opened in soft, surprised query.

He was so fucking perfect. Vitari had the sudden, savage urge to *ruin* him.

Francis gasped and jerked away, then backed up until he bumped into the wall, unable to flee any farther.

He didn't need to say anything. Disgust was etched into the sneer on his lips.

Vitari laughed at his own idiocy and looked at his bloody hand. He squeezed his fingers, wringing more blood from the cuts, and now he felt the wounds, felt their burn. Pain was all he deserved. Turning his back on Francis, he grabbed a dishcloth, wrapped it around his hand, and hurried back onto the upper deck.

He switched off autopilot and pushed the throttle, demanding more power from the yacht's huge engines.

They'd be on the Spanish coast by midmorning tomorrow.

And there, he'd ditch Father Francis Scott, alive or dead.

His fate was not Vitari's concern.

CHAPTER FIVE

FRANCIS

He wasn't sure what had just happened. He'd been cleaning Angel's hand, and then... something had changed between them. Angel had gone very still, and pale, and quiet, the opposite of everything he'd been so far, and there had been a moment, just a tiny moment, when Francis had thought Angel had been about to... kiss him. Which was ridiculous. It was all in Francis's head, and he'd almost crossed a line and done something that would have ensured Angel threw him overboard.

He'd been about to kiss his kidnapper, a murderer.

These unholy urges were going to get him killed.

It was bad enough he'd dreamed *things*. He couldn't act on them. Men didn't kiss men. Or they did, but it wasn't discussed. Certainly not in the Church. Celibacy was a journey. A journey Francis kept falling down on. He loved God. There was only room in his heart for God's love. Lust was selfish, by its very nature. He lived for God, and that meant there could not be room in his heart or body or mind for desire.

But... when Angel had touched his chin, he'd wanted him to lean in, to press his lips to Francis's, to taste him, to kiss a man. It was forbidden. But it had been so long since he'd been intimate with someone, and it was complicated, a mess in his head and heart, pulled between two impossible things: priestly vows and sinful desire.

It was the stress. Just stress. Brought on by *everything*. He was weak, and in his weakness, he'd lost sight of God.

He bowed over and braced his hands against his thighs. His body was betraying him, his dick had grown thick in the borrowed trousers, and the more he tried not to think about Angel's mouth on his, the more his thoughts veered into dangerous territory. What would have happened if they had kissed? If he hadn't imagined it, and Angel had wanted to?

He had to clear his head. To get these thoughts out. He straightened, headed back into the bedroom, and splashed his face over the basin. He prayed, he thought about all the dull, daily tasks he'd had to perform at St. Mary's, none of which were sexual, and eventually, the desperate need to touch himself faded along with his erection.

He knelt and prayed, and when his voice had grown hoarse he left the bedroom, climbed the steps onto the upper deck, and at the rail, with the smell of salt water and damp wind in his face, he stared at the moonlit horizon.

Perhaps, if he could make Angel see he was a living, breathing human being, worthy of life, then he wouldn't kill him?

Francis had faith in God, and faith in the brief moments of softness he'd seen in Angel's eyes.

This would not be his end.

Besides, if Angel had wanted him dead, he'd had plenty of opportunities.

No, all Francis had to do was befriend a killer. How hard could that be?

Francis woke to the sound of rigging clanging against poles, and as the yacht didn't have sails, they had to be berthed somewhere near other boats. The engines were quiet too.

Had Angel left him alone? That seemed unlikely, but this might be his chance to escape. He put his shoes on—no socks, couldn't find them—and emerged from the lower deck into brilliant sunshine. The bright light stabbed at his sore head, and as he squinted, holding a hand up to shield his eyes, the cut burned anew.

The buildings around this marina were very different from the English apartment blocks they'd left behind. Sun umbrellas dotted the water's edge, each marked with the Spanish name of a restaurant, and hundreds of people sat outside, eating, chatting, drinking wine, laughing.

The dockside was right there. All Francis had to do was step off the yacht and walk away.

"Don't even think it." Angel appeared from the topmost deck. "I have to make a call. Stay here. Or, if you really must run, go ahead. I enjoyed our last chase." He stepped off the yacht and sauntered down the dock. Francis watched him walk away, and within a few minutes, he merged with the crowds, sliding right in among them as though he belonged.

Francis wasn't going to run; he had no idea where this was or where to run to. But if he could find a phone, he'd call the police.

He waited a few minutes to see if Angel reappeared, and when he didn't, Francis walked from the yacht—not running. Although, as he drew closer to the crowds, his racing heart quickened. Angel hadn't struck him as being stupid enough to let him wander around freely, but here he was.

Sunlight warmed his back, through his sweater. Chatter swirled in the humid air. He wove through the outside tables and chairs and entered the nearest building, a relaxed bar. All around, people carried on with their lives, as though everything were fine.

Everything was *not* fine.

He had to find a phone, call the police, and get away.

At the bar, he caught the barman's eye. "A phone? Do you have a phone? It's urgent."

"Teléfono?"

"Yes, si, si. Ugh... urgent. Emergencia?" What was emergency in Spanish? He should know. He spoke Latin, which gave him a basis for understanding some foreign languages, but his brain had turned to mush and panic froze his thoughts. Should he call 999? No, that wouldn't work here. Where *was* here? Spain, Portugal? What was the number for the Spanish police? Dear God, he hadn't thought this through.

The barman handed him a phone.

"Who are you calling?" Angel asked, sliding onto a barstool beside him. He'd found a pair of sunglasses that masked his pretty eyes and smiled as though they were old friends meeting for a drink.

Francis blinked at the phone in his hand while all his hopes deflated. "I don't suppose you know the number for the local police?"

Angel snorted and plucked the phone from his hand.

He reeled off fluent Spanish to the barman, who laughed at Francis's expense and took the phone back, shaking his head as though this was all a hilarious joke.

"Here, put these on." Angel handed Francis a pair of slim sunglasses.

Francis frowned at them and heaved a sigh. They felt expensive. Of course, he'd only brought them to disguise Francis's face from the crowd.

"Don't look so down." Vitari grinned. "I have good news. Sit."

He sat. And put the sunglasses on. And when the barman arrived with two half-pints of something probably alcoholic, Francis glared at that too. He should have run. He could have made it far enough away from the marina that Vitari wouldn't have been able to track him.

"We own the police," Angel said. "So don't go calling them. It just makes everything more complicated, which puts me in a bad mood, which means I'm less inclined to help you."

"I thought you were *Italian* mafioso? Isn't this Spain?"

Angel rolled his eyes and laughed. "You really don't know much about organized crime, do you?"

"No. Because I'm a priest, not a criminal."

Vitari snorted another laugh. "You have a naïve perspective on your own kind, Father."

He thought all of this was so amusing. Francis's kidnap, the dead bodies in St. Mary's, it was all so *amusing* to Angel. Anger simmered inside Francis' gut. "If you knew half of who I am, you wouldn't sit there and call me naïve."

Angel said something in Spanish again to the passing barman, who plucked a paper straw from a box behind him and handed it to Francis.

Francis took the straw.

"For your lip," Angel said.

He was giving him a straw because of his cut lip? Francis had seen him beat a man to death, but he was concerned for Francis's lip? No, this wasn't right, Angel didn't get to be *nice*. He wasn't *kind*. He wasn't *helpful*. He was a horrible person.

Francis tore the straw in half and flung the pieces at Angel. "You suck on it."

He was supposed to befriend Angel, to make him like him, but he couldn't do it, he couldn't grovel to such a terrible person.

Angel flashed his wicked grin, seemingly in high spirits —a stark contrast to their strange encounter last night.

Francis resisted the urge to shove him off his barstool. Violence was not the answer. He would not stoop to the same level as the men who had hurt him. Oh, but he wanted to lash out, to scream, to tear off the sunglasses and throw them at him too.

"Are you done being petulant, Father?"

"What's the news?" He sipped his drink, wincing when the alcohol burned his lip. Angel smiled at that too and it was all Francis could do not to throw his drink over him.

"I've bought us more time to figure out what's going on with you and the DeSica."

"How?"

"I told the boss the DeSica want you alive, so you must know something of value."

"But they were going to kill me."

"We don't know that. They threatened you, yes. if they'd only wanted you dead, then you'd be face down on a grave like the nameless woman in your graveyard."

"Then why were *you* there? What did you want?"

Angel shrugged. "To watch you, initially. I was in your little town for a week before you noticed me."

"That's it, you were there just to check on me?"

He shrugged again. "I just follow orders. Those were my orders."

No, Francis didn't believe it. Angel was a killer. He was there to *kill* Francis. And the DeSica had gotten to him first.

Angel's nice act was a lie. He wanted answers, and when he got them, or when he realized Francis didn't know anything, Angel would kill him.

By God, Francis had to get away from this man.

Was it something to do with the boys' home? When he'd mentioned Stanmore, Angel had withdrawn. More than that, he'd crushed the bottle he'd been holding. Stanmore meant something to him.

There was more to all of this, and perhaps it had something to do with Francis's past at Stanmore.

"We should eat," Angel said. "I know a stunning restaurant a short walk from here." He threw cash on the bar. "Let's go."

"I still have this drink."

"And no straw." He pulled a mock sad face that made Francis want to throw his drink over him again.

The staff in the Italian restaurant knew Angel without him having to say a word. Francis didn't speak Italian either, and even if he did, he wasn't sure he'd catch half of what was being said. They spoke quickly, switching from Spanish to Italian, falling over themselves to offer the best table, a bottle of wine, and a basket of bread and olives.

Angel was having a heated discussion about something

on the menu that involved a great deal of hand gesturing and random barks of laughter.

Francis watched it all as though he'd landed on an alien planet.

Nobody in this restaurant was going to help him. They were far more interested in Angel and making sure he was being served correctly. Half the staff kept glancing over, as though terrified.

"Hm, try the wine."

Francis eyed the wine glass.

"You can sit there and sulk or choose to enjoy one of the finest Italian meals you will ever eat. Your choice." He removed his sunglasses with quick fingers and folded them away. Now those fine eyes were back on display, and Francis admired their long-lashed elegance, and how Angel swept his gaze out the window, scrutinizing all he saw.

Francis turned toward the window too. The ocean glistened under a high sun, and all the shiny boats bobbed. It didn't seem real. Any of it. Perhaps he'd hit his head harder than he'd thought, and he was still in St. Mary's, on the floor, unconscious, dreaming all of this insanity.

"What made you want to be a priest?"

He swung his gaze back into the room at the man seated opposite him. It seemed to be an innocent question, if such a thing was possible from Angel's lips.

"Did you always know, or did you have an epiphany?" he asked, leaning back and swirling the wine in his glass.

And there was the mocking tone again. Angel's watch flashed as he gestured, but below that, Francis noticed the delicate tattoo encircling his wrist. It appeared to be a loop of rosary beads. Or razor wire. He couldn't be sure.

"If you're going to sit in silence," Angel huffed, "this is going to be a very dull meal."

"What made you want to be a criminal?"

Angel poked his tongue into his cheek and laughed. "The thing about criminals, *Father*, is it's not a choice."

"Neither was mine." Francis cast his gaze outside again but caught how Angel's smile fell away, as though cut off at the stem. "You compared priests to criminals, earlier. You implied I was naïve if I didn't see how they were similar. What did you mean?" Francis asked.

Angel picked up his glass of wine and his sharp-eyed gaze danced over the cutlery, the wine glasses, the fine embossed flowers on the tablecloth, but stayed far from Francis. "I can see you're going to be a real pain in my ass."

"Then, maybe," he whispered with venom, "let me go?"

"Ah!" Angel sat back and clapped his hands together as multiple dishes of food arrived. The staff laid the food out, full of smiles and head-bowing and nervous sideways glances. "Father, won't you say a prayer before we eat?"

Francis placed his hands together, breathed out, and closed his eyes. "Merciful God, to whom the secrets of the heart lie open, who recognizes the just and makes righteous the guilty, hear our prayers for our brothers and sisters who know not the crimes they commit, grant that through patience and hope they may find relief in their guilt, and soon atone unhindered for their sins."

When he opened his eyes, Angel peered through narrowed lashes.

"Do you pray for me, Father?"

"Yes."

"I feel holier already. Let's eat."

He considered not eating out of principle, but his stomach grumbled and the food smelled delicious. He hadn't eaten in so long, he couldn't even remember what had been his last meal. Probably some toast, as he'd rushed out of the door and up the street to church, in a world and a dream far away from this one.

"It's good food, some of the best, and I'm starved," Angel was saying, scooping more delicious seafood, pasta, and sauce onto his fork.

"I see that."

Francis chuckled, ate, drank wine, and despite wanting to hate everything about every second, the sun shone through the open-fronted restaurant, people chattered around them, the food was some of the finest Francis had ever eaten, and there were far worse places to be, in more dire circumstances. Angel had said he'd bought Francis more time, so that was a good thing. But more time for what?

"Tell me, Father Scott, why a priest? I mean... we're the same age, you're smart, attractive, you could be anything."

Francis looked up with a fork full of pasta poised near his lips. Angel thought he was attractive? The pasta unraveled from his fork and schlepped into the bowl, splashing Francis's shirt. Angel snickered, in a wholesome, strangely endearing way, and Francis caught himself admiring that half-snorting laugh. When it wasn't full of derision, that laughter held a warmth he hadn't thought a man like Angel capable of. He had a heart under all the threats, snarling, and shallow smiles.

"I had it decided for me," Francis admitted. "But it worked out well, as it's my calling, my fate."

"'Fate', huh. Sounds very final. So you didn't have a choice?"

"I could have left during studies, but I chose to stay. I want to help people, guide them, be there for them, when they need God."

"What about you?" Angel pointed the dessert fork.

"What do *you* need?" He cut into some delicious raspberry dessert cream/tart thing, that had a very saucy-sounding Italian name, and it was good he focused on that, because the question rocked Francis, knocking all possible answers from his head.

"My uh, my needs are irrelevant. My every moment, my every day, is in service to God."

Angel scooped up the raspberry dessert, opened his mouth, and slid it between his lips. He sealed his lips around the fork, withdrew the fork, and licked gleaming sauce from his top lip. Then laughed and used his thumb to wipe away the rest. He licked that off too—put his thumb in his mouth and licked.

Francis picked up his wine. Then put it down again. Goodness, it was hot. Was it hot? "I think uh... some water?"

Angel clicked his fingers, rattled off some Italian, and the staff buzzed like bees, hurrying off to do his bidding. Not because he was a nice person, but because they were scared of him.

The waitress arrived. Her hand trembled as she poured water from a large pitcher, sloshing it over the sides of the glass. She said something in Italian, which caught Angel's eye and earned her his long stare as she left the table.

"Un momento," Angel said. He got up and left the table, then caused some kind of furor at the back of the restaurant.

This was madness. Francis drank the water, wishing he'd never asked for it. Hopefully he hadn't gotten the waitress into some kind of trouble.

Angel returned, carving through the restaurant like a shark on the scent of blood. He grabbed his shades and put them on. "We're leaving."

"What happened?"

"Nothing."

"What did she say?"

"Nothing you need to worry about."

But Francis was worried. Angel grabbed Francis by the wrist and pulled him along. He tried to search for the woman among the staff, but they stared after him, their faces fearful. Had Angel done something to the poor woman? What if he'd hurt her because Francis had wanted a glass of water?

He pulled Francis outside, into glaring sunlight, and almost dragged him down several steps. Francis snatched his arm back. "Stop!"

Angel whirled. "Do not bark orders at me. We need to go."

"Did you hurt her?"

He curled his lip. "What if I did?"

Francis had forgotten, just for a little while, the man he'd enjoyed a fine meal with was in fact an unashamed killer. And that was Francis's fault—he'd let the food and the atmosphere distract him. "Then I will pray for you."

"Pray for me? Jesus Christ." Angel laughed, then seemed to realize they'd drawn the attention of several people seated nearby, drinking their cocktails by the water. His laughter died, and all the warm humor on his face turned to ice. "Will you stop with the righteous bullshit? C'mon, we need to move before we're seen."

Francis *wanted* to be seen. He wanted to stand still and shout so everyone saw him. He planted his shoes on the ground and grabbed the rail leading up the steps into the restaurant. Angel shot him a look of pure rage and grabbed his wrists again.

"No."

Angel pulled.

"No." He wasn't going. Angel couldn't kill him here, in front of a dozen witnesses.

"Chi cazzo credi di essere?" Angel snarled, then added vehemently, "Vaffanculo!"

Francis had no idea what any of that meant, but by some nearby gasps, he assumed it wasn't good. Then Angel pushed in, chest to chest, and pinned Francis against the rail. "That woman knew who you were. She said help was coming, but don't get excited Father, she was fucking DeSica, in my goddamned favorite restaurant. Trust me, you do not want the help she is offering."

"Trust you? I'm not trusting you. I will never trust you. You're a vicious, lying, unrepentant killer. Let me go!"

Angel's glare darted around behind his glasses. He let go, then flung up his hands and backed off. "Have it your way."

The restaurant staff had gathered at the door to watch, still without their female colleague.

"Call the police," Francis said, then yelled. "Polizi!" He knew that one. "Polizi!"

Angel spat in the dirt, turned on his heel, and marched away. In seconds, he vanished, swallowed by the crowd.

Relief lifted like a thousand-pound weight removed from his soul. Francis crumpled on the steps and covered his mouth to keep from sobbing. Someone touched his shoulder. He flinched, and said, "Will you please help me?"

The woman nodded.

Good.

It was almost over.

He just had to wait, the police would come, and everything would be fine. "Praise God." He rocked. "Praise God, praise God, praise God."

He was going home.

CHAPTER SIX

VITARI

This was for the best. He should never have gotten tangled up in the priest anyway.

Giancarlo had told him to bring Francis home. He'd be pissed now Vitari was about to return empty-handed. Luca would probably be sent to finish the job, and Vitari would get a beating. Maybe lose a finger. Shit. No, that wouldn't happen. Giancarlo loved him.

Vitari walked down the pontoon toward the gleaming yacht. He gripped the smooth chrome rail and took a single step onto the boat. A grubby boot mark dirtied up the glossy black step. A print that pointed into the yacht, not outward.

Someone was aboard.

He took the knife from his pocket and eased up the steps, then crossed the deck and made his way below. Water lapped against the side of the yacht, but otherwise, it was silent on board. Nothing appeared to have been disturbed, but his senses tingled, hairs lifting on the back of his neck. This was bad. Someone had been here.

He backed up, and without checking the rest of the yacht, hurried off.

The yacht was compromised.

Someone in Puerto Banus was searching for them, which meant Francis was in danger. Since the DeSica already knew he was here, they'd track him down, torture him, and it would make what happened at St. Mary's look like fuckin' communion, or whatever priests did for fun.

Why had the fool dug his heels in at the restaurant? Why did it have to be so fucking difficult—

A plunge of heat scorched his back, as though someone had thrown boiling water over him. A sudden blast sent him sprawling. He skidded face down on timber slats and buried his head under his hands. The roar washed over him in one breathless wave, then withdrew just as fast.

Ears ringing, he twisted over and stared at the flaming wreckage where *Dolce Vita* had been moments before.

Metal and burning timbers rained all around, splashing into the water and hammering other boats.

Vitari's heart lodged in his throat. Jesus, that had been close. The DeSica were going to fuckin' pay!

He stumbled to his feet, winced around a few sharp pains in his shoulder, and limped along the pontoon. Screams peppered the sound of crackling flames, and distant sirens. The police would arrive soon, but in the chaos, Vitari had to find Francis. He couldn't have gotten far. Vitari had only been gone a few minutes.

He fought against the surging, terrified crowd, toward the restaurant.

Francis wasn't outside where Vitari had left him. He

climbed the steps and asked the panicked staff if they'd seen the man he was with. Nobody had. Vitari cursed them all.

The DeSica woman would know.

He limped into the kitchens. "Open it," he barked at one of the assistants, nodding toward the huge freezer. The kid hurried over, opened the freezer, and Vitari glared at the shivering woman inside.

"Where are they taking him?" he asked in Italian, but from her wide eyes and the shake of her head, she was more scared of her employers than she was of him. That was her mistake. "I'm going to give you one chance to help me, and then I start breaking bones. You know me, huh? L'Angelo della Morte? You've heard of me?" He stopped close in front of her, and from the widening of her eyes and the muttering of a prayer, he figured she did know of him. "You know why they call me that, right?"

"P-please," she begged, trembling. "I have children. I d-do what they say or they will hurt my babies. Please don't hurt me."

"Just tell me where they are, and nobody needs to know the information came from you."

She blinked and a single tear clung to the ice crystals on her cheek.

"You're praying? The man I'm trying to protect is a man of God. A priest. If you don't want to help me, then help him."

"The priest, yes. He's on the n-news. That's how I knew it was him."

Francis was on the news? Well, that made things more difficult. But one problem at a time. "Last chance. Where is the priest?"

$$———$$

CHAPTER SEVEN

The sight of the Spanish police arriving in their all-black garb with *Policía* printed on the front should have been reassuring, but the two men were built like bodyguards, and there was nothing reassuring in the way they hauled Francis to his feet. Or the guns holstered at their hips.

"English?" he asked. "Do you speak English? I was kidnapped."

"Si, si," one of them said, attempting to placate him. Their gazes didn't meet his eyes. They said something else, something about a car; Francis knew that much. They'd take him back to their police station, he supposed.

"Come... with us," the smallest of the two men said in broken English. Although small was relative. His thighs were as wide as Francis's waist.

They steered him away from the waterfront, between two more bars, and took a right onto a one-way street where their marked police car waited. One of the men's radios blipped, as though someone were trying to reach him. A distant voice said something, and the man answered with one short, sharp word into the receiver.

They'd passed into the shade of the building now, and while traffic flowed back and forth at the far end of the street, and the bars still bustled near the waterfront, this part of the back street was empty. Nobody was around.

Francis chewed on the inside of his bottom lip. This didn't feel right.

An explosion thundered overhead. Francis staggered against the police car and stared back the way they'd come. A plume of thick black smoke rolled into the blue sky above the rooftops.

That explosion had to be something to do with Angel, didn't it? Which meant it was to do with Francis too. What if Angel had been near that explosion? What if he'd been caught in it?

Perhaps that was a good thing. God punishing those who deserved it. But Francis didn't want more deaths. He hadn't wanted any of the deaths. "Do you need to go there, see if anyone is hurt?" Francis asked the police.

They hadn't flinched, and looked at him as though nothing had happened.

They'd known it was coming.

Hadn't Angel said his people owned the police? So then, perhaps, the DeSica owned some too? Angel had warned him...

Francis swallowed. The larger of the two officers lowered his right arm, toward his gun.

Francis bolted, and free of the robe, he ran like the wind, ran so fast there was no chance of them catching him. A gunshot rang out. Francis ducked, heart in his ears, beating in his lungs, and everywhere. Adrenaline throbbed through him. He ducked left, between two apartment buildings, then right. Another shot rang out. Why were they shooting? He had to get somewhere public, maybe back by the water. Not even the police would shoot him out in the open. He vaulted a low rope slung between two golden poles and collided with a set of bistro tables and chairs, but it didn't matter, because everyone else was running too.

The yacht. *Dolce Vita* was in pieces, smoke rising from what remained of its hull.

Had Angel been aboard? Francis's heart missed a beat. He glanced behind him. The police were bearing down, guns out, pointed down. He'd lose them in the crowd. He pushed through the fleeing people, half mad with panic, and as he glanced behind him again, the police were still coming, closer now.

He spotted the restaurant where he'd clung to the rail. And there, by some Heaven-sent miracle, was Angel, limping his way down the steps. His hair was a mess, his clothes dusty. He looked over, and his eyes blew wide, then skipped past Francis to the police behind him. Angel's expression fell, losing all emotion, and he ducked back inside the restaurant.

Francis ran up the steps, burst through the door, and fell against the counter, panting, wheezing, burning up. "The—police—they're—"

The first of the police pushed through the door into the restaurant, his murderous glare fixed on Francis. He didn't see Angel to his left, waiting to ambush him.

"Please, don't shoot!" Francis thrust out his hands.

Angel grabbed the man's gun, ripping it from his hand, jammed it under the man's chin, and pulled the trigger.

It was horrific—the blood, the noise, how the man jerked and fell, dead before he'd hit the ground, where he lay, twitching. Shock muted Francis's thoughts. The second policeman plowed through the door and swung his gun toward Angel—too slowly.

Angel aimed, fired, and just like that, in the space of a few seconds, another human being was dead, discarded as though his life were nothing. Gone, with a boom of the gun.

Angel hadn't even blinked.

"Oh..." Francis clung to the counter. It was so... horrible.

Angel barked in Italian at the staff, grabbed Francis's arm, and ushered him through the restaurant, through the kitchens, and out via a back door, into the street behind the restaurant, away from the chaos. The heat beat down on him, and the choking smell of blood—he could still see it, still taste it. Every time his lungs expanded, his throat squeezed closed. His body convulsed around fear and horror.

"Keep yourself together, Father," Angel said, voice flat.

He couldn't do this. No, he couldn't. Those men, Angel had... And they were dead, because of Francis. Angel had shot them. They'd come apart. He'd seen bits of them paint the windows.

He couldn't breathe. The air wouldn't come. His throat closed. His lungs burned.

"Hey." Angel clasped Francis's face in both hands and held him still, so all Francis saw was his eyes and how they narrowed, how they pierced Francis's soul and found it already full of holes.

"I can't, I can't..."

"Yes, you can. I've got you. We need to keep moving. Do you understand? Find God or whatever you need to get through this, but we have to keep moving."

Francis breathed in through his nose, then out, then in.

He clutched Angel's arms, grounding himself. Angel had killed them, but they'd tried to kill Francis, hadn't they? They'd shot at him. Why? "Why?" he wheezed. "I don't... They tried to..."

"Are you all right? Yes? Say yes, Francis, so I know you're in there." Angel's eyes finally warmed, turning human again.

"Yes." His breathing slowed, his heart too, so its thumping no longer filled his ears. "Yes, I'm all right."

"Good. C'mon, I have a garage not far from here. If it's not being watched, we'll be on the road soon. Fall apart later."

They hurried down the street, took a confusing number of turns, and came upon a garage door in the side of an old shop. It wasn't being watched, and without really knowing how, or why, Francis climbed into a car with Angel again, and they drove far out of the town, where the roads were lined with golden grasses and the sky was a washed-out blue.

He stared at the passing scenery and the aquamarine sea, when it came into sight. He couldn't think, because that opened the door to a cascade of feelings and pain and things he couldn't carry, not with everything else in his head. So he watched the sea roll by until the sun began to set, until Angel pulled the car off the road, onto a dirt track.

Dust plumed the air behind them, erasing their tracks.

They arrived at a villa with arches and a pool and no nearby buildings, just a house and the sea and the sky, with nothing between them and the rest of the world.

Francis stared at the white-washed house. He was just... numb. Inside and out.

Angel left the car, and with a phone to his ear, he kicked over a nearby plant pot, uncovered some keys, and unlocked the gate. Francis blinked at the house, the gate, the sky. And stayed in the car. He just... couldn't do anymore. He didn't want to get out. Not yet. Later. He would sit, and wait, and listen to his heart. And he'd pray for those poor men.

Angel glanced over but said nothing. He walked down the path that ran the side of the villa while unleashing a slew of angry-sounding Italian into the phone, then vanished out of sight.

Angel's voice faded, and now there was nothing. Just the sound of crickets and the *swish* of the distant ocean.

And Francis's sobs.

CHAPTER EIGHT

Vitari

He flung the phone down onto the table and marched to the back of the villa, tearing off his shirt. Sal was as pissed as him, especially about the yacht. They'd all liked that perk. Now it was gone. What Sal didn't say was how the DeSica fuckers were going to feel the pain of that misstep. Nobody came after Vitari unless they wanted to lose their goddamn lives, their children's lives, the lives of their fucking pets. Don Giancarlo would see it done. The Battaglia did not suffer disrespect. An attack on one was an attack on all.

Vitari stopped at the bathroom mirror, twisted at the waist, and winced at the bloody scratches on his back. The cuts were minor. They just needed to be cleaned out. His leg was the bigger problem; it had been burning since he'd walked away from the smoking yacht.

He stripped and tried to get a look at the back of his thigh. A throbbing suggested something wedged in there, probably a piece of wood from the explosion. He'd have to get Francis to pick it out. Francis had taken a vow to help people, even people like Vitari. He'd do it. Just not yet. Best to leave him in the car, his face as pale as death. Vitari had never seen a living man turn so white.

He'd get over it.

Vitari showered, threw on a fresh shirt, and wrapped a towel around his waist, then ventured out into the open plan lounge/kitchen area.

Francis sat on the couch, leaning forward, head bowed in his hands. At least he hadn't run.

"You good?" Vitari asked.

"I threw up by the car."

"It's normal." Vitari shrugged, hoping to ease the man's trauma. "You get used to it."

"Get used to it?"

Vitari had been reaching for a glass in one of the high kitchen cupboards but the vehemence in Francis's words had him expecting a knife in his back. He lowered his hand and glanced over his shoulder.

The fury on Francis's face was raw and visceral. He hadn't known Francis would be capable of such loathing, but it was right there. He fucking loathed Vitari.

It would have been unusual if he didn't. Perhaps now wasn't a good time to ask him to fix the wound in his leg. It wasn't so bad anyway, just a scratch. "I need to get supplies. Stay here. If you leave the villa, you'll only get lost, and there's one road. I'll see you on it."

"Fine." Francis sneered.

Vitari returned to the bedroom, pulled on a clean pair of trousers, grabbed the car keys, and left the villa. Francis wasn't going anywhere. He was in shock. He'd be all right.

The nearby town had one convenience store. Vitari tossed the basics into a basket, grabbed some medical supplies, and queued behind an old woman at the counter.

A familiar face smiled out at him from the front pages of the newspaper rack. In Spanish, the headline read: 'Young Priest Missing.' They'd used a photo of Father Francis Scott in his vestments, his bright face laughing as he shook someone's hand.

Vitari picked up a paper. These rural parts of Spain were devout Catholic. It was no surprise they'd be interested in a missing priest, especially one as photogenic as Francis. Vitari paid for the supplies, and after returning to the car, he read the article.

Two further bodies had been discovered in St. Mary's, in addition to the Jane Doe. The two dead men, known criminals, had links to London gangs, but there was no mention of the DeSica by name. A brief biography of Father Francis Scott's life, all twenty-four years of it, took up the rest of the two-page spread. There was mention of his being adopted and how he'd gone on to serve God. The way it had been written, it seemed Father Scott was the poster boy for Roman Catholic priests everywhere. Even an archbishop commented on how devastating it was that their beloved Francis had been taken. There was no question of his having left or run away. He'd without-any-doubt been taken, and the perpetrators would be brought to justice, in the eyes of the law and God.

Francis had the perfect life. But nobody was that saintly. Not even Francis. Stanmore Boys' Home didn't churn out real angels, just broken ones like Vitari.

He returned to the villa and found Francis on the couch where he'd left him. He was having a hard time getting over events at the marina.

"You're famous." Vitari dropped the newspaper onto the cushion bedside him.

He blinked out of his dream and down at his smiling photo. There was very little chance of anyone recognizing this Francis as the missing priest in his black robes. Out of his robes, his appearance was very different, and now that his hair was all mussed and his face bruised, he was another man.

"You even have an archbishop worried."

Francis gazed through the article as though he didn't see it, then picked it up and began to read.

Vitari busied himself unpacking the supplies, occasionally checking Francis was still there. He was so damn quiet, but quiet was bad—quiet meant he was inside his own head —and while they were as different as chalk and cheese, Vitari knew too much time lost in thought made everything much worse.

"You want some breakfast, or lunch, whatever the fucking time is?"

Francis lifted his gaze and those soft brown eyes of his were crying out for help. Vitari only knew two ways of forgetting. One, get blind-drunk. Or two, fuck like there was no tomorrow. Francis didn't seem the type to stoop to either option. Breaking his celibacy vows would likely make him feel worse, on top of everything else.

Although, Vitari would absolutely top him.

All that righteous, pent-up fury, and from the glimpses Vitari had seen, it seemed as though he had a fine body beneath those clothes.

Fuck, what kind of religion stopped a handsome piece of ass like him from getting his rocks off? The Catholic kind. It was all about sacrifice and devotion through pain, yaddah yaddah. Vitari had never put much stock in God, seeing as no true God would ever let kids live the life he'd had.

"Why don't you take a shower, I'll make breakfast—"

"What are we doing here?" Francis asked.

"There's an airstrip a few miles east. A plane will land in a few days. We just have to sit tight, and we're out of Spain."

"Going where?"

"Italy."

His eyes widened, and his jaw dropped. "I can't go to Italy."

"I hate to break it to you, Father, but you don't have a choice." Vitari downed his beer, then grabbed the eggs. He'd make an omelet. Food was a great comfort. Once Francis was fed and showered, he'd relax. If he didn't, this was going to be a long few days.

Francis poked his omelet around his plate, then mumbled about taking a shower. Vitari left him alone to deal with his trauma, and after ditching their food in the trash, he carried an ice bucket and beers outside to the chairs beside the pool.

When Francis didn't emerge after an hour, Vitari checked inside and found him wrapped in a towel, face down on the bed, passed out from exhaustion.

Vitari folded his arms, leaned against the doorjamb, and watched him sleep. The muffled sounds of his light snoring tugged on Vitari's smile. Francis's smooth back and shoulders were as pale as Vitari had imagined, but his body was leaner than he'd expected, with a slim dip at his waist and a firm, peachy ass, hugged by the towel. Father Scott was criminally cute—a sentence he'd never believed he'd say about a priest.

Francis could have been on that boat when it had been destroyed. If he hadn't left the yacht to make his ill-advised call to the cops, the DeSica would have found him, slit his throat, then blown the boat, destroying the evidence. If Vitari hadn't run by the restaurant, the Policia would have shot Francis and dumped his body out at sea, never to be found.

That doe-eyed smalltown priest wasn't made for shit like this. He wasn't going to survive. It was a fucking miracle he'd lived this long.

And that was a problem.

Vitari backed away from the room, scooped up his phone, and with the sun setting over the ocean, he stepped from the villa, sliding the glass doors closed behind him. He dialed Salvatore.

"Angel, you at the safehouse?" Sal asked. Club music thumped in the background, along with indecipherable chatter.

"Yeah, we're good. Listen, I need you to do something and keep it quiet, all right?"

"Sure, frá. What is it?"

"This priest, find out more about him? Anything in his past that would make him a target for DeSica? There has to be a reason they're all over him."

"Can't you ask him?"

"He doesn't know."

"Ask him *harder*."

"He doesn't know, for real, Sal. He's like a lost Labrador in all this. It's fuckin' tragic."

"All right, fine. Anywhere I should start?"

If he asked Sal to look into the boys' home, he might uncover the fact Vitari had grown up there. Although, as far as he knew, there were no real records for the group of kids he'd been among, just unmarked graves in the local churchyard. Only Giancarlo knew the truth about Vitari's origins. As far as most people were concerned, Vitari was half Italian, one of a string of bastard sons Giancarlo denied existed. An open secret. "Yeah, the DeSica asked where he was born. Find that out, eh? It's important."

"Doesn't the bastard know?"

Vitari glanced back through the closed doors, checking Francis was still out of earshot. "He was adopted. Spent some time at a children's home in Essex. Just... do some digging. Oh, and hey, that girl the priest found in his graveyard, find out who she was. There's too much about all this that doesn't add up. I don't like knowing less than the DeSica."

"You're just jumpy, fratello."

"Maybe."

Someone—a woman—tried to ask Sal if he wanted another drink. Typical. He always had a lover on the go. "You got this?" Vitari asked.

"Yeah, give me a few days."

"And Sal, hey, uh... don't tell Giancarlo, okay? This is between you and me." He didn't want Giancarlo thinking he was going behind his back or undermining him in any way. That was how bullshit rumors started.

Sal's disgruntled huff sounded down the line. "Certo. You owe me one."

Vitari snorted and hung up. He'd covered for Salvatore

a hundred times, usually when he fucked the wife of some prominent politician.

He sat back down at the poolside table, but the call and all the unanswered questions had left him restless. There was more to all this, and it loomed large, as though he was tangled in it too. He eyed the pool's inviting water and began to unbutton his shirt.

CHAPTER NINE

Francis was going to have to hurt Angel. Not kill him—murder was out of the question—but he could knock him unconscious, steal the car, and drive until it ran out of fuel.

He'd never hit someone before. He'd gotten into a fight once, at the boys' home, when he was eight. But that had been the other boy's fault. Francis had mostly been in the way.

What else was he supposed to do? If Angel took him to Italy, he'd likely be killed there. His body would never be found. He didn't know much about the Mafia, but he was pretty sure they didn't fly strangers into their home, have them see all their faces, and let them go scot-free after.

So, attacking Angel was the only way he could survive.

Crickets chirped outside the villa windows and the night was hauntingly quiet. Hopefully, Angel was asleep, and all Francis had to do was find something heavy enough that it would do most of the work when he swung it.

After buttoning up his shirt and trousers, he snuck through the villa, searching for a vase or knife block he could pick up and wield, but as he entered the lounge, the light from the outside pool illuminated Angel about to dive off the pool's edge, into the water. Angel raised his arms, bent his knees, and dove like an arrow beneath the surface.

Francis froze.

At least Angel had worn shorts. Although he might as well have tossed them too, for all the covering up they'd done. They'd clung to his firm ass as though painted on.

Francis looked away and reached for the kitchen counter, but the image of a near naked Angel, illuminated by shimmering light, scorched his mind. Angel had a body defined with muscle, like a sportsman: lean, sharp, masculine, and brutally beautiful. His back had been a work of art, and as he'd raised his arms, light had licked over his muscles, pooling in every curve.

Francis closed his eyes.

It had been a long time since he'd seen a naked man with his own eyes, not a picture. He avoided all images, had set up his laptop to block all adult content, so he wasn't tempted to go searching during any of his low points—and there had been many. He'd been doing well, but now God had placed temptation in his path and lit him up like a stage show.

Was this a test?

If it was, he was already failing.

He should leave, go back to bed, and wait there until Angel retired for the night. But even as he knew leaving was absolutely the correct course of action, he lifted his gaze and watched Angel swim the length of the pool, dive underwater, and swim back again. Lust was a sin. Sex was a sin, if its sole purpose was pleasure. The only time sex was considered Godly was between man and wife in the pursuit of a child. As two men didn't create life with their lustful pursuits, all homosexuality was also sin.

He'd been through this during his studies, confessed his frowned-upon urges and sought guidance from the Church, but rather than help, he feared the Catholic teachings may have complicated matters. Not least because of... his past. And the reason for the solicitor's letter sitting unopened on his desk in St. Mary's.

Angel spotted him through the glass doors. He braced against the edge of the pool, and those sultry eyes fixed on Francis. Men like Angel were aware of the power of their beauty. He knew he was desirable, and the way he peered through wet lashes at Francis now suggested he knew every filthy thought in Francis's head.

If ever there were a man made of sin, it was Angel.

He raised a hand and waved him over, and when Francis didn't move, he laughed, pushed from the edge of the pool, and swam a length, even with the small wound Francis had spotted on his thigh.

Francis couldn't hide from this. If he returned to his room, he'd only spend the time thinking about Angel, and alone in his bed, he'd be free to act out on the inevitable urges. Better to be out here, where he could wait for Angel to tire and go to bed, then bludgeon him and be done with this whole ordeal.

He slid open the doors and ventured onto the patio.

"Join me?" Angel asked.

Francis's heart pounded. "I don't swim."

"Is this like an *I don't drink* scenario?"

He sat at the table. Everything was going to be fine. He just had to get through this. "I *can't* swim."

"They don't teach swimming in priest school?"

Angel was mocking him again. Francis plucked a beer from the ice bucket and tried to crack it open on the side of the table, as he'd seen Angel do in the yacht. But the top remained stubbornly stuck. He tried again, with no luck. Then, to compound the horror, Angel emerged from the pool, walking up the steps like temptation personified. Water cascaded down his gorgeous body and dripped onto the patio. He strode closer, grabbed a beer from the bucket, popped the lid on the side of the table, and handed it over.

It was as though Adonis himself had just cracked open a beer for Francis. The tiny shorts did *nothing* to cover his manhood.

Heat flushed Francis's face. "Thank you," he mumbled.

"It's all in the wrist." Angel's right eyebrow twitched, pulling his smirk sideways at some innuendo Francis had missed. Francis took the drink and watched as Angel turned and dived into the pool.

Thankfully, the pool lights were so soft, Angel probably hadn't seen the flush in Francis's face. He could get through this. He just had to sit very still behind the table, drink a beer, and pretend all of this was normal. Angel wouldn't suspect anything, and later, he'd fall asleep, letting down his guard. Francis just had to not think about how the tight shorts had hugged the man's groin as he'd approached, or how they'd been glued to his buttocks when he'd turned around. How the water droplets had gleamed on his golden chest. Or how his whole body had moved like a symphony of muscle and masculinity.

Francis took a drink to try to moisten his dry mouth and slow his fluttering heart. There was no hiding the bulge in his trousers, but Angel couldn't see his lap from the pool. His erection would ease soon, once Francis got control of himself. *Lord, give me strength to resist temptation...*

"You don't swim, you don't drink, except in extenuating circumstances. What do you do for fun, Father?"

Angel propped his chin on his folded arms on the side of the pool. Without his watch on, the delicate tattoo stood out around his wrist. Definitely razor wire. It was the only deliberate mark on him, apart from a few scars and the fresh cut on the back of his thigh. Francis had always been fascinated by tattoos, and why people marked their skin for life. That razor wire must have a deep meaning.

"I uh... I don't know. I read, I suppose," he stammered. When would this ordeal end?

"Okay, what do you read? Thrillers, fantasy, crime... no, wait, *romance*?"

"Psalms."

Angel snorted. "Fuck off, you read more than that."

A smile pulled at Francis's lips. "I read some fantasy," he admitted.

"Yeah, what kind? Vampires and werewolves, that shit?"

He plucked the most well-known fantasy series he could think of from his memory. "*Game of Thrones*."

"Fuck that ending, man." Angel's eyes sparkled with humor.

"Not the TV series, the books. And the ending hasn't been written yet."

"That old guy's never going to finish writing it."

"Have you *read* the books?"

"No, I watched the series." He ran a hand through his hair, making the dark locks spike. "Don't tell me the books are better—that's what Sal says."

"They are." Francis smirked and took a swig of beer. "Who's Sal?"

"Just someone... I work with," he said, his humor fading. "A friend." Angel pushed from the edge of the pool and drifted on his back. Water lapped at his chest, his waist, between his thighs. Francis looked away and tried to swallow his racing heart. Was Angel deliberately flaunting himself? No, this was how men behaved altogether. It was normal to swim with almost nothing on in front of other men. It was only people with minds and desires like Francis's that twisted acceptable social behavior.

He'd tried not to like men. One of his mentors had said it was a choice, and he just had to choose not to. But it didn't work like that for Francis. He hadn't chosen anything. Life carried him along, and most of the time, he tried to stay afloat while drowning.

"You have other friends?" Francis asked, when the quiet had gone on for too long.

"I have family," Angel replied.

"What about... girls?" Francis asked, and hoped it didn't sound as awkward as it had in his head. More heat flushed his face. Which was ridiculous. It was a simple, innocent question.

"Girls?"

"Women. Lovers. Companions. A Mrs. Angel?" Francis gulped more beer. The taste was bitter, but he needed something to do with his hands, to keep his mind off Angel's body.

Angel's grin lit up his face, full of teeth, and his eyes sparkled with mischief that seemed to indicate he'd smelled blood and was about to bite down on whatever juicy victim he'd singled out. "You think someone like me does relationships, Father?"

"I just—"

"You think I'm going to settle down behind a white picket fence and spawn a few kids?" He snorted and swam to the main steps, then climbed out.

Angel was every lustful dream, every fantasy, every forbidden desire Francis had ever had coming toward him, glistening wet, smiling as though he owned the world, with eyes that could melt glaciers.

"I mean, I just, I assume..." He picked at the beer label. "I just thought, it's, you, you're..." he mumbled, not having a clue what he was saying. Lust tightened his breath and pooled heat in his groin low, filling his dick all over again, but harder. So hard, it hurt.

He shifted in the chair, trying to ease the pressure, then pried some of the tight fabric away, but the act of touching himself poured another surge of needful heat down his spine.

Angel flopped, wet and slippery, into the opposite chair and grabbed the last beer, splashing water on the table. "No woman with half a brain is going to want me. I mean, they're good for a fuck, but what's the point in anything else, yah know?"

Francis almost asked why he thought nobody would want him, when he was obviously attractive. But Angel's reply hadn't been anything to do with attraction, it was about who he was *inside*. Francis *knew* that. He also knew the kind of man Angel was. Angel was right, no woman should want him. Or man, for that matter. Francis's physical reaction wasn't about love, or devotion, or any kind of relationship. His body thought it needed the pleasure and desire Angel could give him. Francis was still a man, even in service to God. Resisting temptation wasn't supposed to be *easy*. The journey, the plight, the struggle was meant to hurt. That was the point.

And right now, it was throbbing.

Angel said something, but Francis barely heard him

behind his mental efforts to stop himself from combusting on the spot. "Sorry, what did you say?"

"What about you? I mean, I know you're supposed to be all about loving God and all that, but c'mon, you still get yourself off, right?" He made a pumping gesture with his right hand and smirked.

Francis's heart stopped. "No," he lied, remembering the night they'd met, when he hadn't been able to banish the vision of Angel kneeling at the altar, and how it had morphed into him kneeling in front of Francis, his eyes pools of dark desire as he'd slipped Francis's dick between his lips and sucked him down.

"Right," Angel drawled. "What, your dick's so holy it never gets hard?"

Lust, desire, fear, confusion, and anger all spun in his head—in his heart—tangled in a mass of emotion. He knew he was breathing too hard, and soon Angel would notice, but how could he stop himself *wanting* the terrible man in the chair opposite?

He stood and hurried from the patio, might have run, but it was dark, and Angel wouldn't see how hard he was. He didn't owe him any kind of explanation. His personal battles were nothing to do with Angel; they were private.

Lord God, make this night end.

Now, he just had to find something hard enough to bash over Angel's head. That would solve the problem of desiring a man he could never, ever have.

CHAPTER TEN

Father Francis Scott was clearly going through some things.

Vitari finished his beer alone by the pool and ran through the conversation again, in his mind. They'd been getting along fine, he'd thought, until Vitari had mentioned dicks. He probably should have known better, with the priest being celibate, but he'd never been able to resist poking at wounds. Naturally, Francis had some triggers.

Chuckling at the priest's reaction, he carried the ice bucket and empty bottles inside, dumped them into the sink, heard the shower running, and veered toward his own room. He brushed his teeth, towel dried his hair, and fell into bed wearing only briefs. Francis wasn't going anywhere, and Vitari hadn't slept much in the last two days. He'd catch a few hours, and tomorrow, maybe Sal would have some clues about the priest's past that would satisfy the horrible, unsettling squirm of dread in Vitari's insides.

He tossed and turned a while, too hot to sleep and too

wired to dream. He'd never been very good at sleeping. A few hours here and there were all his racing mind allowed him.

The bedroom door creaked open. Vitari kept his eyes closed. Soft footfalls whispered against the tiled floor, coming closer.

Vitari leveled his breathing, made it seem as though he were sleeping, curious to see what Francis was plotting. He didn't have it in him to—

He heard the *whoosh*, twisted, reached up, and grabbed Francis's wrist. The priest loomed, his face white with shock. He dropped the rock he'd been about to land in Vitari's skull, and it bounced on the bed next to Vitari's shoulder, then rolled to the floor with a heavy *clunk*. Vitari had to give credit where it was due; he hadn't expected that.

But now he had Francis by the wrist, and far from being the victim, Vitari had his prey right where he wanted him. Realization dawned on Francis's face, and his shock waned. He was going to try to justify his actions. His gaze skipped down but darted back to Vitari's face. The shock was back, widening his brown eyes. He hadn't yet tried to pull away.

If the priest wanted to play games, Vitari was willing. He yanked, unbalanced Francis, and as he toppled forward, Vitari twisted out from under him. Francis let out a startled cry, then froze on his back with Vitari poised over him, still holding his wrist.

He writhed some, then stopped wriggling and glared. His nostrils flared. "Get off me."

There was that delicious fire. "You attacked me, Father."

He writhed again, his hips brushing Vitari's knees. Vitari dropped his stance, trapping Francis against the mattress, and once more, Francis froze. He breathed as though he were furious, and his eyes burned with righteous priestly rage. Vitari should probably let him up. He had no intention of hurting him, but then there was the feel of Francis's tightly strung body sandwiched between Vitari's knees, and the firm beat of his pulse against Vitari's hand, and maybe, just maybe, somewhere in that perfectly innocent head, Francis *wanted* this.

The way his eyes had turned mean when he'd watched Vitari earlier in the pool, and how snide he'd become afterward... He got snappy when he was scared, or confused, like now.

What if Vitari tested him some, a little tease... that was all?

He lowered his head, mingling Francis's racing breaths with his slow ones. Francis's eyes widened, lashes fluttering, and his lips parted, just like they had in the yacht's galley kitchen when Vitari had swept his bangs from his eyes. Vitari wet his lips, nice and slow, and Francis's big brown eyes tracked the motion, drinking it in like a man parched. All right, this was... something, and it was fucking hot. Was Francis hard? Because Vitari was. Would he lose his mind if Vitari reached down and touched him? Did he want that? Vitari hesitated, but only because this anticipation felt good —the desire, the moment before boundaries were drawn and lines crossed. So far, they were just two men; nothing had happened, just a foolish attempt by Francis to knock him out.

"What do you want, Father?" Vitari whispered, almost sure he knew the answer. The words skimmed Francis's lips. He could turn his head; he could say no. Vitari wasn't stopping him from speaking his mind.

Vitari stroked his lips over Francis's, nudging a little, to see if he responded. Their breaths mingled, faster now.

Vitari's skin buzzed, and his dick hung low in his briefs, brushing hot fabric. He hadn't yet ground his cock against Francis, sensing that might be a step too far. But if the priest wasn't already hard, his blown pupils suggested he was well on his way to it. God, Vitari ached to touch him. He was right there, pinned down, trapped, belonging to Vitari. All he had to do was say the word and Vitari would give him a night he'd never forget. A night like no other. All the ways he could make Father Francis Scott pant and moan and beg for more.... Would he take it in the ass? Would he let him flip him over and fuck him hard into the mattress? The thought alone had Vitari's dick weeping.

"Get. Off. Me."

Vitari stroked the tip of his tongue over Francis's lower lip, and Francis's strangled moan might have been the sweetest damn sound Vitari had ever heard. That wasn't a moan of fear, or disgust—that moan was a sound borne of pure, desperate need.

Vitari dropped his hips, dug his cock against the hollow of Francis's hip, through his clothes, and fuck if he didn't feel the hard nudge of Francis's dick probe his groin. Now he had something, now he had proof Francis wasn't as sweet and innocent as he tried so hard to be. He was just a man too, full of weakness and desire, riddled with faults and fuckups. And Vitari wanted to lick every inch of his sinful body clean. Did he want to fuck? Would he suck his dick between those sweet lips? A sixty-nine?

Fuck, Vitari was getting too far ahead. Francis was petrified of Vitari, or scared of how they were both hard and what that meant.

Vitari might have more luck going gently, but it was going to kill him not to lose his fucking mind and tear all Francis's barriers down.

"Not so innocent, are you?" Vitari sucked Francis's lip between his, then nipped. Father Scott twitched. His breaths sawed hard through his nose, but it was his grinding hip action that had Vitari biting his own lip. Francis's dick rubbed Vitari's. Did he know?

When was the last time someone had touched him?

Vitari persuaded Francis's mouth open with his tongue —sucking, biting—but as Francis didn't seem all that interested in chasing a kiss, Vitari trailed his tongue down his jaw, swirling it under his ear. And with every breath, Francis shuddered or twitched or ground his dick harder against Vitari's. They weren't even doing anything, were barely touching, and it was the hottest damn petting Vitari had ever experienced.

He freed Francis's wrist, and Francis released a staccato sigh. That sigh was a surrender. He'd been fighting his own battle for a while. But while Vitari could suck on him all night, and it seemed Francis's hips had the right idea, the rest of him clearly wasn't in the game.

Vitari had freed his wrist, but he still hadn't moved. And when Vitari pushed up on his hands, Francis stared through him, through the ceiling and onward.

He could go down on him, but with only half of Francis in the room, it didn't feel right.

It was time to back off, even though it pained him, or pained his dick more. Still, he had his own hand to finish himself, and with the taste of Francis on his lips, and the priest filling his head, his hand would be more than enough.

Vitari sighed his own surrender, straightened onto his arms, and pushed away.

Francis's thin fingers clamped around his wrist, over the razor wire tattoo, and pulled Vitari down. His other hand claimed the back of Vitari's neck, and suddenly Francis's mouth scorched Vitari's. His tongue thrust, wild and lashing, and fuck—it was as though some switch had been flicked in Francis's mind. He'd come alive, and he was fucking ravenous.

Vitari clutched at his face, then his back, hauling him into his arms. Francis moved with him, rocking closer, seeking more. Vitari needed him naked, needed to feel him trembling under his hands, his mouth, needed to kiss his heart's beat.

He straightened, straddling Francis's hips, and made quick work of the shirt buttons. With his chest exposed, Vitari dropped and licked low, near the hollow of his hip bone. Francis's fingers thrust into his hair and twisted, directing him downward, toward his cock. Vitari needed no more encouragement. He opened the fly of Francis's trousers and mouthed the firm heat of his dick through his underwear. The sweet smell of his pre-cum destroyed any notion of going slowly.

Vitari yanked Francis's boxer shorts down, exposing the fine length of his dick, and sucked him into his mouth. Francis bucked, arching off the bed. He flung his hands either side of him and gripped the sheets, scrunching them in his fists. God, he was a vision, lost and found at once, giving himself to Vitari like a sacrifice, like Christ on the fucking cross. And Vitari took him, sucked him, stroked him, tongued his head and pumped. Vitari wanted him to come and wasn't going to stop until he had him wrecked.

Francis panted; his lithe body shivered and trembled.

Vitari licked him low, sucked on his balls, and worked his tongue up the dense shaft, finding Francis's intense stare on him every inch of the way. Goddamn he was hot, glaring at Vitari like that, as though he hated him, even while Vitari sucked him off.

Vitari grasped his own dick in his free hand and pumped. He needed it, needed the relief, and as he sucked and worked Francis between his lips, he chased his own high, alternating between lavishing attention on Francis's cock and his own. Pumping and licking, and fucking his fist, and sucking Francis's cock, harder, faster.

Then Francis threw his head back, his moans coming in waves now. Enough fucking around. Vitari squeezed his shaft in his fingers and pumped, wrapping his tongue around him at the same time, sucking hard. Francis tried to resist, but not even God was saving him from coming.

Salty cum hit the roof of Vitari's mouth. He swallowed, pulled off, and pumped the rest of Francis's release, watching creamy cum spurt from his cock. Francis shuddered and gasped, his orgasm riding him.

Mindless, Vitari grasped his own dick. It didn't take much, a few rapid stokes, and he came so fucking hard, spilling over Francis's trousers, his thigh. He liked seeing the cum on him, wanted to lick it off, but then he caught Francis's wrought expression coming down on them like a slamming door.

Francis leaped from the bed, stumbling over his own feet, and ran from the room.

Vitari stared at the open doorway, still fucking buzzing. What the fuck had he done that was so wrong? He rubbed at his chest, over his heart. Francis's guilt was his own problem. Vitari had no such qualms.

At least with Francis, everything they'd just done would be kept between them. There was no way Father Francis Scott would tell a single soul how he'd lost his load to Vitari.

He flopped onto his side and buried his face in the pillows, breathing Francis's lingering scent. It didn't matter anyway, it was just sex, something to pass the time while they waited for the pickup.

He rolled on his back and sighed, then licked his lips, tasting cum, and smiled. He closed his eyes, fucked and spent. Sleep carried him off in seconds.

———————

CHAPTER ELEVEN

———————

Francis

It didn't matter how long he stood under the shower's hot jets, his sin wasn't washing off. Guilt set in, like it always did. He should have been better, stronger. He wasn't worthy. He'd never be worthy. He was broken. He'd always been broken. He'd thought being a priest would fix him. That was what he'd been told. God would fix him; he just had to study hard, obey his superiors, and kneel in service to God and the Church.

But he wasn't fixed. He was the same as he'd always been.

He closed his eyes and saw Angel sucking his cock. He tasted him on his lips, could feel his fluttering kisses under his ear, down his neck. And he was hard again. His damned body was conspiring against him! Why couldn't he control himself?

This was punishment for doubting God, for doubting everything, and for giving up.

He'd let Angel have him. Francis had been under him, and he'd tried to say no, he really had, but Angel had been on him and naked and hard, and God, he'd been desperate and weak. He couldn't even claim Angel had overpowered him. Francis could have said no. At any time. Those dark eyes, they'd looked at him, begged him, taunted and tempted him. But they'd also asked permission. And Francis had said yes with his body.

He couldn't blame Angel for this. It was all on Francis.

He hardly slept, and when he heard Angel clattering around the kitchen, he squeezed his eyes closed and hoped the bed would swallow him. But he'd have to face the man whose cum stained his trousers, who'd had Francis's dick down his throat.

Maybe he wouldn't say anything. It would be just a thing that had happened. If neither of them mentioned it, then it didn't have to exist at all.

As Francis emerged from the bedroom, the ocean view beyond the windows had turned grey and angry, the sea a choppy dark blue. Angel was on the patio, talking on his phone. The wind tugged at his open shirt and swept through his hair, and glimpses of his perfect chest and abs sung to Francis like a siren song. Why did he have to be so *fucking gorgeous?*

Francis flicked on the coffee machine and listened to it gurgle. Focusing on that meant he didn't have to watch Angel strut back and forth, or admire how his low-slung pants clung to his narrow hips.

Francis should have hit him over the head with the rock.

He hadn't even been able to do that!

The glass sliding door hissed, and Angel returned. He didn't look smug. He wasn't smirking. No smile at all. "So, we know who the woman was," he said. "Does the name Victoria Chance mean anything to you?"

"No, I don't think so."

He winced. "No, I didn't think it would. She is—was—a prostitute, escort, whatever. Normally she's in London and serves a certain clientele. Politicians, celebrities, the like."

The poor woman, she'd likely had no choice in her life either. "Organized crime?"

"Yes. She's connected to the DeSica, the same people who are after you." He began to pace. His shoes clipped the tiles, like they had back in St. Mary's, when he'd knelt at the altar. Francis's sleep-addled brain unhelpfully provided the image of Angel going down on him. He turned his back on him and fussed with making coffee.

"But there's a reason she was there, and a reason they killed her in your graveyard."

"People come to church for all sorts of reasons, but most come for help." Francis glanced behind him and found Angel approaching.

He handed Angel the coffee. There didn't have to be any motive behind it. None of this needed to be weird, or uncomfortable. Just two men. Drinking coffee. "I don't know how many sugars you take, but as you're a long way from sweet, I gave you uh... two."

Angel frowned, took the cup, and smiled as he sipped. "Two is... fine."

This was... okay. It was normal-ish. They didn't have to mention last night. Better to focus on their situation than any mistakes they'd made. It hadn't meant anything; it was just a... trip along the path of life.

"The DeSica weren't in your town before me, but I suspect Victoria was," Angel continued. He leaned against the counter, relaxing. "I think she was coming to you for a specific reason, and they killed her for it. Now they've got a dead body and police, and they've shown their hand, so they had to make their move in questioning you. You're sure you didn't know her?"

"No." He recalled her face when he'd tried to turn her over in the grass. Now he knew the life she'd been embroiled in, he wished she'd made it through the church doors. He could have helped her. There was something about her though, some niggling little tic at the back of his mind. As though... maybe he did know her, but from where? "I suppose she may have been familiar, but I've no idea where from."

"She didn't have anything on her? No personal items?"

"I mean... not that I saw, but it's not as though I rummaged through her pockets—"

"A phone or purse might have told us more, like why she was coming to you, specifically."

Francis left Angel in the kitchen area and sat on the edge of the couch, preferring to have distance between them so he could think without all that *distraction*. "What about Stanmore? Could it have anything to do with this?"

"No," Angel said, then paced again.

"They asked where I was born, as though that was important."

"They were only trying to make sure you're the right priest, the one they'd had orders to question and kill. It's nothing. But they *really* want to get their hands on you. So you either know something that they don't want revealed, or you *are* something they don't want out there. But you don't have any ties to the mob, right?"

"No." Francis sipped again. "I mean, right."

"Either you do or you don't."

"No, I don't. I said I don't. I'm just a priest."

"It's pretty fucking important. There's nothing, you're sure? You didn't, I don't know, take a confession from a mob boss?"

Why did he feel as though he was on trial? "Only you," he muttered.

Angel stopped pacing and cocked his head. "I didn't confess to you."

"You were about to."

What sin brought you here?

You did.

"No, I... wasn't," Angel scoffed. "I don't need some higher power to forgive me. You get that, right? You and me, we're not the same. I do what I do because I like it. I don't know why the fuck you do what you do because it seems to make you fucking miserable every day of your life."

Angel knew *nothing* about him. And he was wrong. Francis wasn't miserable. "That's not true."

"Isn't it? You forget, Father, I watched you for a week. And that was all it took to know you hated putting on that robe. You said yes to everyone when you wanted to tell them all to fuck off. You were done. That night I prayed at the altar, you know what I prayed? I prayed for you, because your life looked like Hell."

Francis's heart rattled his ribs. How had Angel known, how had he seen... the truth? "You don't know anything about me. You're a thug, you don't even have a soul worth saving—" Francis cut himself off suddenly, ashamed and distraught he'd even said such things. He stood and wanted to take the words back somehow. "I didn't mean—"

Angel gave one of his careless laughs and croaked, "The

difference is, I know my soul is shot. What happened to you, huh, to ruin yours?"

"Nothing." With nowhere to go, Francis sat back down and hugged his coffee. *Everything.*

"Don't worry, this will all be over soon. I'll shoot you myself to put us all out of your misery."

"What?"

"A figure of speech." His smile was back. The flimsy look-at-me one. Full of lies. "I'm not going to shoot you."

Did Angel think this was a joke? He had kidnapped Francis, brought him here, done terrible things to him. Francis slammed his coffee down, sloshing it over his fingers and the table. "I should have hit you with that rock!"

"Then I wouldn't have blown you." Angel lunged, shoved Francis in the chest, forcing him into the couch cushions, and braced over him, his face inches away. "Is that cum on your trousers, Father?"

Francis bared his teeth in a sneer. "You took advantage of me."

"You're right, I took advantage of your cock down my throat."

Francis swung an open-handed slap and landed it hard across Angel's face. Francis gasped, and in the moment between one second and the next, Francis's heart stopped. His palm burned. He'd hit him *hard*. Angel slowly leveled his gaze, then licked the corner of his lip. Blood glistened on his tongue.

"Oh Father, you shouldn't have."

He lunged. His mouth slammed against Francis's. His tongue thrust in. Francis gasped, tried to pull away, turned his head, but then Angel's mouth was skimming his jawline, his little teeth nipping, and a cascade of treacherous shivers trickled down Francis's spine, gathering in his cock. He didn't want this. He screamed but no sound came, because the larger, rabid, more desperate desire overrode that tiny voice of denial.

He needed this; he needed it so much he was going to crawl out of his own skin to get it. He wanted Angel on him, in him, wanted to be fucked and bitten, and he wanted Angel on his knees again, looking up at Francis, begging him, as Francis buried his cock between his lips over and over. He wanted to fuck Angel's smiling mouth, to fuck like an animal.

He clutched at Angel's open shirt, tried to push him off, but yanked him close. "Oh God." And he kissed Angel, smashed his lips, fucked with his tongue. They rocked—mad, rough, shoving, grabbing. He was scared too, scared of this and its insanity, and scared of Angel and these strange feelings he had for a vicious, murdering, sinful man.

Angel tore free, straddled Francis's thighs, and whispered in his ear, "I'm going to fuckin' ruin you, Father."

The gasp that fluttered out of Francis was the kind of breathless animal whine grown men shouldn't make. This was so wrong, even the words were wrong, implying terrible, wonderful things. He *wanted* to be ruined. Oh God, Angel was going to take him straight to Hell, and he'd go there of his own free will.

Angel held him down, his hot hand on Francis's chest. With his other hand, he unbuttoned his own trousers, then grabbed Francis's left hand and shoved it into his boxers. Firm, warm, erect cock filled his grip. Angel smirked and began to move, and then Francis moved too, sliding his grip over Angel's dick. And it was right there, between them, flushed pink and leaking pearly cum. He wanted to taste it, to lick it, but he was trapped, pinned under Angel and at his mercy. Somehow, that made all this a thousand times worse and more maddening. Yet also better. Nothing made any sense. It was all madness.

Angel threw his shoulders back and closed his eyes. He rocked his hips in time with Francis's pumping hand, sliding his dick between Francis's fingers and thumb—so wet they didn't need lubricant. Angel was beautiful like this. With his eyes closed, he didn't see how Francis watched every little tic of his sinful smile and how his tongue swept out, touching his lips. He was free, freer than Francis had ever been. That freedom was all over his face. Bliss. He didn't hate this; he wouldn't feel guilty when it was done. He fucked Francis's hand with abandon.

Jealousy was a sour barb in Francis's gut. He'd never been that free. He hated Angel anew, but wanted to be him too. To be so free that nothing mattered. To be so at peace with himself that he could smile as though the world owed him a thousand favors.

Maybe Angel was right. Francis had been in Hell.

In a rush of hate, maybe fear, and a whole lot of need, he half shoved Angel off but guided him downward too, laying Angel on the couch. And with Angel curiously peering up at him, Francis shuffled down and took the thick, veined cock between his lips, where he'd needed it to be. Angel tasted warm and was broader than he'd expected. What if he gagged? What if he couldn't accommodate it? Angel thrust, and all those concerns vanished, pushed out as Angel's dick surged down his throat. He gagged, withdrew, then licked saliva and pre-cum off Angel's hot cock.

Angel had used his hand and mouth on Francis's dick last night, and Francis did the same now, making him moan.

"Fuck, Father, who knew you gave such good head."

He didn't want to talk. He wanted to make Angel come so hard he lost his mind.

Francis sucked hard, rubbed, pumped, listening to Angel's broken breaths and how he shuddered. He was close, and he had his eyes closed. He gripped Francis's shoulder, guiding his pace, quickening it.

"Fuck yes." Angel's eyes opened and he peered down himself, at Francis, and grinned. "You goin' to swallow?"

There was that mocking tone again, daring Francis to do it. He bobbed his head, working Angel's dick. His hand burned from the repetitive action, but Angel wasn't winning this. Yes, he was going to swallow. Angel must have seen the fire in Francis's eyes, and it was the final nudge, tipping him over the edge. Angel's own rhythmic pumping stuttered. Salty cum hit Francis's tongue. He gagged and swallowed out of spite, pretending to hate everything, when in actuality his own cock stood upright and demanding, as hard as it had ever been, its pressure unbearable, as though he might come with a single stroke.

Angel jerked out from under Francis, hauled him onto his knees, and thrust his tongue into his mouth, where his own cock had been seconds before. Angel's tongue swirled, and Francis pushed back, taking as good as he got, and then Angel grabbed his dick and gave three devastating fast pumps that shot a bolt of wild lust through Francis's veins. He came hard, clutching at Angel's arm to keep from collapsing against him.

Angel squeezed, wringing him, making it hurt but in a weirdly good way. Francis hissed and shuddered, pulling his dick free of Angel's cum-soaked fingers.

Angel raised his fingers and licked, dark eyes absorbing the shock on Francis's face.

Francis didn't know what this was. It felt like hatred as

he watched Angel suck his own fingers clean of cum, but it also felt like freedom, felt as though he'd crossed a line and didn't want to go back.

Whatever this was, he might just be lost to it. And maybe he didn't want to be found.

CHAPTER TWELVE

Vitari

Father Francis Scott might have been the best fuck he'd ever had, and all they'd done was blow each other. There was something poetic in the priest's eyes when he came, as though his surrender meant a thousand times more than Vitari's typical fuck-me-fast encounters behind seedy bars.

He didn't want to get lyrical, but Francis damn well fucked with all his emotions on his face, out there for Vitari to drink in. And he hated what they were doing. He hated Vitari most of the time too, but he also needed sex, like a starved man needed sustenance. And so Vitari was going to give it to him. Repeatedly.

"That didn't happen. It can't happen again," Francis said. "Ever."

He wanted it. But right now he was having a crisis, brought on around the time Vitari had lapped up Francis's cum.

He shoved Angel off him and staggered to his feet but

had nowhere to run. It wasn't even night, so Francis's sins were in the room with them, in broad daylight. His face was flushed, his freckles bold. He growled as though he might break something. Angel leaned back in the couch and watched the priest bounce about the room, pacing back and forth, each step like a hammer on a nail. He was definitely going to shatter something, maybe himself. The man was unravelling and perhaps Angel should feel some guilt for his part in that, but all he felt was satisfied.

Francis scooped up the coffee mug and hurled it at the glass doors.

There it was. The rage. He kept it buried deep, so deep that the world rarely saw it. But Vitari witnessed it now.

The mug exploded. Coffee splattered across the toughened glass and onto the floor. "Never again!" Francis yelled. "Understand?"

"Sure." Angel tucked his dick away. Maybe he did feel something squirming inside, something like guilt? They'd had their fun, until the next argument erupted. He headed outside, leaving Francis to pace, mutter, and pray.

The grey clouds from earlier had cleared, leaving the ocean sparkling like diamonds on blue silk. Now Vitari was getting all poetic. Francis must have been rubbing off on him. He laughed at his own joke and sauntered off the patio, taking the old overgrown path down the slope, toward the cliffs. He'd always hated this house. It was too isolated, too lonely. But today, despite Francis losing his mind back there, Vitari felt strangely at peace. Probably endorphins from having his cock sucked by some of the sweetest lips out there. Those talented lips proved Francis was not a virgin. Vitari had wondered—with the whole priest deal—whether he'd been closeted his whole life. Not much time to fuck around and find out if you're in priest school. Or maybe there had been, because Francis had not been new to sucking dick.

Maybe priest school was exactly where he'd learned it.

He knew firsthand how priests weren't all the shiny examples of celibacy they claimed to be. Vitari sniffed, kicked a tuft of grass, and squinted into the sun, but even in this faraway place, he could still hear the deadbolt clanging like a bell tolling from his past. He flinched. Just a memory. It didn't have to touch him here, when he was having a fucking moment, admiring at the sea, his body still wired from sex.

He hadn't planned on screwing Francis again. Last night had been interesting, but today he'd needed to focus on getting in touch with Sal, to find out what was really going on with Francis. Then Francis had dragged himself out of bed, all sleepy-eyed and floppy haired, and made Vitari coffee, saying some nonsense about sweetness that had done weird things to Vitari's insides. After that, shit went downhill, ending with the slap, which still burned. And there was no way Vitari was going to let some doe-eyed priest slap him around. So he'd kissed him, because right then, it had seemed like the right thing.

It was beginning to feel as though whenever he got close to Francis, he wanted to fuck him instead of kill him. Which could definitely *not* be an ongoing occurrence.

Something glinted in the grass farther down the slope. He narrowed his eyes, peering into the ocean's glare.

Someone was down there. They either had a scope or binos. If it was a rifle scope, Angel was fucked. There was no cover, and he stood out in the open. But as he was still breathing, whoever was out there either didn't want him dead—yet—or he wasn't the intended target.

He sniffed again and ambled in the general direction of

their guest, careful not to tip them off he'd spotted them. He didn't see the glint again. Maybe it hadn't been anything, just a bottle discarded in the grass?

The bushes rustled and a figure bolted.

Vitari sprinted after him, leaping over a few rocks, and gained on the fleeing man.

He veered left, Vitari lunged, cutting him off, and tackled him to the ground. He punched him once, hard in the gut, winding him, and pinned him down. He frisked him for weapons.

No gun or binos. He could have dropped them. Either way, Vitari had him now. "Who are you and what the fuck are you doing spying on me?" The prick glared, lips sealed. "Oh, you wanna play that game? Sure, let's play." Vitari scrambled off him. The guy flung a fist and earned himself a punch to the gut that knocked the fight out of him. Vitari grabbed him, hauled him to his feet, and marched him back to the villa.

He found Francis on his knees in the living area, brushing bits of broken mug into a pan. He looked up, startled to find they had a guest. "Who is he?"

"Good question. Let's find out." Vitari shoved the man onto the couch, turned on his heel, grabbed a shard of broken mug off the floor, and marched back to the prick. A knife from the kitchen would have been easier but not as dramatic. He slashed the jagged bit of porcelain across the man's cheek, opening up a thin, bloody line.

Francis's gasp yanked at Vitari's nerves. Ignoring the priest's judgment, Vitari scrunched his fist in the man's hair and held the edge of the porcelain to his gritty, sweat-slick neck, where the artery throbbed. "Let's try this again. Who are you and why the fuck are you here?"

He was darker skinned, darker than Vitari, with a short,

well-kept beard. His face wasn't familiar, so maybe he didn't know Vitari or his reputation, because there was a distinct lack of begging coming from the man's lips.

Vitari poked the shard of mug between his fingers, clenched his fist, and punched the prick in the gut, jabbing him with the sharp edge. He gasped, and now fear showed in his eyes. "Yes, I will absolutely fuck you up."

"Oh God," Francis moaned.

His tone grated against Vitari's resolve. He was *trying* to work here; he didn't need Francis's righteous glare weighing on him.

"Go outside and look for a gun," Vitari ordered.

"What?" Francis replied. He came around Vitari's side, still holding the dustpan. What the fuck was he going to do with that? Scoop up the man's insides? Because the way shit was going, this bastard was not surviving their meeting.

"His gun, go find it. Walk down the path from the pool. It's out there."

Francis held his gaze. He knew he wasn't being sent to find a gun; he was being sent off so he didn't have to watch Vitari gut this man.

"You don't have to do this," Francis said.

"Go," Vitari growled.

The priest glanced from Vitari's face to the bleeding man, and if he damn well refused, then they were going to have a problem, and maybe Vitari would have to reconsider letting Francis have his freedom. But he turned away and stepped through the patio doors.

Vitari watched Francis walk far enough away that he wasn't going to hear what came next, then he eyed the man he'd stabbed.

The intruder grinned. "Faggot."

Vitari smiled. "Been watching us a while, have you? Did you get hard, huh? Seeing me suck a priest?"

The man spat, and the globule smacked into Vitari's already sore cheek. Goddammit, he just needed to refrain from killing this homophobic dick long enough to get answers out of him.

"Giancarlo doesn't know his son sucks dick," the guy said.

"Giancarlo?" He shouldn't be hearing that name, not on this prick's lips. What did Giancarlo have to do with this? Vitari swallowed. "You're Battaglia?"

The idiot smiled and clamped his lips closed.

Fine then, this was the part where the screaming started. Vitari grabbed the man by the forehead and pressed the jutting bit of mug toward his right eye. He struggled, and the shining eyeball swiveled, seeking a way out. "They want you gone!" he blurted.

Vitari's veins turned to ice. "What?"

"That bomb was meant for you."

The bomb on the yacht? "You're lying." There was no way the family would turn on him. No fucking way. This was some kind of DeSica ploy. What if this guy was distracting Vitari while a partner was still out there, in the grass? Shit, he hadn't considered there might be more of them. And Francis was wandering around like a lost lamb.

Jesus.

Vitari pushed off the prick. "You're DeSica. I'd know your face if you were family."

The guy smirked and wiped his cheek, then poked at the shallow stab wound in his gut. "Not DeSica. Would DeSica know you're here?"

No, he was wrong. Maybe they'd tailed them, although

Vitari had been sure to check the car mirrors for tails when they'd left Puerto Banus.

He studied him and waited a few beats, needing time to realign his thoughts around this new information. "Who told you where we are? Who sent you here?"

He shrugged.

"Not fucking good enough!" Vitari grabbed him, threw him to the floor, and stamped on his hand. Bones shattered under Vitari's heel, and the man's screams filled the villa. Francis may have heard, but it was done now, and why the fuck did Vitari care what Francis heard?

The priest was a goddamned distraction.

Vitari dropped his knee into the man's chest, grabbed him by the neck with his left hand, and raised the jagged piece of mug in his right, locked between his fingers, the point showing. "Right in the neck, you'll bleed out in three minutes. Is that what you want?"

Now, he was afraid. About fucking time.

"Who sent you? Was it Sasha?" The DeSica boss. It had to be.

"You're not... listening..." the prick wheezed.

"It wasn't my fuckin' family!" Vitari barked. He squeezed tighter, making the prick gasp for breath. His face darkened, and his eyes wept, turning bloodshot. Vitari eased off, and the prick gasped and gulped air. "Try again."

"Salvatore!"

"Now I know you're fucking lying, you piece of shit!" He drew his arm back and eyed the man's pulsing artery in his neck.

"Don't!" Francis barked.

Vitari hesitated and raised his gaze to find Francis stepping through the patio doors, a rifle at his side. Francis wasn't supposed to be here, about to witness Vitari kill yet another person. And he definitely wasn't supposed to be carrying a hunting rifle.

None of this was supposed to be happening.

"Francis," Vitari hissed. "Let me do my job."

"He doesn't have to die." Francis swallowed so hard, Vitari heard the click. And then he raised the rifle and sighted Vitari down the scope. His finger rested on the trigger.

Vitari laughed. "Put the gun down so I can finish this."

"No."

Why now? Why did Francis have to pull this shit *now*?

"I let you kill those men in St. Mary's," Francis said, "and you killed the police. I'm not letting you kill him."

"I killed those men to save you, you fuckin' idiot."

Francis sneered. "Don't put this on me."

"Is the safety even off?"

Francis blinked. He didn't know where the safety was. But he didn't lower the gun, and Vitari couldn't see the safety from his angle. And now Francis's hand trembled. He still had his damn finger on the trigger. If that gun was primed, it wouldn't take much pressure to fire it. "You're not going to shoot me, Francis. Put the gun down."

"Let him go."

"You're holding the gun he was going to use to *kill you*!"

"But he didn't, and he doesn't have to kill anyone, and neither do you."

Vitari pursed his lips. He didn't want to die because Francis didn't know how to use a gun. He'd known he'd be a pain in the ass. "Mi hai rotto i coglioni," Vitari muttered, and the DeSica spy snickered at his crass words. "Shut the fuck up."

Francis would back off if Vitari refrained from the murder threats, and once he lowered that gun, Vitari just had to take it from him. He straightened and climbed off the would-be assassin, then tossed the bloody bit of mug onto the coffee table.

Francis still had the damn gun on him, and by its angle, the round would hit Vitari in the gut. He'd seen enough stomach wounds to know he did not want to die like that, clutching his insides in his hands. "Francis, the gun?"

"Shut up!" Francis screamed.

Vitari pressed his lips together and raised his hands. He may have underestimated how much the last forty-eight hours had messed with Francis's head.

"Where are the car keys?"

"Where are you going to go?"

"Anywhere. The keys!?"

"Kitchen counter." He watched Francis scoot around the furniture, his finger still skimming the damn trigger. "Watch the gun, Francis. I'm doing what you want, and your finger is real close to that trigger."

Francis snatched the keys off the counter and hurried back toward the patio doors. He met Vitari's gaze, then glanced at the prick on the floor before bolting.

Vitari lowered his hands and sighed. He could let him go, but the cops would pick him up, and either the Battaglia or the DeSica would pry him out of their hands before the British cops could arrive to rescue their missing priest.

The assassin eyed him from the floor, waiting to see what he'd do—go after the priest or kill him.

"Fuck!" Vitari sprinted out of the door, veered around the side of the villa, and heard the car's engine roar. He pumped his legs, ignoring the burning wound in his thigh, burst through the gate, and slammed into the car door. The car lurched forward, then backwards, and mounted the grass bank. Vitari grabbed for the door handle, got his fingers in, and yanked it open.

Francis spun the wheel and accelerated, whipping the car around, kicking up dust and grit, and throwing Vitari off. He lurched out of the way, then coughed in dust as the vehicle sped down the track. He could try running after him, but Francis wasn't slowing.

He'd lost him.

Vitari planted his hands on his hips and watched the car bounce along the track. "Fucking priest."

Remembering the assassin, he dashed back down the path, into the villa, but the assassin had fled.

"Fuck!"

Vitari stood on the patio and scanned the barren hillside.

Jesus, what a clusterfuck. He was no closer to knowing why Francis was such a hot target, and now the DeSica were playing fucking mind games with him. Everything had gotten so much *worse*. He'd lost Francis, had no idea what the DeSica wanted, and now the assassin had vanished— and he'd witnessed Vitari fuck Francis's hand. Shit like that could get him killed.

Vitari threw his hands up. He was done with priests. Fuck the lot of them. And fuck Francis.

He returned to the villa and pulled his phone from his pocket.

It was time to go home.

CHAPTER THIRTEEN

Francis

He'd done it. He was free.

He shivered behind the wheel, despite the heat. His teeth chattered. But he was free. Had no idea where he was going—*but he was free* and that was good.

The rifle lay across the passenger seat.

He'd almost pulled the trigger. Almost shot Angel. He'd wanted to.

Didn't matter.

He was free.

He'd drive, and... get far away. Just drive.

The car rumbled on for a few hours, until the sun set and road signs displayed place names in Spanish that Francis couldn't read. Then there were streetlights, and two lanes of traffic. He'd driven in England, but not abroad, where they drove on the opposite side of the road.

He made it through a bustling town and continued into

another patch of countryside without drawing attention to himself. He could have stopped and asked for help, but given his experience at the marina, with the cops who had tried to shoot him, he just wanted to keep on driving and get as far away from *everything* as possible.

The fuel indicator dipped below the orange warning bar, and outside there was... nothing. He passed by a few tin-roofed shacks and an occasional wandering dog. Did they have wolves in Spain? No. He didn't think so. Coyotes? Why didn't he know these things?

The car spluttered, coughed, continued on for a little longer, and died. He rolled it to the road shoulder and sat behind the wheel, headlights on, peering into darkness. This was another test then. A leap of faith. He had faith. God wouldn't abandon him. God didn't ever abandon the devoted. He gave them the tools they needed when they needed them. Right about now, Francis could have used a phone. Or a flashlight.

It was fine.

Everything was fine.

He'd stay with the car and wait until sunrise before walking onwards.

He'd be safe in the car.

At least he had a gun.

Knuckles rapping on the window woke him and a kind-faced old woman peered inside the car. She rattled off fluent Spanish and smiled, showing gaps in her teeth.

"Telefono?" he croaked.

"Si." She nodded, then her smile fell away. She'd seen the gun on the passenger seat.

"Oh, no, that's just—that's not mine." He laughed nervously. "I'm a priest. I don't do... guns."

She hurried back across the road and down a meandering track toward a distant farmhouse. What if she was also getting a gun?

"God, grant me strength."

He was going to have to walk. If he took the gun, he'd look like a crazy person. If he left the gun, a child might find it. If the police found him *with* the gun, they'd probably shoot him.

He stashed the gun under the seat, left the car, and started walking.

Waves of heat beat down. But he was alright, considering the last few days. It could have been much worse.

So... He'd walk until he found someone with a phone, and then he'd call St. Mary's. Julia would probably pick up, but that was fine, she'd call the police, and eventually they'd organize someone to come and find him out here... Wherever here was.

He glanced behind him. No cars, nothing in the blue sky. Just glaring daylight.

He didn't have water or food.

What if Angel found him?

No, he wasn't thinking about *him*.

Sirens wailed far off. Then grew louder. He squinted into the heat haze rippling off the road.

They couldn't all want to kill him, could they?

Police cars appeared over the hill, one after another. Six in all. A lot. Maybe the kind old woman had called them and said he had a gun.

He stopped and raised his hands, trying to appear as nonthreatening as possible.

The cars screeched to a halt. Armed men spilled from

inside in green flak jackets with GARDIA on the front. They swarmed around him, barking orders in Spanish.

"Oh God." He didn't understand what they wanted. "My name is Father Francis Scott," he stammered. "I'm a priest." He just had to stay calm, talk slowly. "I was kidnapped." His heart raced. Fear clogged his throat, trying to choke him.

They drove him to his knees, yanked his arms behind his back, and slapped cold cuffs on his wrists. Why were they armed? Did they think him dangerous? What if he ended up in a Spanish prison? No, they'd have to have translators. They couldn't arrest a priest without cause and throw him in jail, could they?

"I'm Father Scott. I'm English. I was brought here by a man... a man who works for the Battaglia."

"We know who you are, Father," a woman said in accented English. She strode from the ranks of officers, wearing the same bulletproof vest, but her smile was kind. She crouched in front of him. "It's all right, Padre. You're safe. Let's get you clean, si? And you can tell us about the Battaglia."

"How are you feeling, Padre?"

"Much better, thank you." Nobody had tried to kill him yet.

"This is good, good." The police officer, who Francis now knew as Catalina Diaz, was a specialist in organized crime and appeared to be the Spanish equivalent of a chief inspector, so a higher rank than most at Marbella's large police station. She wore her long, wavy dark hair in a no-nonsense ponytail and conversed with her staff in a sharp, commanding tone. Francis had always been intimidated by powerful women, but when she smiled, which she did often, her ruthless streak faded. "There is a liaison from the National Crime Agency on their way from the UK. Before they arrive, Padre, would you answer some questions for us, si?"

"I'm not under arrest?"

"No, no. A courtesy," she explained. "To help."

He sat in what appeared to be an interview room, but there were no recording devices. Just comfortable chairs, a water cooler, and a window overlooking Marbella center. "All right, it's just... There were some police in a marina—a port," he explained, unsure if she could understand all he was saying. "Somewhere, I don't know. It was a few hours from where you found me. They uh... they were corrupt, I think. I don't know who to trust." He shifted, uncomfortable. Somehow, he'd gotten sand or grit in his shoes, probably from the villa track, and it had rubbed into blisters. Everything hurt. In truth, he just wanted to go home. He placed his hands on the table and picked at his nails. "It's erm... it's been a difficult few days."

"I know, and I am sorry for all you have been through. Once the NCA take you to England, we will lose our chance to speak with you, and it's the corrupt police you mention I am interested in. And the Battaglia."

He nodded. People were dead. Justice had to be served. "All right, yes, that's fine. I'll help."

"Thank you, Padre."

She lifted a briefcase onto the table, flicked its latches open and removed a stack of photographs from inside, then laid them on the table in rows. "Tell me if you recognize any of these men."

He watched each picture land and studied their stoic

mugshots. "Oh yes!" He pointed at the photo of one of the police who had shot at him at the marina. "That one, he was one of the police."

"Not policia," Catalina said, gravely. "DeSica."

"But who are the DeSica?"

"One of two large criminal organizaciones, operating from southern Italia. DeSica are smaller, but as dangerous. Battaglia is Mafia, you know the term, sí?"

"Yes." Unfortunately, Angel had enlightened him to the fact the mafia weren't a product of Hollywood and were in fact very active.

"They traffic people, drugs, guns, counterfeit products. Australia, Canada, London. And España. What happened to this man?" She tapped the DeSica man's photograph. He looked down at the placid face and vividly remembered how Angel had held a gun under the DeSica man's chin and blown his brain matter all over the restaurant ceiling.

If he told her, they'd be able to charge Angel, arrest him, convict him. With Francis's help, as a witness. It was the right thing to do. Angel had killed them. He hadn't hesitated. He should be arrested. Should be behind bars. But then there was the Church to consider, and Francis's placement at St. Mary's. A scandal like this would be frowned upon, regardless of the fact none of it had been his fault.

They'd support him, he hoped.

And then there was Angel... and what they'd done. Together. If Francis accused him, he'd reveal how they'd been... intimate. Francis had only been a priest for a few months. A scandal like that would ruin his entire life.

"Padre?"

"I er... I don't... They chased me and the uh—there was a bomb, and the boat... it, well, it exploded, and they were—

it was confusing, lots of people running." He rubbed his sweaty forehead. "I'm not, I don't, it's a lot to take in."

"It's all right, Father." She smiled, and his pounding heart slowed. "What about *this* man?"

She'd placed more photos down while he'd been going over the painful last twenty-four hours in his head. Images of more suspects, more blank faces, but there was Angel, his expression bored, staring into the camera as though daring whoever had taken that photo to use it against him. Even there, with its stark white background, his black hair and black lashes, combined with those haunting eyes, arrested Francis. "I uh…"

"Is this the man who took you?"

She had to know it was. "Yes," he said, quietly.

"Angel, si?"

"Yes, he said his name was Angel."

"Si, si." She sat back in the chair. "This man… He is Vitari Angelini, Angelo della Morte, Angel of Death. Don Giancarlo Ciani's son. You are very lucky. Vitari Angelini is a very dangerous criminal."

Yes, he'd come to that conclusion himself. But he had no idea Angel—Vitari—had been a Mafia boss's *son*. He'd been taking Francis back to Italy for *his father*.

"Were they going to ransom you?" she asked.

"Ransom me?" Who would pay? He couldn't imagine the Church would sully itself with such things, and he had no family, very little money. "I don't know. He didn't say, really. He seemed to want to keep the DeSica from finding me, more than anything else. They were the ones who came to my church. In England. The bodies… I… They…" He touched his forehead again, and the scabbed bruise where he'd struck the pew. That seemed like weeks ago, not a mere few days.

His heart fluttered like a trapped bird in his chest. He couldn't do this, not yet. "I'm sorry, everything is a blur."

A knock at the door jolted him, and a younger woman poked her head in, said something in Spanish, and was gone again.

Catalina gathered her photos up and sealed them away inside her case. "I would like to speak with you some more, perhaps when you are settled back in England? Si?"

He really did want to help, it was just... a lot. "Yes. I'm sorry, I'm feeling a bit... overwhelmed."

She seemed sympathetic, and in the face of that genuine smile, Francis tried not to sob like an idiot.

"All right, your liaison is here."

He was handed over into the care of a curt woman from the NCA, which seemed to be the UK's government agency dealing with organized crime gangs. She introduced herself as Priti Sharma and explained how she'd take him to the airport right away, as it was important they leave Spanish soil, implying he wasn't yet safe from the Mafia's clutches.

They left the police station in a motorcade of marked cars and arrived at a small airport, where an unmarked twin-propeller plane waited. He boarded, and within an hour, they were in the air. It all felt surreal, like a dream. But nothing had seemed real since he'd found Victoria Chance's body in the churchyard. Maybe even before that—when he'd knelt in front of the line of bishops in Westminster Cathedral, about to be ordained.

He stared out of the window and Spain shrinking beneath them.

Would he ever be free?

They landed at London City airport just as the sun began to set, painting London's skyline in late summer's red glow. As the plane touched down on British soil, Francis sighed out the rest of his rattling nerves. Almost home.

"We will want to ask you some questions, Mister Scott," Priti said, either forgetting he was a priest or preferring to ignore the fact. He couldn't blame her; he didn't look or feel particularly priestly.

She gathered her bags and nodded for him to walk ahead. "But as you'll be in safe hands, we're quite happy to have you take a day to get yourself back on your feet."

"'Safe hands'?"

"Father... Hawker, I believe his name is, has come to collect you."

"Father Hawker." Why did Francis feel as though he'd stepped from one hornets' nest into another? Father Hawker had been nothing but kind and helpful. Francis should be relieved he was here for him.

They descended the steps from the plane into frigid London air, and as Francis followed Priti, he cast his gaze ahead and spotted Father Hawker standing with his hands clasped in front of him by one of the terminal's service doors. The wind tugged at his cassock, rippling it around his ankles, but the black cloth hugged his overweight middle. He brought his arms up as Francis approached and embraced him without hesitation. "My goodness, you look terrible, Francis." He patted his back as they separated.

"I feel terrible, honestly." He hadn't expected a hug. Or to see Father Hawker in London. All this fuss, for Francis.

"Let's get you inside," Father Hawker urged, eager to get out of the cold wind.

They entered the building together using a service

tunnel, which seemed a little strange, but Francis's mind had frayed at its edges from stress and lack of sleep, and very little of anything made sense.

He waited on a plastic chair like a misbehaving boy outside the headmaster's office as Priti and Father Hawker discussed the hotel Francis would be staying at and the number to call if there were any problems. He must have dozed off, because when Father Hawker gently nudged his knee, Priti was gone and it was just the two of them in the long, cold tunnel.

"Francis, I know you've been through a lot, and I'm sure you just want this whole ordeal to be over with. But I'm afraid there's quite the crowd of reporters at the front of the airport, and it seems the archbishop would like you to be presentable when he greets you in front of the cameras."

Very little of what he'd just said made any sense.

Father Hawker held out a stack of folded black cloth and grimaced. "Sorry."

Not just cloth, a cassock.

He wanted Francis to wear a cassock, now? They'd only landed moments ago.

"Uh, I uh…" Francis stood, and took the weighty cassock. "Now?"

"Yes."

His own clothes—the ones he'd borrowed from Angel— were filthy. At least the trousers were so stained that any incriminating marks were no longer noticeable. "A shower, first, surely?"

Father Hawker frowned. "Archbishop Montague is waiting."

Montague was here. Francis's heart raced again and somehow thumped in his ears *and* his chest.

Father Hawker checked his watch. "He's been waiting for quite some time."

Francis didn't have a choice. It was that simple. He was to put on the cassock and be the priest everyone expected him to be.

"Yes, yes," he mumbled, aware of Father Hawker's growing impatience. Gathering up the robe, he tossed it over his head and wriggled it downward. It buttoned close to the neck, so nobody would notice he wasn't wearing white underneath. Father Hawker handed him the stiff white collar. He took it and flinched at the sharp memory of Angel throwing his old collar into the trash at a rest stop.

"Francis?"

By God, he just wanted this over with. "I'm fine. Yes. I'm fine." Cassocks were always heavy, but this one seemed particularly so. He strode onward, assuming Father Hawker would steer him the correct way, and caught his reflection in the walls of glass. Apart from the cut on his forehead, and the bruising, and the fact he wasn't wearing socks, nothing had changed. He was still Father Francis Scott, newly ordained, fresh out of priest school—as Angel would say.

A strange little bubble of laughter tried to leave his lips, which definitely would not do. He had to greet the archbishop with poise and grace, apparently in front of journalists.

What do you want, Father? Angel had asked, in that way he did, his words like landmines to Francis's mind.

What Francis wanted had never mattered.

"Are you going to be all right?" Father Hawker asked, trailing by several steps while puffing to catch up.

"Why wouldn't I be?" Francis pinned his usual smile to his lips.

The background hum of many people chatting signaled he was getting closer to the exit. Archbishop Montague was waiting. He was Francis's mentor, his patron. The man he'd vowed to obey in all things, beneath only God. And Francis was about to greet him having witnessed multiple murders, while his trousers carried the dried cum stain of the man who had killed them.

Nausea wet his tongue. The edges of his vision throbbed.

He just had to get through this, just sidestep the mess in his head and heart and get it done.

Francis pushed through a door into a gallery of faces. Hundreds of people stood behind a thin barrier, and all of them turned their heads toward him. Then the cameras came up, and a hail of flashes blinded him, each one piercing through to the back of his skull.

He clung to his smile like a life raft and swept his gaze left, following the barriers, and there was Archbishop Montague, with his salt and pepper beard and smiling eyes. Francis glided toward him, and as the archbishop's hand came up, Francis went down onto one knee and kissed the pontifical ring. Cold, hard, metallic. His gut heaved. He swallowed bile and smiled up at the archbishop. The thudding in his head turned to screaming, but he wore his smile like a shield.

"Father Francis, what was it like being held prisoner?" one of the journalists called.

"Father Francis, are you glad to be home?"

"Were you tortured?"

"Was there a ransom?"

"Father, a quick photo of you and the archbishop?"

Montague placed his hand on Francis's head and said a

prayer, and as Francis closed his eyes, he dreamed he was back in a small Italian restaurant on the Spanish coast, watching boats bob on sunlit waters.

Because even dinner with a murderer was better than here.

CHAPTER FOURTEEN

Vitari

The wine had gone to Vitari's head, but it wasn't important, he still had enough of his wits to eye Luca and make sure the little prick wasn't about to do or say something that would earn him a punch to the face. Since Luca's older brother had been slammed behind bars, little Luca Esposito was so damn desperate to make a name for himself.

The staff refilled Vitari's glass over and over, and Sal was laughing in that way he did, chortling about some idiot who'd cut him off in Rome traffic, so Sal had chased him down and threatened to cut off his balls. The barking laughs and rumble of family conversations filled the night air.

Vitari plucked his damp shirt from his chest. Giancarlo had chosen to move the feast outside on the patio to make the most of the evening breeze. He seemed comfortable at the head of the table, deep in conversation with Sal's father, Antonio—Little Toni.

Everything was just as it should be. Except Vitari couldn't shake the feeling everything was *not* fine. Since he'd landed back on Italian soil a day ago, he'd had a niggling itch at the back of his mind that he couldn't scratch. By now, he should have been half drunk, shooting cans or getting high with Sal. They'd usually walk into Le Castella, maybe take a yacht up the coast, pick up women, Vitari would pretend to get sucked off, then they'd cruise the beachside bars, maybe start a fight. If a night didn't end in bloody knuckles, it wasn't worth remembering.

But none of that felt right tonight. He was too wired, too alert.

"You seem down, fra." Sal grabbed his shoulder and dropped his bearlike muscular bulk into the chair next to Vitari. "That priest get to you?" He smirked. His glassy eyes suggested he was as drunk as Vitari should have been.

"Not him—the DeSica. They were all over this, and it fucks me off."

"Let it go. You're back, it's done. Drink more wine." He chinked his glass with Vitari's.

Sal's father, Toni, caught Vitari's eye and summoned him over with a wave.

Sal grunted an apologetic sound, and Vitari rose, then sauntered over. He'd avoided having to deal with his father all day, but the encounter was inevitable.

"We're putting Luca on the priest," Toni said.

Vitari held the older man's gaze just long enough to know the idea was a terrible one, then dropped his chin. "Whatever you think is best." Luca was nearby, probably listening in, thinking he'd won.

Toni glanced at Giancarlo, then both men levelled their glares on Vitari, and it was like being stared at by two lions who'd yet to decide whether killing him would be worth getting off their rock for. They wouldn't kill Vitari. He was blood. A whore's unwanted problem, but whatever, Giancarlo was still his father. But there were more creative ways to hurt someone than by killing them.

"We're sending you to South America to oversee operations there," Giancarlo said. He spoke slowly, with gravitas, knowing he was the king of his world and everyone else was beneath him.

Vitari did what he did best and went down on his knees. He took his father's hand and kissed the ring. "I have failed you, and for that I am sorry. I will make it right. I love you, father. You are everything, and I owe you my life. I will forever be in your service." The words fell out of him in a rush. "And in service to the Battaglia—" He paused, to moisten his throat. "—I beg you, please do not send me to South America."

Sending him to Venezuela was punishment. He'd be out of sight, out of touch. He'd prefer Giancarlo take a finger than send him halfway across the world to the fucking jungle.

Giancarlo smiled and covered Vitari's hand with his own. "Good boy." Then his fingers clamped shut, crushing Vitari's hand. He gasped. Giancarlo grabbed him by the back of the neck, hauled him into his lap, and sneered, "Fail me again, like the whore's son you are, and you will not return from Venezuela." He let go and smiled and laughed, and everything was fucking right with the world as Vitari stumbled to his feet, hand burning, face even hotter.

The prick Luca—with his flash of dyed blond hair—grinned from his seat and stuck his middle finger up, like a fucking child.

Vitari vowed to break Luca's legs with a crowbar. Later. Since nobody wanted to associate with him, now he'd fallen out of favor, he left the table and hurried across the grass, leaving the house gardens behind.

"Angel," Sal called, hurrying to catch up. "Fuck Luca. He knows he's not you, so he has to be a dick."

Vitari waved him off so Sal didn't see how raw Giancarlo's words had made him, how much it hurt to be called all the things he knew himself to be by his own father. "I'm good, go back to the meal."

"Let's go to town." Sal flung his arm around Vitari's shoulders, stumbling into him.

Vitari shoved him off. "Fuck off, Sal."

Sal lunged in again, grabbed Vitari, and yanked him close. "No way, you need me."

Sal's antics summoned a reluctant smile. "You need to sober up."

But they were already halfway down the winding road to town, and Sal wasn't going to leave now he'd latched on to Vitari. He never did. He was probably the only true friend Vitari had. Everyone else wanted to get close to him because he was Giancarlo's son, thinking they'd climb another rung of the Battaglia ladder, not realizing Vitari was at the bottom.

He strode into town with Sal, and after a few more free drinks in the bars, the sting from his father's words faded. Giancarlo just got like that. His anger was a whip. But once its blow had been dealt, it was over.

"Is that your priest?" Sal asked, nodding toward the small TV playing on silent in the corner of the bar.

Father Scott looked good in his spotless black robe. It swept from his shoulders and flared at his hips in long, sleek lines. So fucking poised and graceful. Nobody knew he'd sucked Vitari's dick. Except the missing assassin. That guy needed to die. Vitari was going to have to get on that.

"Yeah, that's him."

The ticker along the bottom of the screen read: *Beloved Priest Found by Spanish Police. Archbishop Greets Father Scott.* Francis went down on his knee and kissed the archbishop's ring, just like Vitari had done with his father. Maybe they weren't so fucking different, except Francis belonged somewhere, and Vitari didn't.

The archbishop, a bearded man in his fifties, smiled to the crowd with his hand on Francis's head, and as the camera panned, Vitari saw the man's eyes. His stomach dropped, and he reached for the bar. He knew him. More than *knew* him. The sound of the deadbolt clanged in his mind like a warning bell, and his vision swam. He was no longer in the stifling bar but back in England, many years ago.

Sal grunted something about being right back and stumbled over to a pair of women, dialing up the charm. He didn't notice Vitari's sudden episode.

Vitari leaned against the bar and watched how the archbishop placed his hand between Francis's shoulder blades and guided him out of the airport. Cameras flashed, the reporters yelled questions like bullets, and Francis didn't even flinch. He smiled as though everything were fine, but he'd worn that same smile when Vitari had watched him in his parish. It was fake.

Good.

Let him suffer. Let them all suffer. Pretentious fucks.

Father Scott was Luca's problem now.

Sal was in the process of convincing the two women to

join them. Vitari sighed at the ceiling, forcing his heart to slow. The panic waned too. The past ambushed him sometimes, especially on nights like these, when he hated himself. But it always passed.

The women joined them, and they hit the next bar, then the next, getting louder with every drink that went down. Nobody dared stop them. They owned this town.

Sal disappeared with his date, leaving Vitari with the beautiful young woman he'd been flirting with all night. She was probably half aroused, half terrified. The local women knew better than to get involved with Battaglia men, so this one and Sal's were likely from some other town, come to enjoy the ocean view, sample the bars and the men.

He couldn't delay the inevitable any longer and steered her from the bar, turning down a cobbled side alley. Vitari raised the bottle of expensive beer in one hand, almost taking a gulp, but hesitated as he slumped against the wall, eyeing a pathway consisting of too many uneven steps. His date leaned in and tried to thrust her tongue between his lips. He hated this part, but it was necessary. There was always a chance she'd been put up to this, or she'd talk later, and he needed to keep up appearances. He kissed her back, putting casual effort into it. Then cradled her head, sinking his fingers into her hair. Faking it was easy, to a point.

She slid down his body, kissing his chest through his open shirt, and he sipped his beer. No offense to her, but she might as well have been a plastic doll for all it did for his dick.

He was so damn tired of failing.

He dug into his pocket, flipped open his wallet, and pulled out a few hundred euros. "Here, take it."

Her face got all puzzled and offended, but also relieved. He wasn't an idiot, and neither was she.

"We fucked, it was great," he slurred. "Tell your friends you fucked Vitari Angelini." So he didn't have to do this dance again for a few more months.

She plucked the notes from his fingers, adjusted her low-slung blouse, and stepped back, checking to see if she was allowed to leave or if this was some twisted game.

"Boo!"

She flinched, and Vitari laughed. He'd thought so. She wasn't about to suck him because she wanted to, it was all about the family, the name, and behaving. "Fuck off," he growled.

She cursed him out and marched away, heels clicking. Vitari snickered, then wobbled, almost falling off a step. Jesus, he'd drunk too much and now this step seemed like the perfect place to rest a while.

He slid down the wall while the alleyway spun, downed the rest of the beer, and flung the bottle at the far wall, watching it smash into a thousand glittering pieces. His insides tightened, folding inward. He pulled his knees up and hugged them close. But the feeling got worse, as though all the ugly parts of him were drowning his heart in darkness, and he couldn't make it better because the broken bits were *inside*.

He sobbed, then laughed, and scrunched his hands into his hair.

A dead bolt clanged down. He sprang from the wall and fell against the opposite side of the alley. A gate creaked open, and a black cat trotted from inside. Its owner closed the gate again, and the bolt rammed home.

Air tightened in his lungs. He doubled over, clutched his thighs, and then his body rejected everything, and he threw up an evening's worth of alcohol. And now he hated himself even more. Maybe he should just put a fucking gun to his head and do the family a favor.

He clung to the wall at his back and looked up, at the watery stars.

Maybe Francis should have shot him. Then the damned priest would go to Hell, where Vitari already was.

CHAPTER FIFTEEN

Francis

He closed his cottage door and walked up the quiet street, passing the postman, who tried to stop and ask a thousand questions. St. Mary's stood where he'd left it. Of course it did. The Catholic church was immovable, immortal, indominable.

Francis pushed through the gate and walked up the cobble path.

It was all going to be fine.

He was back where he belonged, and he'd do things differently. He'd be worthy.

Everything that had happened was... a journey. He was merely starting out and hadn't yet reached the destination, that was all.

Father Hawker had counselled him, taken his confession, although Francis hadn't told him the worst of it all. He would unburden his soul, just not yet. Father Hawker had been so accommodating and helpful; he didn't want to have the man bear the weight of all the terrible things Francis had seen and done. He'd pray and seek God's guidance, but more importantly, he'd serve God and his parishioners because he knew now how important they were.

St. Mary's was his sanctuary.

Everything was going to be all right.

He bid Julia a good morning and tried not to think about the sadness in her eyes. She'd been the one to find the dead men and alert the police to his absence. He'd speak with her about it, when they were both ready.

"A cup of tea, Father?"

"A fabulous idea. Thank you."

"I saw you on the news looking very handsome."

"Erm, yes." He pulled the chair out from behind his desk and sat. This felt right. It felt like a fresh start. Like a second chance. Angel had been a test, and a lesson.

Francis had learned to be grateful for all he'd been given.

He opened the top drawer and froze.

The Private & Confidential letter sat on his diary. Open.

He stared at the jagged pieces of torn envelope. "Julia, did you open this?"

"Here you are." She placed his cup of tea down, rattling the saucer, and peeked into the drawer. "No, that was already open when I put it there. I assumed you had opened it?"

His smile twitched. "Yes, probably." He hadn't.

Julia ran through the day's events, reeling them off one by one, but her voice faded behind the dread thumping in his head.

Francis slammed the drawer shut. Someone had opened it. Someone had *read* it. He hadn't had a chance to open it before he'd been taken, but he knew what it said. "Was there anyone else in my office while I was gone?"

"Uh..." Julia shuffled from foot to foot. "The police were here. Lots of police. And Father Hawker, I suppose."

No, Father Hawker wouldn't have opened a letter marked *PRIVATE*. The police wouldn't open letters, would they? Perhaps they had, to see if it was relevant to his disappearance. He'd have to find out.

"Anyone else?"

"There were some other people from the Church here. You'd best ask Father Hawker about them. He spoke to them a lot."

"Did they have names?" he asked, instantly regretting the sharpness in his voice, but this was important.

"Father, is everything all right?"

No, nothing was all right! Why had someone been through his personal items and opened a private letter? "Can you please give me a moment, Julia?" He looked at the door, at her, and at the door again. She cleared her throat and hurried outside, clicking the door closed behind her.

He steepled his hands against his lips and sighed through his nose. Someone knew his secrets. Someone knew his past. He opened the drawer, pulled out the letter, yanked out its pages, and clasped the letter in both hands.

Historical Abuse Claim

Notice of Intent to Submit a Legal Claim/Outcome

Claimant: Father Francis Scott

Defendant: Archbishop Charles Montague

Francis read on, absorbing only half the words. ... *strong case against... additional evidence... witness testimony.*

He set the letter down. What was he doing? This would cause a scandal. It would blight everyone he'd touched, ruin St. Mary's and Father Hawker and all the priests he knew to be good people. And there were many. It had been his fault. He hadn't said no; he could have stopped it. After everything he'd been through, the bodies left in his wake, this letter seemed... trivial and pointless.

The phone on his desk rang—its incessant shrilling found its way through the fog in his mind—and he picked up the receiver.

"Father Scott, St. Mary's—"

"I didn't think you'd answer."

Angel.

Francis's heart leaped into his throat. He slammed the receiver down.

It rang again.

"Do you want me to get that?" Julia called.

"No!" He picked up the receiver and had the words on his lips to tell Angel to leave him alone, but they wouldn't come, and when Angel didn't say anything, neither did Francis. He heard his soft breaths, felt them again on his neck, whispering into his ear. *I'm going to ruin you, Father.*

Francis slumped in the chair and rubbed his forehead, still listening to Angel's soft breathing. But his name wasn't Angel. He'd deliberately used that alias to rile him. "Vitari."

"Ah, they told you my real name—"

"You can't call me here."

"Then where?"

"No, never. You can't call me ever." He should hang up now. But didn't. Something about Vitari's voice smoothed out Francis's frayed nerves and took him far away, back to that table by the window overlooking the Spanish marina. He rubbed some more at his head, trying to push out a growing ache. The line was quiet but for an occasional sigh of Vitari's expensive clothes.

He could see him in his mind—see him so clearly, kneeling at the altar, wearing those expensive clothes, his watch glinting. "What does the tattoo mean?" Francis asked.

"What tattoo?" he asked in return, his voice soft, slightly muffled.

"On your wrist."

There was a rustle, as though he'd looked at his own arm to remind himself. "It's a symbol."

"Of what?" Francis asked, harshly. He had to know. He wasn't even sure why.

"Commitment. Imprisonment. Life."

He loved the way his voice clipped off at the end of every word, and how the luscious sound of it poured into his ear, sliding through his defenses.

Vitari chuckled again. "What are you doing, Father?"

"How did you get this number?"

"There's this amazing thing, I don't know if you've heard of it, it's called the internet. I typed in your name and your church, and there it was—"

Renewed hate and frustration simmered in his gut. He shouldn't be doing this, shouldn't be talking with him. "What do you want?"

"Maybe I want to confess?"

"I think that ship has sailed."

"Oh, listen to you, so angry. Are you in your robe? I saw you on TV. I'd forgotten how good you look in black."

Francis hung up. There was a way to block numbers, wasn't there? He'd ask Julia to do it.

The phone rang again.

He snatched it. "Do not call me, do not think of me, you and I are done."

"I wasn't aware we'd begun," the wicked man purred.

"You're terrible."

"I know. Tell me again, just let me get somewhere private so I can *really* enjoy it."

Was he... Was he going to... touch... himself? Heavens, no. Not on the phone. "I'm hanging up."

"But you're not."

"Go away."

He laughed again and that sound poured warm lust down Francis's spine, until it found its way to his dick. Francis bit into his lip. *God, grant me strength.*

"Fuck, I'd forgotten how much fun you are. But seriously, you need to listen. This isn't over. You can sit behind your desk and in your little church and pretend everything is fine, but the family wants you. I failed, so now they're sending someone else."

No, why wouldn't this nightmare end? "I can't do this again."

"They get what they want, Francis. You need to—"

"I haven't done anything to you or your family! Why don't you just leave me alone?"

"That's a good question. Maybe you should find out?"

Francis hung up, then knocked the phone off the hook, but then he wasn't sure if the call was still connected, and in a fury, he pulled the line from the wall, wound it around the phone, and tossed all of it into the corner of the room. Now Vitari couldn't call him. Nobody else could either, but that was fine. He'd fix it later.

He grabbed his head and squeezed, pushing out all the unclean thoughts and Vitari's devilish voice, and when he stopped hearing him whispering in his ear, he dropped the solicitor's letter in the trash and prayed and prayed and prayed, until all he was, his heart and mind and flesh and thoughts, were prayer.

He had a duty to his church. He was not going to live his life in fear.

Then he smiled his painful smile and left the office to begin the day.

CHAPTER SIXTEEN

Vitari

Vitari rarely smoked weed—didn't like losing control—but it was that or shoot up, and he wasn't yet too far gone to disappear down *that* black hole. He'd spent the day making preparations for Venezuela. The plane left at near midnight from a private airfield. He had—he checked his watch under the glint of the streetlight—two hours.

The earlier call to Francis had been interesting. When he'd tried to call back, the line had rung out. Still, he was pretty sure he'd gotten under the priest's skin in the most deliciously wicked way. Francis's words got all clipped and sharp whenever he was trying and failing to stay calm, and those edged words had sounded like sweet music to Vitari's ears.

He dragged on the joint, tilted his head back, and blew smoke into the air.

The village was quiet. Middle of the week meant the weekend tourists hadn't arrived.

Sal had said he'd meet him here, but the prick was a no-show.

Maybe Venezuela would be a quick one-week trip. But it was unlikely. Something was off, someone was working against him, or maybe he'd just fucked up too many times and this was all on him?

A whistle drew his eye toward three of Luca's crew making their way up the street toward him. Vitari straightened, hairs on the back of his neck rising. He looked left, and sure enough, there was Luca with another of his allies.

Vitari smirked and took the time to finish his joint as they closed in like sharks scenting blood. This was how it was going to be, huh? The farewell party. Vitari flicked the stub and began to roll up his sleeves.

"Thought we'd say goodbye," Luca said, all smiles and swagger now he had the numbers on Vitari. "You know, get intel from you on the priest, as you were *so close.*"

Vitari kept his smile but slid it sideways. "Get out of my face, Luca."

Luca smirked, shoulders high, so full of confidence. The idiot was all arms and legs, skinny as though he had an eating disorder, or a drug habit. He leaned a little too hard on the product for Vitari's liking. "You still think you're on top," Luca sneered.

Vitari sighed through his nose. The others had encircled him. If they laid a hand on him, they were dead men, all of them. Giancarlo would see to it. "Is this going to take long? I've got a plane to catch."

Luca nodded, and the guy to Vitari's right moved in—too slowly. Vitari ducked the lazy swing and jabbed the prick in the nose, startling him backwards. Another idiot thought he could have a go. Vitari danced to the left and cracked his knuckles across the prick's chin. But then the bag came down over his head, arms grabbed his, yanking them behind his back, and his knees slammed into the ground.

"Don't worry." Luca pressed his mouth to the bag, and pushed the words into Vitari's ear. "You'll make your plane."

Vitari struggled, but the multiple hands tightened. "Fuck you, Luca, you prick!"

Luca's laugh was all the reply he had. Then the hands hauled him upright and marched him down the road, then bundled him into a car. He kicked at the seat in front of him, but it made no damn difference. Vitari sat back, saving his strength, and tried to make out any shapes through the burlap sack.

The sound of twin props running revealed they'd taken Vitari to the airfield early. He was grabbed again, marched from the car, and dumped into a chair. Someone tore the sack off and Vitari scanned the hangar full of shipping crates. Product.

Luca knelt in front of him, still wearing that fucking ear-to-ear grin. Vitari glared back. This would be over soon; he'd get on a plane, and he'd plot his revenge, but right now, Luca held the cards. He wouldn't do anything permanent; he didn't have the balls.

Luca reached into his pocket, removed his phone, and swiped his thumb across the screen, then held it out in front of Vitari. The photo showed Vitari straddling Father Scott on the couch in the Spanish safehouse. Vitari had his head thrown back, and it was pretty fucking clear where the priest had his hand.

Vitari snorted, mind working fast. It was going to be difficult arguing he'd been torturing him from that angle.

The assassin had filmed them. The fucking assassin Francis had *let go*.

"Did you let the priest go after he rubbed your dick, Angel?" Luca asked.

Vitari kept his mouth shut but his smile was getting too heavy to hold for much longer.

Luca thumbed the photo away, displaying a new one of Francis. His ass in the air, head down, as he sucked Vitari's dick on the same couch.

Vitari twitched an eyebrow. He remembered it well. Francis had a very forgiving mouth.

He lifted his gaze to Luca's smirking face.

"You're going to go to Venezuela and you're going to stay there," Luca said, "or Giancarlo gets these pictures of his faithful son with his dick down a priest's throat."

It wasn't often Vitari was lost for words, but he didn't have any now. Luca had him by the balls.

Shame ate away at the edges of his confidence, and he hadn't felt humiliation in a long time. Those images wouldn't only ruin Vitari, they'd destroy Francis. That was how Luca was going to get Francis. He wouldn't have to physically threaten him. There wouldn't be any bodies left behind in St. Mary's. Francis would have to go with Luca or those photos of Instagram's most photogenic Catholic priest blowing a mob boss's son would go viral.

"I think we have an understanding." Luca straightened. "Get on the plane and don't come back, fra."

"I'm not your fuckin' bro."

Luca was on him in a second, his fingers around his throat, squeezing hard. He thrust his snarling face in front of Vitari's. "You're whatever I say you are. I knew you were fucked up, but I didn't realize how fucked up you are,

Vitari. What you are"— he raked his glare over him—"is cock-sucking filth."

Vitari tore free, but Luca's men swooped in. Fists rained too fast for Vitari to deflect. He couldn't do a damn thing but curl up and take the beating.

CHAPTER SEVENTEEN

Francis

The September air had an autumnal bite to it and the leaves on the trees surrounding the local playing field had turned amber and red. Most of the townspeople braved the chilly weather to celebrate the harvest festival, wrapped in thick coats.

Francis had ensured the church provided donations for local charities, which had the added benefit of keeping himself busy. A focused mind left no room for dwelling on the recent past. With the festival in full swing, he did his rounds, speaking with those who knew him, and introduced himself to some new faces too. The struggling young men and women of his parish appeared to appreciate the fact he wasn't much older than them. Unemployment was rife. Depression common. He helped ease their burdens, said prayers with them, and listened to their woes.

Children played. Some of the older kids kicked a ball at

the far side of the field. God's grace had granted them dry weather, even if it was cold.

It was a good day. An honest, relaxing day, and one of the best since his ordination.

If only he could extricate himself from Mrs. Roe and her distaste for the local bus timetables that she seemed to believe he could fix. Francis's mind wandered as he listened to her bemoan council services. His gaze drifted over her shoulder, toward the queue around the burger van. A man stood alone, off to one side, wearing a grey hooded top with the hood up. He turned his head, hiding his face, and sauntered off, disappearing behind the van.

"Father?"

"Oh? Yes. My apologies, you were saying?"

Mrs. Roe continued to explain how the diminishing bus routes were making it difficult for her to visit her son, some twenty miles away, and as she didn't have a car...

Francis scrutinized the crowd. People chatted and laughed, children played chase, and everything appeared as it should be. Why, then, had a chill touched his spine?

He'd told the NCA about the call from Vitari, and they'd assured him should Vitari Angelini or any of the Battaglia's known entities enter the country, they'd inform Francis, and if they deemed necessary, they'd send protection. He hadn't heard anything from the NCA, or Vitari, and it had almost felt as though life were returning to normal. As normal as it could be.

The man in the hood was probably just an innocent visitor to the fair. Recent events were making him jumpy.

Francis excused himself from Mrs. Roe, much to her dismay, and ordered a takeaway hot chocolate from the animal shelter's charity stand. A hot drink would warm him through and chase away the unease. He sipped and spoke with Carol, the charity's manager, about not disturbing log piles this time of year, to save any hibernating hedgehogs.

"It's cold enough to freeze your balls off, don't you think, Father?" a stranger said beside him, his English heavily accented. Francis glanced over, caught the stranger in the grey hood's smile, and dropped his gaze to the phone in his hand, tilted toward him.

The picture on-screen jarred with the festival's friendly ambiance and thrust his mind back into a Spanish villa, when he'd sucked Vitari's cock so deep he'd gagged.

His heart stopped, but also thumped louder. He stopped breathing too and flicked his gaze up at the stranger's face. Thin, deep-set eyes, a shock of blond dyed at the tips of his otherwise black hair.

"Would you like a hot chocolate?" Carol asked him.

"La ringrazio, ma per questa volta no," he said, sounding gracious and polite.

Carol blinked at him, at a loss. "Oh, not from around here, are you." She giggled.

"My name is Luca," he said, dropping his phone into his pocket. "Come with me, Father. We have much to discuss."

He had to get this man away from these people, not just because of what he had on his phone, but because whenever his sort crossed Francis's path, people died. There were families here, children, innocents.

"Yes," he said automatically, and fell into step beside Luca. Who was he? What did he want? To blackmail Francis? To hurt him? Where had he come from? Were there others nearby? A new question landed with his every step. Were there more, was Vitari here, was this DeSica or something else?

"We're going to walk to the cars over there as though we're old friends. If anyone sees you, smile. Nothing is wrong. We're just taking a walk in this beautiful little town."

Francis still had hold of his hot chocolate. Its heat burned through the paper cup, into his cold fingers. Someone called his name.

"Turn and wave, as though you're returning soon."

Francis swallowed. This man was going to put him in a car, just like Vitari had done. Francis would *not* be returning soon. Vitari had been different to this one. Luca spoke softly, calmly, but his eyes were cold. Unlike Vitari's eyes. They'd always had soul.

Francis turned and waved, then hurried on. He couldn't do this again. His heart raced. He couldn't go with him. But the picture... Luca would have more incriminating photos. If those photos were ever made public, his entire reason for living would be destroyed. He'd be laicized.

"What do you want?" Francis asked, surprised to find his voice calm.

"Only you," Luca said, as though polite and charming. "You're not going to be a problem, are you, Father?"

"No. No problem."

What if he called the police? But how to get away without risking that photo and others like it becoming public. "I don't have any money, and the church will not pay a ransom. I am of no use to you."

"Father." Luca sighed. "I'm just here to take you where you need to be."

"I don't know anything. This is a mistake. I told Vitari —"

"Giancarlo will decide what you are." He stopped alongside a gleaming black BMW and opened the rear door.

Francis stared at the back seat. His heart hammered so

fast it began to choke him. Cold sweat trickled down his back. "I... I'm not going."

"Father, I can type out a text message and have that photo on the internet in under two minutes. Is that what you want? How does the Catholic church view homos? And those celibacy vows? Hm, it does not look good for a new priest such as yourself."

Francis's biggest fear was on that man's phone—not that he'd be exposed as gay, that was inevitable, but that Archbishop Montague would go on, untouchable, beyond reproach. If the Church laicized him, Francis would no longer be *inside*, and he'd lose his means of revealing the truth, lose his access to everything that gave him a voice. If he was no longer among the Church, he was silenced. He was nothing.

He wasn't ready. It was too soon. He needed more time. "Father?"

But if he got in the car, he might never escape. Once had been enough.

He could not go through it again.

He peered into the steaming hot chocolate. Whatever he did here would determine his destiny. But he wasn't being taken without a fight, not like before. With a surge of rage, he flung the hot chocolate at Luca's face. The man yelped, recoiled, and Francis spun to flee. He'd make it back to his house and call the police. They'd protect him.

Luca grabbed his arm.

Francis reeled and swung an openhanded slap, landing it hard across Luca's cheek. His palm burned. The blow rang out like a gunshot. The whole town must have heard it. Luca stumbled against the car, hand on his face. "Oh, you will regret that, you filthy ass-fucker!"

Run. He had to run! The sounds of tires skidding on

loose gravel almost didn't register behind the pounding in his ears.

"Francis!"

Vitari.

Francis whirled again, and there he was, behind the wheel of a sleek white car, the passenger door flung open, engine revving. He wore sunglasses, hiding his eyes. "Get in!"

He knew he shouldn't, even as he ran for the car and threw himself into the passenger's seat. Common sense told him Vitari was no better than Luca, but his heart knew that to be a lie.

"Put your belt on, this is going to get lively."

The car lurched, the passenger door slammed from the sudden acceleration, and Francis thrust his belt on.

"Fuck me, Father, did I just see you hit Luca Esposito?" Vitari laughed, rammed the gear shift down, and roared the little two-seater sports car through the town. He reached up and adjusted the mirror. "He's following. It's fine, I'll lose him."

Vitari demanded more from the car, making the engine scream. He changed up a gear and raced along twisting, lurching country roads.

Francis clung to the seat. They were going to die. He's escaped one madman by choosing another. He had to be mad too. This was all madness! He prayed, closed his eyes, then opened them again and found Vitari looking over and smirking in that way he did. His smart mouth hooked into his cheek. His lip was cut, and the sunglasses hid a shadow of a black bruise around his eye. He'd been beaten, and now Francis had seen that mark, he saw other bruises on him too. His jaw, his neck.

Vitari threw the car around bends, almost losing control.

"Slow down, please?"

"Can't do that." He tightened his fingers on the wheel and grinned.

He was insane. "Do you want to die wrapped around a tree?"

"Beats getting caught."

"No, it doesn't! Do you hear yourself?"

"Did you miss me?"

"No. I hoped to never see you again—Slow down!"

The car slid sideways, crossing the white line into the opposite lane on a blind corner. Francis squeezed his eyes closed and prayed, and breathed, and wished he was far, far away, and not back in a car with Vitari Angelini.

Vitari didn't slow. Not around the lanes, and then, when they reached the freeway, he slammed the accelerator to the floor and raced the car at high speed, passing other motorists as though they were sitting still. It felt like forever until Vitari finally slowed, changing down gears, and veered the car into a side road signposted for a local airfield.

They sped along the road to what appeared to be nothing more than a warehouse with a single large twin propeller cargo plane on the runway, engines already spun-up and whirring.

Vitari skidded the car to an abrupt stop, flung the door open, jumped out, and barked at Francis to hurry.

He stared at the big plane, ready to take off. Nobody was around, although there had to be people here running the airfield, didn't there?

"Francis!"

He left the car and jogged after Vitari. He'd clearly had this planned. It wasn't by chance the plane had been waiting for him. How had he gotten here so fast, and where was he going?

Vitari jogged up the metal steps, toward the open passenger door.

Francis placed his shoe on the first step, his hand on the cool rail, and stopped.

The engines roared, propellors spinning, whipping his cassock around his legs, chilling him to the bone. He lifted his gaze and found Vitari on the top step.

"Father?" The backdraft from the engines churned Vitari's short hair and flapped his shirt. "Hurry, Luca won't be far behind. We need to leave."

Leaving with Vitari was the wrong thing to do. He felt it in his heart. He couldn't run forever. He should call the police and have them deal with all of this insanity. They said they'd protect him. Vitari was the devil in human form, the epitome of temptation and sin. Wherever he went, people died.

Vitari descended a few steps and tore off his sunglasses, exposing the extent of the bruising on his face. His eye was black, the brow split. He offered his hand. "Francis, come with me."

"Almighty and most Merciful God, graciously hearken unto our prayers and free our hearts from the temptations of evil."

The plane engines thundered, the wind tore at Francis, and it seemed as though he stood on the edge of a precipice, as though this moment were the final test and there would be no return from this.

"Did he show you the pictures?" Vitari shouted over the roaring engines. "Luca owns you. If you don't come with me now, he'll destroy you. Come with me, Francis." He licked his lips. "I'll keep you safe."

"Why?" Francis shouted back.

Vitari's smile fell away. His lashes fluttered down,

before he stared at Francis with renewed intensity. No more lies. Whatever he said next was the truth. "Because we're both fucked, because I need to find out why you're so special, because I... because I don't want to go alone."

What if this test wasn't about Francis? What if it had never been about him? What if the man who pleaded with him now was the real reason Francis was here?

He'd vowed to help people, and right now, with his hand out, Vitari needed help. His words weren't the whole truth, but his eyes were honest. He did not want to be alone.

Francis reached up and grasped his hand. Warm fingers closed around his, and Vitari hauled him up the steps and guided him inside the cargo hold. Rigging rattled around stacks of wooden crates. There were no windows, and nothing in the way of comforts.

Vitari slammed the door closed, locked it, and nodded toward the small seats bolted to the side of the plane. "Sit, it's going to be a long flight."

The fuselage trembled, the engines roared, gaining momentum, and the plane rumbled along the runway.

Francis sat and buckled himself in with fumbling fingers. The crates were all unmarked. What was it the Spanish policewoman had said? The Battaglia trafficked people, guns, drugs...

Vitari slumped on the floor, drew one long leg up, stretched the other out, and rubbed at this forehead. He caught Francis watching and smiled. "First Class to Venezuela."

CHAPTER EIGHTEEN

Vitari expected Francis to lose his shit and try to escape the plane, but whether he'd had enough of running or if he was in shock, he didn't reply, just stared at the crates, his cheek twitching.

It hadn't been easy, getting here, greasing palms, using his name while it was still good to get back into UK airspace, and then have a plane loaded with product sit idle in a nowhere airfield like a honeypot to feds everywhere.

But Luca wasn't winning this, and now Vitari had Francis, Luca couldn't get to him. Nobody could. DeSica, the cops, even Giancarlo. Maybe Venezuela would be a good thing. At least he could control his life there.

He'd been sure Francis had been about to run again on the steps. He'd heard his prayer about evil and read much of it on his lips. Francis was probably right, he *was* evil. He'd been told it often enough in the small dark room from his childhood. Evil, broken, good for nothing.

The plane left the ground and climbed, then levelled out. They were on their way. What the fuck was he going to do with Francis once they landed?

He hadn't planned to have the priest tag along to the coca farms. Francis would be alright. He was a lot tougher than he looked or gave himself credit for. He was resourceful, quick, and hid an angry streak that saw him land that beautiful backhand on Luca. That little prick had it coming.

But then, Francis had always been different. From the moment Vitari had laid eyes on him, he'd known the man was special, he just couldn't figure out why.

They didn't talk, and after a while, the plane's engines lulled Francis to sleep.

Vitari rested his chin on his knee and watched Francis's head loll to the side. The black robe clung to him—his armor. Once he took it off, he'd be vulnerable again. Vitari knew that much. Those robes protected him, but also weighed him down. The rectangle of white collar was back around his neck, like a noose. Vitari imagined plucking it free for a second time, then he'd straddle Francis's lap, tip his chin up, and kiss him. He'd kiss him until Francis's eyes were no longer full of pain, until he was free of that noose.

It was a stupid dream.

Men like Vitari didn't get happy endings. And they definitely didn't get the good guys.

He was fucked anyway. They both were.

Unless they could pin down why Giancarlo wanted Francis, why the DeSica wanted him. Why two of the largest crime syndicates in the world were so fucking interested in a priest. What could he have seen? What had he done? Something important enough to risk exposure, to lose enforcers over, for Vitari's father to banish him to Venezuela for.

Vitari hugged both knees to his chest, then propped his chin on top and let the thrumming plane and swinging rigging lull him somewhere close to sleep. With any luck, Venezuela would be a walk in the park compared to the last few weeks.

It couldn't get much worse.

Vitari woke with a jolt. The plane's engines were powering down as the plane rumbled and bounced down the runway.

Francis sat rigid on the seat, his robe folded on his lap. His civilian clothes jarred again with Vitari's impressions, casting aside the man of the cloth, and all the pomp that came with it, leaving just a man in black slacks and a plain white button-down shirt.

He glowered back at Vitari, which was better than the thousand-mile stare he'd been giving the crates when they'd left England.

Vitari climbed to his feet and stretched out sore and bruised muscles. "You good?"

Francis nodded, croaking, "Yes."

"All right." Vitari grabbed the rigging by the door and watched Francis get to his feet, with the robe tucked safely under his arm.

He still looked like Father Francis Scott, *the infamous English priest,* but hopefully nobody this side of the Atlantic was paying attention to the international news. "You're going to need a different name."

"Why?"

"Because you're famous and a target for every guerrilla sindicato in Caracas."

"But I like my name."

Fuck, he was so wet behind the ears he was going to get himself shot. "Just pick a name," Vitari snapped.

"I don't know... Justin?"

He wasn't a Justin. "Not that one."

"You pick one then," he growled back. Sweat gleamed on Francis's face.

Jungle humidity had begun to seep into the plane, now the air-conditioning was off. Vitari plucked his own shirt from his back. He hated the jungle. Jesus, what was he doing here *with Francis*? The door clanged from the outside.

Vitari side-eyed Francis. "Frankie." He tugged his collar away from his neck, then unbuttoned the top few buttons. "Keeps things simple."

Francis pulled a face. "Frankie?"

"Shit is different here," Vitari said. Why was his heart pounding? He wasn't usually this nervous greeting the locals. "Stick with me, don't do anything stupid, and you'll be fine."

The door opened and a blast of superheated jungle air washed in, like walking into a sauna. Carlos's people stepped out of the way and the man himself grinned, thrusting out his hand for Vitari to shake. Behind him, two men wearing camo gear and carrying assault rifles stood guard.

"Ahn-hel," Carlos greeted, grinning from ear to ear.

They shook. Vitari slipped into his role as Battaglia rep and introduced Frankie as an important *friend* in Spanish.

Carlos and Francis shook hands, while Francis blinked and smiled and had no fucking clue what was happening, then Carlos plowed into a breakdown of the key areas of the business. They descended the rusted old steps from the plane, as the plane's cargo door groaned open. An army of locals swept in and began to unload product by hand toward a convoy of parked trucks.

Carlos and his armed men escorted Vitari and Francis toward a row of shiny black Toyota Land Cruisers, and Francis gawked at the operation, his eyes wide and face pale, like a lost deer in headlights.

Carlos took a gold nugget from his pocket and tossed it into the air. Vitari caught it and smiled, weighing the golf-ball-size nugget in his hand. "Nice." He dropped it into his pocket and climbed into the front of a waiting Land Cruiser. Francis fiddled with the seat belt in the back, trying to dig it up from where it had been wedged between the seats. Nobody used belts; they got in the way of a quick exit should the convoy get ambushed. Vitari could have told him, but watching him struggle was more fun.

As they got underway down a jungle track, Francis must have noticed nobody wore their belts and gave up trying to fish for his. Vitari hid a smile behind his hand and peered out of the window at the sweating jungle. The track widened, then joined a gravel road, and as the sun rose over the jungle-clad mountains, the convoy trundled into the town of El Cristo. The guarded escort trucks peeled off, no longer required since the de Vincente Sindicato owned El Cristo, and the Battaglia owned the Vincente. They were as safe here as back home in Calabria. Maybe safer.

Carlos showed them to a newly constructed house situated halfway up a hill on a plot of land among swaying palms, overlooking the town. Vitari made all the right kind of impressed noises, hoping he could take a shower before diving into business. But then Carlos invited Vitari for breakfast with the family—an invitation that couldn't be refused.

"You should stay here," Vitari told Francis in English,

while Carlos rattled off orders for his men to inform his housekeepers they had company.

"Here?" Francis stood in the middle of the living area—damp shirt clinging to him, his hair sticking to his face, with the fan swishing above—looking lost. "What is this place?" He clutched his robe like a talisman. He'd gone from his quaint English village to the wild Venezuelan rainforest in less than twenty-four hours.

"Relax, Frankie. I'll be back later."

He nodded, eyes wide.

Vitari held his gaze, and something like guilt squirmed in his gut. It wasn't his fault Francis was here, so why did he feel responsible for him? "I'm a king here. Nobody is going to hurt you." Vitari smiled, hoping some of his confidence might put Francis's mind at ease.

Francis swallowed, blinked a few times, and nodded, but appeared to remain unconvinced. He just needed a few hours for the culture shock to wear off. He'd be fine.

Vitari left the house and walked with Carlos down the hill. When he glanced back up the hill, Francis stood on the veranda, watching them leave.

There's nowhere to run here, Father.

That thought should have eased Vitari's guilt, but instead inexplicably made it worse.

CHAPTER NINETEEN

FRANCIS

The next few days passed in a blur of men with guns visiting the house, and Vitari leaving for most of the sweltering days. One night he didn't come back at all, and Francis convinced himself Vitari was dead in the jungle, abandoning Francis in the middle of a foreign country with no way out.

Every morning, he woke covered in sweat from the humidity and fear. He made his own breakfast from the supplies, then prayed for guidance for himself and for Vitari.

On the third day, Isabel the housekeeper arrived, and while she didn't know any English, and he only knew a few very basic Spanish words, they managed to strike up an awkward broken conversation. He made her a drink after feeling guilty while she toiled to clean the house in the heat. He learned she had a family—two young boys. She showed him photos, then through some deciphering and gesturing, he also learned her husband had been killed in the mountains. He didn't ask why but could guess that most men in the town worked for Vitari's organization.

He prayed with her, which she seemed to appreciate, and when she left, the sinking sense of loneliness and isolation crept back in.

Was this his life now? On the run in a faraway land?

At least the view of the mountains was breathtaking. He tried not to think too long about what went on beneath the jungle canopy. Illegal gold mining, for sure, since he'd seen the gold nugget Vitari's contact had given him when they'd arrived. Drug factories. Cocaine, perhaps. Exploitation of the locals.

Isabel returned in the evening, a few days later, and as she restocked the cupboards, she asked about Francis in broken English. He couldn't tell her who he was, but he told her the truth otherwise. No family, no wife, nobody really to speak of. His family was the Church, he told her, but didn't dare say any more. She mentioned the town had a little church, and how her son was sick, so he prayed with her as she clutched her rosary.

It felt good, helping her. Gave him an anchor in the swirling storm that had become his life.

Vitari stumbled in as they finished praying, finding them both on their knees at the coffee table. His scathing glare and dilated pupils warned that something bad had happened. He barked at Isabel in Spanish, clearly terrifying her so much that she hurried from the house.

"You've been here less than a week and you're praying with the fuckin' housekeeper?" Vitari grabbed an unmarked bottle from the cupboard, ripped off the top, and poured the clear white liquid into a glass. He gulped it back and eyed

Francis though dark lashes. "Does she know you're a priest?"

Francis hadn't missed the handgun tucked against Vitari's lower back.

"No." He sensed that if she did, he'd never see Isabel again. "Her son is unwell—"

"I don't care." He took another deep sip of his drink and maneuvered around the kitchen counter, keeping a hand on it to steady himself. "You don't even speak the same language."

"God is universal."

Vitari laughed, sounding callous and cruel. "God?" he mocked. "There's no God here."

Francis straightened. Vitari was a dangerous man, even more so when out of control. But he didn't *look* dangerous right now. He slumped against the counter, eyeing Francis, as though waiting for judgment, daring him to comment. Whatever he sought, he must have found it, because he snorted a laugh, swaggered through the living room, and stepped out onto the veranda.

Francis waited a while, then joined him outside, where he sat on a lounger, sipping his drink. "There's a church here," Francis said. "I'd like to visit—"

"Do what you want." Vitari waved a hand. "Just stay in the town. Wander too far into the jungle and someone will mistake you for a tourist and cut your ears off to ransom."

Was that true or was he just being dramatic? "I can leave the house?"

"I said yes, didn't I? You're not my prisoner. Jesus."

After being trapped for days, he eyed the road outside that snaked down the hill and wanted to leave immediately, just to stretch his legs and to look at something other than the same view and same walls. But the state of Vitari held him back. Right now, sitting on the lounger, staring at the mountains, an aura of sadness hung around him. The drink was a crutch.

"What happened today?" Francis asked. He sat on the second lounger, far enough away to give Vitari space.

"Nothing." He continued to stare at the mountains but his cheek twitched as he ground his teeth. He glanced over. "You think I'm going to confess my sins?"

"No—"

"Jesus, do you get off on knowing everything about everyone? You enjoy listening to all their juicy, fucked-up secrets, Father?"

"It's not like that, at all." If he knew the toll it took to bear the weight of so many sins, he wouldn't snarl like he was now. If he knew the times Francis had buried his face in his hands and cried under that weight, he wouldn't judge him with that cold glare. But this wasn't about Francis.

Vitari eyed him side on. "What's the worst secret you've been told?"

Francis stayed silent.

Vitari grinned, teeth bright in moonlight. "All those sheep in your flock. I bet they get up to all sorts of filthy shit, and they tell you all about it the next day so they can go and do it again. It's a fuckin' joke."

Francis pressed his lips together and stared out at the mountains too. Vitari couldn't be reasoned with when he was like this. He had too much going on in his head to see the damage his words were doing. "I understand your anger."

"No, you don't."

"You're in pain. Will you let me pray for you?"

Vitari arched an eyebrow. "Go on then. Let's hear it."

Francis closed his eyes, bowed his head, and prayed.

"Lord God, be near us in my time of weakness and pain. Sustain us by your grace, that our strength and courage may not fail. Heal us according to your will, and help us always believe what happens to us here is of little account when you hold us in eternal life, my Lord and God. Amen."

Francis expected a snide remark, some lashing rebuke, but Vitari just smiled and faced the jungle again. They fell silent together, listening to frogs croak and crickets chirp. A warmth embraced Francis's heart, and he knew God was there with them.

"I watched a kid get blown away today." Vitari's expression tightened as he fought to hide his hurt. "The stupid prick was stealing gold. He'd been caught before, so..." He took a drink to drown the words.

The loss of human life was always terrible, but the loss of a child's life, even more so. Francis closed his eyes and bore the weight of that confession. When he opened his eyes again, he asked, "Could you have stopped it?"

Vitari stilled. He swallowed hard. "Maybe. No. It's complicated."

The silence returned.

"Kids don't deserve that," Vitari whispered. "Grown men can fuck each other over, we know what we're getting into, but that kid was just trying to get by. He wasn't stealing gold because of greed. His mother is sick—I found out later. Doctors out here are expensive." He rubbed his face. "We're supposed to look after these people, that's how it works. We own them, they help hide our operation from the police, and we look after them. We care for them. I didn't come here to execute fuckin' innocent kids."

Something ice cold and viciously sharp shone in Vitari's eyes. He stood, then grabbed for the lounger.

Francis reached out and caught his hand, helping to steady him.

Vitari peered at their entwined hands and frowned. The depth of pain in his eyes went soul deep. Francis felt it too—the agony of loss and guilt.

"I'm going to bed." Vitari eased his hand free and staggered through the living area, vanishing into the back of the house.

Francis stayed on the veranda, listening to the jungle chirp and rustle, and sometimes, the occasional laugh brought to him on the breeze as it swept through the town. The warmth was still there, in his chest. A comfort, and a purpose.

He gazed down at the town's twinkling lights and wondered if all of the trauma, all the woe and tests, had brought him to the one place on Earth he needed to be.

Tomorrow, he'd visit the church.

Weeks went by, then months. Francis saw little of Vitari, and spent most of his time at the tiny church, helping where he could. Vitari spent days and nights away, doing whatever he did in the jungle. They orbited one another, aware of each other at a distance. One night Vitari announced he'd be gone for a week, and the next morning, he'd left. Vanished like mist under the sun. While he was away, Francis threw himself into helping those who needed God's guidance. *Blanco Padre*, they'd begun to call him. Father White.

There was no harm in it. He liked them. They were good people, honest people, caught in a world of violence and politics and crime that had its roots in many previous generations. He couldn't fix that, but he could give them solace and spiritual guidance.

He returned to the house, weary from the day's work but uplifted too, in a wholesome way he'd rarely experienced in England.

"What are you doing?" Vitari said. He leaned against the far wall, in the lounge with the lights off, arms crossed, like an ambush. After days without him, he reappeared like a stranger in Francis's life, just a silhouette of someone he'd almost known.

A shoulder-holstered gun contrasted with Vitari's white shirt.

"I don't—"

"Blanco Padre?" Vitari pushed off the wall and swaggered closer. "What the fuck? Do you want Luca coming here? Do you want to be found, is that it?" His angry eyes flashed in the gloom.

He had no reason to be angry. He just didn't understand. Francis raised his hands. "They don't know who I am. It's just a name."

"You can't help yourself, can you?" Vitari snorted. "You just gotta be the center of attention, got to polish your halo where everyone can see." He stopped in front of him and raked his derogatory glare over Francis.

Francis stood firm and clenched his fists. Why was Vitari being like this? "I like the people, I like helping them. What else am I supposed to do? Sit here and wait for you?"

"This isn't a vacation camp," he snarled, and the viciousness in his eyes was real. "There are at least eight criminal syndicates who will gladly shove you against a wall and put a bullet in your brain. I'm trying to protect you, Francis."

"*You* kidnapped me. You brought me here!"

"I didn't kidnap you." He snorted. "You got on that plane with me of your own free will. This isn't my fault. You chose to be here."

"To help you!"

Vitari recoiled. "I don't need your fuckin' help."

"Yes, you do, Vitari. You're a mess, you're in pain, and I can help you." Francis moved closer, offering his hands, trying to make him see and understand. "This isn't you, any of it. This whole life you're embroiled in, you pretend to love it, but you're afraid, every day."

"Back off, Padre. I'm not your charity case." Vitari moved as though to turn away, then lurched and thrust a finger in Francis's face. "You're the one who needs to save everyone because you can't save yourself. You're the one fuckin' trapped, not me."

The torrent of anger washed over Francis. Vitari was hurting, and that was when he lashed out. He didn't need rage from Francis, he needed someone to listen, someone to tell him everything was going to be all right. Vitari wasn't here because he wanted to be. He *was* trapped. How could he not see it?

"Goddamn you, Francis," he snarled. "Don't go back to that church."

Francis frowned. "I'm going back."

He barked a strained laugh. "They will find out who you are."

"I don't care. I'm helping people. I'm making a difference here."

"What about you? What about me?" Vitari tapped his chest, his hands getting more animated by the second. "Don't you get it? We're fuckin' dead men. The *family* just has to say the word and we'll be executed like that stupid kid. I'm here because I didn't kill you when I should have, you're here because Luca has pictures of you sucking my dick, and the DeSica are convinced you're important. Keep your fucking head down, Francis, or I can't fucking protect you."

No, he wasn't obeying Vitari. He'd spent too long on his knees, obeying others. This was his life, and he could make something here. "What else is there? Why am I here? You don't understand, I have to do this. I have to make things better. I have to help them."

"Why?"

"Because..." The words stuck in his throat like razor wire. Because he was broken inside, because this was the only way he could lighten his soul, because for the first time in forever he felt as though he might be redeemable.

Impatience flashed across Vitari's face. "Why do you have to risk both our lives for strangers, Francis?"

"I'm a priest."

Vitari laughed. "No, you're not, remember? You're Frankie, a nobody who the jungle will chew up and spit out. I should fucking shoot you myself."

"Fine, then do it!" He lunged for Vitari's gun.

Vitari—lightning fast—drew the weapon and aimed between Francis's eyes. Francis froze, gulping hard, and raised his hands.

Vitari's top lip curled. He pressed the gun under Francis's chin, tilting his head back, and stepped in close. His firm chest burned against Francis's shirt. He breathed fast too. "Don't try me, Francis," he hissed close to Francis's cheek, gaze flicking up. Francis closed his eyes. The cold pressure of the gun increased as Vitari leaned into it. Vitari wouldn't shoot him, they'd come too far, but the gun digging under his chin made a mockery of any sense or reason.

"You drive me fuckin' crazy," Vitari whispered. The

words skimmed the corner of Francis's mouth. "You're so fucking good, all the time."

Vitari's lips skimmed that same place, and then his tongue teased and the gun still dug in, and Vitari's heat scorched Francis's body. He could smell the cool metal, and Vitari's cologne, the gel he used in his hair, and his sweat. But it wasn't fear making him tremble.

"I will fuck you up and drag you down in the dirt with me." Vitari's mouth skimmed his cheek, delivering the words into his ear, where they pierced all his barriers and slid inside. His wretched body strummed with lust, helpless when it came to Vitari. He knew how to undermine Francis's strengths and expose all his weaknesses.

He couldn't open his eyes; if he did that, he'd fall into Vitari's gaze and there would be no escape. Like this, rigid, eyes shut, nonresponsive, Vitari would get bored.

The gun's hard muzzle stroked down Francis's neck, down his chest, and Francis's heart pounded harder the lower the weapon dove. He was hard. It was wrong. Everything about this was wrong. But he was weak, just a man with needs and desires, and a long, long way from the perfect priest Vitari seemed to believe him to be.

Dreaded lust made his cock ache.

"Don't," he croaked out.

Vitari ignored him, and the gun's cool, firm muzzle stroked against Francis's dick, trapped awkwardly in his slacks. Vitari shuddered a sigh against Francis's mouth; not a touch, not really, and not a kiss, just a promise of one. But the not-touching made everything sharper, crueler, more real. The hardness of the gun rubbed him, and Francis squeezed his eyes tighter. He could withstand this. It was just lust, just animal need. When Vitari grew bored and stopped, the savage needs would fade.

"I feel your heat. You want... to... fuck." He dragged the words down Francis's neck, made them slow, made them torturous.

Francis's breaths stuttered out of him. His dick twitched, flexing, seeking more friction. If Vitari put his hand there, Francis wouldn't be able to resist. But Vitari wasn't touching him with his hands, just with his mouth, and the gun.

"How many times have you dreamed of me on my knees, Francis? I know you like me there."

"Please..." The gun ground against him, and Francis was wet for it. It was deviant, getting off on a gun like this, but... it felt so good, felt like relief, and the more Vitari rubbed the gun over him, the harder he wanted it.

"Please what, Padre?"

Please stop, please don't, please harder, please more, please fuck me, suck me. Please ruin me.

Francis opened his eyes, and Vitari's blown pupils shone like black diamonds in the dark. He was there, everywhere at once, and Francis couldn't escape. Didn't want to. God, he was going to come. He tried not to move, not to jerk his hips, tried not to seek more and more, faster and faster. Was he fucking a gun? Was this happening?

Vitari's wicked mouth ghosted over Francis's. His shoulder jerked from the rubbing action, and his smirk grew into a wicked grin, a grin Francis wanted to eat right off his lips.

"Your heart's racing. You goin' to come?"

Francis bit into his own lip, stifling a whimper. Vitari rubbed harder, faster. The gun clicked mechanically. What if it was armed?

Hot lust poured down Francis's spine, and liquid need

surged into his balls. Why did these violent thoughts torment him?

Vitari sucked Francis's lower lip between his teeth, pinched it there, and gently bit down, and with the action of his vicious rubbing, the assault became too much to fight, too much to hold back. Ecstasy thundered toward him, blinding bright. He cried out, jerked, spurting cum, and Vitari thrust his tongue between his lips, muffling his cries, kissing them away. He tossed the gun, swooped an arm around Francis's waist, and crushed him close. Vitari's hard dick dug into Francis's hip, nudging him as Vitari jabbed his hips, trying to fuck him with their clothes still on.

"No." Francis got his hands between them. "No, stop." He shoved, and Vitari staggered back. He grinned, wiped his mouth on the back of his hand and snorted, then adjusted his trousers around his obvious erection. That filthy self-satisfied gaze of his made Francis want to hit him —and kiss him.

"Cock tease," Vitari growled. He gestured at Francis's middle. "You got a little cum there, Padre." He picked up his gun. Francis couldn't take his eyes from the weapon and watched as Vitari re-holstered it and sauntered toward the back of the house. "I'll be in the shower dealing with my blue balls."

"Don't do that again!" Francis called, loathing how his voice trembled.

"Sure," Vitari called back. Even though Francis couldn't see the smirk, he heard it.

He stood motionless in the dark, uncomfortably wet *down there*. The sound of water running filled Francis's head with images of Vitari standing naked under the jets of water, his dick in his pumping hand, head thrown back, as free as any man could be. He wanted to do that, to reciprocate, not because he felt like he should, but because he wanted to see the delight on Vitari's face and to know he'd been the one to give him that peace, just for a little while.

He sighed and stared at the walls, the furniture, the mountain view from the window. He was pretty sure there was nothing in the Lord's teachings regarding men who fucked guns.

This was his life now.

And tomorrow, he was going back to church.

CHAPTER TWENTY

Vitari

Venezuela wasn't so bad. The Vincente operation ran like a well-oiled gun, churning out cocaine from the coca plantations and well-hidden processing camps, while the gold mines buried deeper in the hills brought in steady profits. The Battaglia provided guns and safe routes to ship the product out of Venezuela to Europe. The Vincente provided the product.

Here, Vitari didn't have to think about the shit waiting for him back home. As he was *still* here, and Luca hadn't shown his face, Giancarlo had to be pleased with the Venezuelan operation.

The convoy of Land Cruisers rumbled back into El Cristo around dusk and veered left, avoiding a colorful procession of people. "What's going on?" Vitari asked Carlos.

"Ah, the celebration." Carlos went on to explain the religious celebration was a local tradition that began as a holy day, then ended as an all-night gathering of food and wine.

Vitari watched the colorful parade through the SUV's tinted windows, and of course there was Francis holding a bunch of big-blossomed flowers in the middle of the towns-people, chatting animatedly. A little kid clung to his leg, peering up at him as though he was her fuckin' messiah.

That idiot. Vitari was going to have to remind him of the conversation they'd had several nights earlier. The conversation in which Vitari had made it very clear Francis wasn't to go back to the church. They had a good thing going here. Francis needed to keep his head down.

They decamped from the Land Cruisers and Carlos explained how his family would be at the celebrations and almost everyone in town would be on the streets. Vitari agreed to meet him later, then returned to the house, grabbed a bite to eat, and from the veranda, watched the procession lights trail through the village.

He changed clothes and sauntered into the town. Some younger townsfolk accosted him with gifts of drinks and food. After the first few ambushes by shy-eyed girls, he spotted Francis among the fray, talking and laughing with a family. A little girl handed him a yellow flower, and while Vitari couldn't hear the words, he saw how Francis grinned as though that tiny flower was priceless. He knelt and said something to the girl that had her big-eyed and full of awe. He didn't even speak Spanish. How had he gotten off a plane from England and stepped into life here as though he'd always belonged?

Blanco Padre.

Vitari snorted and gulped whatever spiced wine he'd been given.

He carved his way through the carnival-like festivities,

trying to make his way to Francis, but as Francis saw him, the sparkling joy snuffed out of his eyes and his broad grin tightened. He straightened, squaring up and shutting down at the same time. His reaction shouldn't have mattered. It was sensible to have his guard up. Most people did around Vitari. But for some reason, this time, seeing Francis shut down eroded the evening's warmth.

"A word," Vitari suggested.

Francis thanked the family in Spanish and fell into step alongside Vitari. "I'm not stopping," he said.

"I see that."

The party atmosphere grew as they walked toward the main street. A band played an upbeat drum and guitar number, drinks flowed, people danced in the dirt, with fairy lights strung above them.

"Where are we going?" Francis asked.

"For a drink."

Francis side-eyed him, waiting for the catch. Vitari smiled back, trying to keep the mood between them casual. They'd been in Venezuela for months and had barely held a normal conversation, which was Vitari's fault. He'd been busy. Not tonight though. He couldn't avoid Francis any longer.

They fought their way into a packed shack-type bar. The man serving drinks recognized Vitari and refused payment, then handed over two unbranded bottles. Francis took the drink but stood rigid, eyeing his surroundings as though he'd entered a den of sin. It wasn't the people that had him on high alert, it was Vitari.

"Is something wrong?" Francis asked, catching Vitari's eye.

"No." Vitari chuckled and leaned a hip against the ramshackle bar top made of scaffold boards.

"Then why are we here?"

"Relax. Can't we just have a drink?"

Francis narrowed his eyes, looking for the trick, then reluctantly perched his ass on the barrel stool and sipped his drink. Now Vitari had him here, he wasn't sure what to say. Scolding him for his church activities would drive him away. Francis wouldn't want to talk about the business; they'd only argue. So what was left? God?

"I started reading *A Song of Ice and Fire*," Vitari blurted, grasping the first nonbusiness, generally safe thing that came into his head.

"You have?"

"Yeah, I mean, I've only read thirty pages. I'm more of a visual arts kinda guy. Not very good at sitting still."

That got a slight smile out of him, and it stayed too, lighting up his face and making his smattering of freckles deepen. The warmth was back in Vitari's chest. As though Francis's well-being meant more to Vitari than he'd realized.

"It's not the same reading it when you know the big twists," Francis said.

"Like when Stark gets his head separated from his neck? Fuckin' idiot. He was way too naive."

They chatted about the books and TV series for a while, and Francis lost his rigid stance, becoming more animated. He'd probably believed he'd been about to get yelled at, and maybe that would still happen later, but for now, Vitari enjoyed just spending time with him. "You're picking up some Spanish?"

Francis cleared his throat and butchered a Spanish phrase that had both of them snorting more laughter. "Maybe work on that."

Vitari suggested they move outside, where the music was louder, and the night was alive with people and fairy lights, thudding drums, and spirited guitar. A sultry male voice sung in rich, deep Spanish. Jungle heat beat down, making Francis's face shine. His eyes shone too, their earlier ice all thawed.

"When you're like this, I forget who you are," Francis said, relaxing against the little table they'd found on the fringes of the festivities. He smiled his soft, almost shy smile. His *real* smile.

"And who am I?" Vitari teased, curious.

"Ah, there's the question." He laughed a little and studied the beer bottle in his hands. Warmth touched his face, probably from the potent alcohol, or the evening's heat. "You really want to know?"

"I know, but I want to see if *you* know."

They sat close, side by side, Vitari facing out toward the crowds and couples dancing, while Francis faced in, his back to the world. The opposite angle meant Vitari could see him in the corner of his eye as he watched the party. And he couldn't take his eyes off him, not this night.

"I don't know, we've talked about this, I guess," Francis said, still shy.

"Have we?"

"Yelled, mostly." He chuckled and looked up, finding Vitari's gaze on him. "You're caught up in all this, but I don't think it's where you want to be. Neither of us do."

This would usually have been the moment they'd argue, but his words didn't rile him this time. "I thought you liked it here?"

"I do, that's not what I mean."

Vitari stood, spun the chair, and sat facing away from the party, closer to Francis. The celebrations went on, but in their corner, the music wasn't as aloud, and it was just the both of them, in their own small bubble. "What do you mean, Blanco Padre?"

Francis chuckled again. "I had nothing to do with that name."

When he laughed, all the pain in his eyes vanished, leaving them soft and open and honest and so fucking perfect Vitari wanted to reach out and skim his fingers across the soft, tawny lashes. Their knees touched; Francis likely hadn't noticed, or he'd pull away. But the touch burned Vitari, making his skin simmer.

Vitari tore his gaze away and stared into the overgrown brush at the back of the nearby shack. This was... a lot. He was pretty drunk, so maybe it was the alcohol fucking with his heart. But being here with Francis, no insanity, no rage, just the two of them—it felt like a slice of normalcy Vitari rarely experienced.

"I wanted to ask, can I... I mean... Is this my life now? Can I stay?"

He *wanted* to stay? In Venezuela? "Fuck, I did not see that coming," Vitari chuckled.

"Yeah." He laughed too. "The jungle was not where I saw myself either. But I like it here, like it a lot more than—"

"England? Yeah, I know that feeling." Vitari breathed in, filling his lungs with spice-scented air. "Maybe." He could make it work. "But you have to be Frankie. Father Francis Scott doesn't exist. The family will leave you alone if they think you're dead in a ditch somewhere."

He paled some. He'd forgotten the real reason they were here. Vitari touched his hand resting on the table, earning Francis's glance. Fuck, the way Francis studied him now, through those brushlike lashes, his eyes full, maybe a little drunk, his pink lips soft.

Vitari wanted to keep him safe, but it was more than

want. His heart thumped so loud, Francis must have heard it.

Francis's fingers gently opened, touching Vitari's, then they slipped under his and curled closed, holding hands in some kind of mutual understanding. Except Vitari didn't understand this at all.

Just that he'd fight the whole fucking world to protect Francis.

He yanked his hand back and took a generous swig of beer. The fuck? What was he doing? What were *they* doing?

Francis withdrew his hand and rested it on his thigh. He faced away, clearly embarrassed.

Fuck, fuck, fuck, this wasn't some fairy-tale romance. Vitari's place among the Battaglia was at risk, and Luca had them both over a barrel with the incriminating photographs. The DeSica were still out there, hunting Francis.

Maybe Francis could hide in the jungle, but Vitari couldn't. In a few weeks, he'd be summoned back home, and whatever romance was blossoming here had better die on the vine.

"Sorry," Francis mumbled, thinking it was his fault for touching his hand after all the shit Vitari had done to him, taking his guilt like he took everyone else's.

"Whatever." Vitari shot from the bench and pushed through the dancing couples. He was a fucking idiot, drinking with Francis as though they were friends. Francis hated him. Like he should. The guy was a fucking saint and Vitari was... unworthy.

CHAPTER TWENTY-ONE

Francis

Vitari vanished into the crowd, swallowed by the celebrations.

Francis closed his eyes and tried to calm his spinning thoughts. He shouldn't have touched him like that, but he'd only meant it as a comfort, and Vitari had seemed as though he'd needed it.

Francis had needed it.

As they'd sat and talked and smiled and laughed, Vitari's walls had crumbled, and Francis had seen the real man behind the cruel bravado and criminal posturing, behind the fake smiles and vicious snarls. The man Francis wanted to know, wanted to spend time with. Wanted to touch.

It was a sin, he knew that, but that was the way of things around Vitari.

He downed the rest of the beer, listened to the singer's smooth, romantic voice and the guitar strum, and instead of relaxing, the rapid beat of the music quickened his heart. His knee bounced. The same knee Vitari had rested against, probably unaware how his touch had ignited Francis. Wanting Vitari didn't feel like a sin, didn't feel wrong. Not anymore. In truth, it had never *felt* wrong. His head had gotten in the way of what his heart knew.

He shoved from the bench, leaving his drink behind, and pushed his way through the smiling, happy people after Vitari. What was he doing? What was he going to say? He'd look like a fool, or worse, Vitari would be angry and yell at him about the church and how none of this was a game.

Francis didn't have any answers, he just knew he couldn't let him go.

He caught sight of Vitari's silhouette on the hill, marching up to the house.

"Vitari!"

Vitari turned and snarled over his shoulder. "What the fuck are you doing?"

Francis slowed, steps unsure. This was what he'd feared. He'd gotten it all wrong. "I just..." He glanced back at the party. "The celebrations are ongoing. I thought—"

"Then enjoy yourself, Francis. You deserve it." Vitari continued up the hill.

Francis stood on the track, halfway between the party and Vitari's retreating figure. He did want to go back and join the festivities, but what was the point without Vitari? He couldn't leave things the way they were; he couldn't let him go back to that empty house and drink alone.

He started up the hill, gaining on Vitari. He'd convince him to return. The hand-holding had been a mistake. It didn't mean anything.

He reached the house just as Vitari slammed the door and stalled again.

Maybe he should go back? Clearly, Vitari wanted to be alone.

This was his fault; he'd crossed a line. The lines between them were so confusing, always shifting. He never knew where he stood. He'd apologize, talk him around. There had to be a way to make this right.

He opened the door, and there was Vitari with his shoulder propped against the corridor wall, waiting. He looked menacing in the dark, hip cocked, one eyebrow raised. "I told you to go back. You never fuckin' listen."

He wasn't going to listen now. Worse than that, he was about to do something insane, something crazy. He stepped inside, then approached Vitari in the unlit hallway.

Vitari's eyebrows lifted as he sensed something had changed, and then Francis, without thinking, reached out and touched Vitari's sharp jaw. He pressed his lips to Vitari's. It had to be quick, or he'd snarl and say something harsh, and this would never happen. But this *needed* to happen. Vitari was in his blood, burning him up, and whenever Vitari hurt, so did Francis. His heart drummed, fear and adrenaline tangled in a heady concoction more potent than alcohol.

He didn't understand it, didn't understand them, but he knew that when they touched, the never-ending noise crowding Francis's head faded away, and there was just the taste and feel of Vitari on his tongue, and the smell of the expensive, light aftershave he wore—the way he smelled and tasted always so delicious, like sin.

Vitari's lips parted, his tongue swept in. He dropped the bottle, it smashed, and then his fingers speared into Francis's hair, and Vitari rocked in, clutching Francis's hip with his free hand. He shoved him against the wall, and the kiss went from careful question to savage demand. Vitari kissed with his body, not just his mouth. He rocked into Francis like a wave, washing in and out again, unleashed and wild.

Francis slid his hands down Vitari's back, pulling him closer, needing to feel more of him, all of him, at once. More, he needed more, needed his shirt off, but his shirt buttons were stubbornly stuck, the buttons too small under his fingers—

Vitari leaned back, tugged the troublesome shirt off over his head, and flung it aside. His naked chest was all the more tempting in shadow. Francis swooped in and sucked his left pec, tasting salty sweat. Vitari made a moaning, needy sound and then clutched at Francis, guiding him lower. Francis's teeth skimmed his nipple; he sucked and teased, and Vitari growled, the sound low and rich, strumming Francis's own need higher.

The music from the town hummed through the house, but the real world was far away. They were lost in some other reality, far from this one. Francis pushed, and Vitari eased off, then laughed as Francis shoved him against the opposite wall and attacked his neck. It wasn't enough. It would never be enough. Now he'd unleashed this need between them, he wanted to *devour* him.

"I want you," Francis whispered during a break in the waves. He met Vitari's gaze, and his eyes weren't mocking now.

He didn't say anything, just stared, then straightened and kissed Francis on the mouth, tipping Francis's head back, making him beg with his lips. They were the calm in the eye of the storm, his touch achingly gentle, so full of meaning and feeling, that Francis dared not move for fear of ruining it. How could this be wrong when it felt so right?

Vitari grasped Francis by the ass and hauled him off the floor. Francis locked his legs around his waist, flung his arms around him too, and kissed him breathless, knowing Vitari could feel how he burned for him, how hard he was. He teased his mouth, nipped at his lips like Vitari had done, and Vitari growled, hissing as he carried Francis into the lounge. They bumped into something, knocked it over.

Vitari dumped him on the edge of the dining table, tore at Francis's trousers, then shoved Francis in the chest, knocking him back so he had to brace on his hands.

Vitari looked up, and between their racing breaths, there was a moment where they locked gazes, and the depth of raw need in Vitari's glare sent shocks of lust to Francis's core.

Vitari grasped his dick, bent down, and his tight, warm mouth closed over Francis's cock, taking him deep.

Yes, he needed this. Needed it so much he couldn't think, couldn't breathe. He wasn't going to last. "Oh God." He couldn't last. It would be over too soon. He didn't want this to end, but he needed the release.

Vitari pulled from Francis's dick, swooped in, swept Francis into his arms, and captured him in a maddening kiss as his hands worked at Francis's shirt, flipping open the buttons until they were naked, chest to naked chest. Hot, slick skin stroked skin. Vitari's mouth scorched Francis's neck. He clutched at him, needing him closer. "More," Francis heard himself demand. He wasn't even sure how they could get closer, or how this could escalate, but then Vitari stepped back, undid his trousers, dropped them, and kicked off his shoes. He straightened, standing proudly naked. Cock hard and jutting. Body gleaming in moonlight.

Francis froze, shocked by the sight.

It was like at the pool, but without the shorts. Vitari didn't care he was exposed, but more than that, he knew how savagely beautiful he was.

"See something you like?" He took his own cock in his hand and stroked.

Francis couldn't find his voice to answer.

Vitari laughed, brought Francis back into his arms, and eased him off the table. With a few confident jerks, he dropped Francis's trousers and gently stepped closer, pressing against Francis's nakedness, switching their rhythm back to a slow, grinding motion. A dance of skin on skin.

God, the feel of firm muscle in all the right places, the soft tease of his tiny hairs, and then, when Vitari pushed so close, their cocks touched, stroked, and Francis rolled his eyes back and muttered a prayer for the Lord to keep him from coming too soon. Vitari's dark chuckle unraveled the last few threads of Francis's control. He was lost, so far gone he didn't care about anything, just Vitari's hot body and all the ways Francis could devour it.

He dropped to his knees, gathered Vitari's dick in his hand, and slipped it deep into his mouth, over his tongue, swallowing as far as he dared.

"Fuck, Francis, your mouth is a sin."

This definitely was. Francis sucked harder, bobbing, licking, using his lips to tighten his hold, then gasped free and licked Vitari's length, tounging the salty head, sweeping up his pre-cum. It still wasn't enough, but he wasn't sure how far Vitari would take this.

"Damn." Vitari clutched Francis's head and fucked his throat. "God, you're going to make me come."

Francis pulled free, gasping for air, and waited for the room to stop spinning. He kissed Vitari's trembling thighs, sinking his fingers into firm, powerful muscle.

"You've been holding back on me, Padre." Vitari laughed.

Francis, on his knees, peered up his fine body, He'd been holding *everything* back, like a dam containing a swollen lake. But, not anymore. He straightened and ground his dick against Vitari's, making him gasp, as though Vitari were the one at Francis's mercy. The power felt good, power to give pleasure.

Vitari grasped both their dicks in his hand and pumped his wet fingers. Francis clutched at his arm, clinging on. Vitari's breaths sawed against his cheek. God, he was going to come all the way undone. He rocked his hips, fucking Vitari's hand and his dick, seeking hot, delicious friction. God, yes. This was it. This was everything.

Vitari clutched his jaw with his free hand and lifted his head. He pumped with his other hand, and Francis fucked, and Vitari's eyes drank him down. "You're a goddamned force of nature, Francis."

His soul had been damned for years.

He fucked harder, then gazed at their dicks trapped in Vitari's hand, and it was the final trigger, the final push. Ecstasy blinded him. He came, sputtering. Creamy spurts landed over Vitari's fingers and up his hip.

"I can't—" Vitari's hand jerked, his rapid pace broken, and he came too, bucking, spilling. Cum dashed Francis's belly. It was filthy, and wonderful, and Francis was spent yet alive, empty but full. His head spun, knees going weak. He clutched at Vitari and rested his head against his shoulder, coming down from the highest of highs.

They panted together, heart to heart, sticky, wet, and trembling.

"If you say we can't ever do that again, I might fucking die right here."

Francis chuckled and lifted his gaze. Vitari looked down, and the electric shiver that ran through him was the same now as when he'd touched Vitari's hand at the table earlier. This was the real Vitari, complicated and lost, just like Francis. Except, impossibly, they'd found something in each other. Francis wasn't yet sure what that something was. He just knew it wasn't bad, it wasn't a sin. It was real, and it lifted his battered heart.

CHAPTER TWENTY-TWO

Vitari

Vitari hadn't done this. This was all Francis. He hadn't held a gun to his head, hadn't threatened him, all he'd done was walk away, intending to leave him at the celebration.

But Francis had followed.

He'd given him another chance to walk away, told him to go back.

And Francis had followed again.

This was happening, Francis had chosen him.

He'd known Francis had buried all his passion. He'd seen it in glimpses of his anger. But he hadn't expected the holier-than-thou priest to blaze like a wildfire, consuming everything in its path. It just so happened that *everything* was Vitari.

Vitari guided him to the shower, since they were both dripping cum, and once Francis stood alone inside the cubicle, he didn't break down or go into a crisis, as Vitari had expected. He washed off, stretching under the water, his dick half hard and hanging low, and then Vitari was the one staring. Francis was slim, with long legs, narrow hips, and a cock that fit perfectly in Vitari's hands and down his throat.

Francis showered, and his hair flattened, making his face lean, almost cruel, but then he'd smile, and damn if Vitari didn't get hard again from watching him.

He wasn't going to hide it either. He'd seen the way Francis had stared at him naked. It must have killed him to see Vitari swimming at the villa months ago. No wonder he'd fled back then.

Francis was pretending not to stare now too, but his cock had noticed, for sure. He gathered up the soap, lathered it all over himself, then hesitated when it came to rubbing his dick.

Vitari didn't hesitate. He opened the shower door and took the soap from his hand. "Let me." He lathered his hand, dropped the soap, and stroked his fingers down Francis's dick. Francis's lashes fluttered, his lips parted, heat flushed his face and chest. He responded so beautifully, so quick to surrender, his face full of desperate need, his body strung tight, ready to be fucked.

Vitari slipped his hand below Francis's balls, cupping them, then kneaded gently. Francis stepped against the tiles, using the wall to hold him up.

Vitari massaged and kneaded, focusing on his balls and shaft, avoiding the head. He didn't want to tip him over the edge too soon.

Water rained down over them both, washing away the suds. He'd never been free to touch another man like this, to relish in it, savor it. His encounters had always been rushed, desperate events, too afraid to be found out, and then later, when he'd learned of how the family treated men who fucked men, he'd stopped altogether.

But here, now, they were both free.

Vitari fenced Francis in, pinning him to the tiles. He captured his wrists and held them at shoulder height, stopping him from roaming his delicate hands all over Vitari. He gently rolled his hips, sliding his dick against Francis's. Skin clung to clean skin, juddering with the motion. What he wanted to do was turn Francis around, lather himself up, and sink deep inside his ass, but since Francis had only just come around to the idea that sex was good, he didn't want to push too far too soon. This wasn't just about sex, it was about silencing all the noise in Francis's head, all the voices from his past telling him this was wrong. Vitari didn't want to give those voices any excuse to be proven right. This was enough; it was more than enough.

Francis's breaths came fast again while he was pinned under Vitari's hands, dicks rubbing, jerking, sliding. Vitari freed one of his wrists, grabbed a bottle of conditioner, worked his fingers enough to gather up a smooth, thick cream, and switched to pumping Francis. Francis dropped his head back, but he didn't close his eyes. He fixed his brown-eyed glare on Vitari. The conditioner greased things up enough to make it last, that and the fact they'd blown off the first wave of lust.

They could slow things down. Enjoy it more. Relish it.

"You do it," Vitari said, letting go.

Francis glowered, clearly annoyed to have his approaching orgasm interrupted. "Me?"

"Yeah." Vitari braced one arm over his shoulder, then had a better idea. "Come on me." He dropped to his knees and peered up at Francis. From their past encounters, brief as they'd been, he suspected Francis got hot for him on his knees.

Francis grasped his own soapy dick, looked down, and

pumped himself, quickening. His wet face was the picture of ecstasy, glassy eyes open, lips full.

"On my face, do it." Vitari had hold of his own dick. He stroked and squeezed, alternating between pleasure and pain to stop from coming too soon.

Francis was beautiful. Vitari didn't deserve him, or this. Francis should make him beg, and Vitari would. He'd beg for that cum. "I'm on my knees for you. I know you like me here. Ruin me, Francis."

Francis gasped, jerked, and let loose a strangled shout. Cum dashed Vitari's face. He closed his eyes, letting it rain, and licked the sweetness from his lips. "Fuck, yeah." He fucked his fist, pumping like a crazed man, and came hard, his cock dribbling as the orgasm burned him up. He swore in Italian and clung on, panting against Francis's leg.

"Are you..." Francis's voice creaked. "Are you all right?"

Vitari flopped his head back and blinked into the streams of water at Francis's adorably concerned expression. "Come to bed."

Francis swallowed, and that shy little smile lifted his lips, simultaneously thrusting a bullet through Vitari's heart. Yeah, he'd fucking die for Father Francis Scott.

The sun was up outside, baking the town. Carlos and the others would be waiting. But Francis was tucked close, breathing softly, fast asleep, and nothing was ruining this moment. His chestnut hair had curled and tangled from Vitari's rough handling. His lips were pink too, his chin a little red from stubble burn. He looked fucking ruined. Vitari's dick twitched. He'd been the one to make Francis lose his mind over and over last night. Francis had fucked

Vitari's mouth like an animal and shouted his name as he'd come down Vitari's throat. He'd had him spilling on his tongue, seen the shock on his face, then that shy smile of his had turned wicked.

Vitari rolled onto his back and sighed. It would make the day easier, knowing he had Francis's cum inside him.

He'd never woken up next to a male lover before. His encounters had all been rushed, desperate fucks, followed by vicious threats so his amore didn't squawk about Vitari Angelini being gay.

What if Francis woke up and hated what they'd done?

Vitari turned his head, watching him sleep.

Francis had been a little drunk, and the party atmosphere had probably gotten to him. What if he thought Vitari had taken advantage of him again? He hadn't though, had he? Francis had come on to him. He hadn't forced him to do anything he didn't already want. But what if it was like everything else, and Francis had just fucked him because he was scared not to?

Vitari swung his legs from the bed, gathered up his clothes, and dressed outside the room, careful not to wake him.

If Francis was going to wake up full of regrets, then Vitari preferred not to be around to see it.

He grabbed the gun, holstered it, tied up his boots, then poked his head back around the bedroom door. Francis had flopped onto his front and snored, bare ass exposed to the air. He could just make out the tiny red mark where Vitari had bitten his right ass cheek. He wanted nothing more than to crawl back into bed, slide his fingers into Francis's ass, and make him gasp all over again. They hadn't gone that far last night. He'd sensed anal play was currently off-limits. But since he now had the finest view of that peachy backside, it seemed like fair play to think up all the things he could do with it.

He was getting hard again.

Laughing at himself, he left Francis sleeping. Today, was his visit to Caracas—a whole day's drive away. He wouldn't make it back before nightfall.

Maybe he should have left a note, like some loved-up boyfriend?

Jesus, he had it bad.

He met with Carlos, hopped into the Land Cruiser, and settled in for a day's driving knowing Francis would be waiting when he got back, and the next night he planned to ruin him all over again and have Francis ruin him in return.

They were both damned, exactly the way Vitari liked it.

CHAPTER TWENTY-THREE

It was midafternoon when Francis woke, with most of the day gone already. Isabel and others from the church would be wondering where he'd gotten to.

He lay on the bed awhile, body still throbbing. Vitari had been... thorough, with his teeth, and tongue, and hands, and... cock. Francis hardened under the sheet again, his dick a rechargeable battery that never quit.

He hadn't expected Vitari to still be in bed with him, and it might have been awkward if he were. Last night had been... "Wonderful," he whispered. He'd never so selfishly indulged, never surrendered so completely. He'd always been on high alert, afraid to be caught, terrified he was doing something wrong, afraid to lose control, and riddled with guilt afterward. There was none of that now. Just... peace in his heart.

If God didn't want him to feel peace, then perhaps God had chosen the wrong disciple in Francis.

Although, God *hadn't* chosen him...

He winced and turned onto his side, adjusting his thoughts. He didn't want the darkness following him here. Just let him enjoy the morning after. The inevitable pain and punishment would come later. Vitari would still try to banish him from the church, and Francis would continue to go. Nobody owned him. Not anymore.

He was free here.

He couldn't spend the entire day in bed. He didn't want Vitari thinking he was so wrecked he couldn't make it out of the door. He showered, dressed, and carried a mug of fresh coffee onto the veranda. The town was quiet, unlike last night, when it had throbbed with life and heat and color. He'd loved that too, being among amazing people who had opened their hearts and homes to him.

A trail of grey 4x4 trucks snaked into the town via the main through-road. It happened sometimes, when the people who worked the mines or the coca fields changed shifts. But these trucks were different. He squinted into the sunlight, shielding his eyes. The men in the back of the pickups carried rifles.

They stood, shouldered their guns.

Gunfire popped, like firecrackers.

Francis dropped into a crouch, but from high up the hill, he could clearly see how the men sprayed the town-houses with bullets, firing in waves. Then the screaming started. A young girl ran from her house, the same girl who had given him a flower the night before. She sprinted, screaming for her mama, and then fell like a doll when bullets strafed her in the back.

"God, no." Francis squeezed his eyes closed. Shock vied with sickness, churning up his insides. He might throw up, or pass out.

A door in the house behind him banged.

He turned.

They were here, men with rifles, the lower halves of their faces covered with masks so only their eyes showed. If he ran, they'd shoot him in the back like the girl. If he didn't run, they'd shoot him where he crouched. He was going to die here, for nothing.

He shot to his feet and raised his hands. "Wait, don't shoot! Por favor."

The men swung their guns toward him and yelled in Spanish, only part of which Francis understood. "Don't shoot. Me llamo Father Francis Scott, I'm a Catholic priest. Your boss will want me alive!"

They yelled some more and ran at him.

"I'm a priest!"

They jerked their guns, gesturing for him to get down. He began to kneel, then they were on him, pinning his arms behind his back. Hands hauled him upright and shoved him toward the door. What if they were going to execute him?

"My name is Father Francis Scott. Please, I'm an English priest! Please, don't kill me."

The rifle butt slammed down, and darkness rushed in.

CHAPTER TWENTY-FOUR

Vitari

Caracas was busy pretending to be a safe city so the American tourists would return. It appeared safe on the surface, even had some of the big franchises on the main streets that Americans would recognize. But the corruption ran deep. Vitari knew, because the Battaglia had a hand in all of it, all the way up to the mayor.

As the cars rumbled through the streets, pedestrians watched on, instinctively aware they were in the presence of royalty. This was what outsiders didn't understand about the Mafia. It wasn't as simple as just another criminal gang. Its influence ran blood-deep; it ran through the veins of a country, keeping it alive, feeding it, nurturing it, while taking from it too. Cut the Mafia out, and the country collapsed. The Battaglia did more good for the people here than the bent politicians and elected government.

And this was where Vitari reigned.

They switched from the beaten-up Land Cruisers to a

fleet of new, sophisticated imported Mercedes. Carlos was taking him to a newly built hotel to show off how far the Vincente had come, and to display some of their best product. Carlos was eager to please. Vitari had no complaints so far. Shit, Carlos and his operation were probably more of an asset to the Battaglia than Vitari was.

They entered the hotel like kings, flanked by a small army of security. Nobody would dare attack them. The security served as a flex. They *were* fucking kings.

Vitari was ushered into a shiny new conference room where, plain as day, several packages of cocaine had been stacked on the table. A crate of guns sat open on the floor, and standing back, a row of four young women finished the presentation, dressed in short dresses with plunging necklines. Two of them were trying not to cry through their smiles.

Vitari hid his sneer. There were some aspects of the business he didn't touch, and people trafficking was one of them. He knew it happened but stayed well-clear. Those young Venezuelan girls had either been bought or were about to be sold.

One of Carlos's eager crew stabbed a pocketknife into a packet of coke and drew a few lines on the table. Carlos wasted no time in taking a hit. Fuck, Vitari hated this part of the job. Best to get it over with. He couldn't refuse without causing an international incident and getting his balls squeezed by Giancarlo again.

He snorted the line and rubbed the dust from his nose, swallowing the immediate tingling. They all jeered each other in celebration—well, almost all. Not the women.

Vitari was given a tour of the new building, with its crystal chandeliers, sparkling beachside infinity pool, and deck area. All bought, paid for, and built on Mafia money. It was almost embarrassing how fucking whipped Venezuela was.

The girls tagged along. They all knew where this party was headed, and it wasn't a happy ending. If Francis ever learned of the deals Vitari did, he'd be disgusted all over again. He knew what Vitari did, but he didn't *understand* it.

The coke had its claws in him, racing his heart, making him loose and free. He really did *not* need to be thinking of Francis at work.

The meeting switched gears, moving to a basement casino, where the drinks and coke flowed. Vitari's girl was a tiny thing, barely through puberty, and there was no way he was touching her. He couldn't save her from the others when he left, but he could make it so she didn't have to be afraid for one night.

When the girl tried to make her move, he couldn't tell her she was cute but did nothing for him without causing a scene, so he played along, letting her corner him while the others gambled, drank, and groped the night away.

"You... with the priest, yes?"

Vitari blinked at her. *How the fuck does she know Francis?* His coke-spinning thoughts screeched to a halt. "What?"

"The priest." She plucked a crumpled photo from between her breasts and held it out. The photo showed a row of older priests, all lined up in their robes, with Francis's face circled in red pen. He didn't need to be singled out; his fresh face highlighted him like a civilian in a criminal lineup.

Vitari snatched the photo. "What the fuck is this? Where did you get it?"

She pointed. "Is in danger."

He stared at her and barely resisted grabbing her and

shaking all the answers out. Shock rattled his high or drunk thoughts. He hadn't expected Francis to follow him to Caracas. This was business. If Francis came into contact with the business, then his admittedly slim cover as Frankie was blown. "How do you know about him?"

"Victoria Chase."

The dead woman in Francis's graveyard? All of that seemed like a lifetime ago. Vitari grabbed the girl and manhandled her into a shadowy corner, making it appear as though they were getting hot and heavy behind a curtain. She stared at him, eyes too bright but far from innocent. "How do you know Victoria? Who gave you this picture?"

"Not Victoria. Adelita... is my sister."

The Victoria Chase name had never felt right, and now he knew why. Shit, did she know her sister was dead? He couldn't tell her, not here, and have her fall to pieces. "Fuck." He had to get her away from the others. "Play along, okay?" He switched to Spanish, repeated the order, grabbed her hand, then veered toward Carlos talking with his men beside one of the blackjack tables. "I'm taking the girl upstairs. We done for the night, Carlos?"

Carlos grinned and slapped him on the back, his eyes glassy from drugs. He told him to meet in the lobby in an hour.

Vitari hurried the girl along the corridors, up a flight of stairs, and tried several closed doors before happening upon one that was open. He tugged her inside, closed the door, and flicked the lock.

The girl whimpered and stumbled backwards, into the room.

"I'm not going to hurt you." He raised his hands, trying to appear less threatening. "Tell me everything you know about *that* priest."

Her big brown eyes widened, unsure but hopeful. "I do not know much. My sister said he'd help me."

How the fuck was Francis going to help her? He wasn't even supposed to be in Venezuela.

Unless it wasn't about now. She was talking about after she'd be smuggled to Europe in a few weeks. Once there, her sister had told her to seek out Father Scott. "Were you told to look for him in Europe?"

She nodded.

"Who told you?"

She bit her lip, shrinking around herself, more and more frightened with each passing second.

"Who told you to go looking for Francis?"

"Adelita."

The dead woman who Francis claimed not to know. "How did—does—she know him?"

She shivered. He was losing her. The girl was terrified. Fuck. He buried his hand into his pocket and dug out the gold nugget Carlos had given him when he'd arrived, then handed it over and closed her fingers around it. "When we are done, you need to walk out of this hotel and keep on walking. I'll tell your handler you're here, sleeping it off. Use this to get out of the country. It's all I can do for you. But you have to tell me how your sister knew Francis."

"They met."

Francis, that fucking liar. "Where?"

"I do not know. Long ago. She trusted him. She said he'd help, she was going to him, but she stopped messaging. I cannot reach her."

Vitari backed off and clenched his hands into fists to keep from hitting something. The coke was fucking with his nerves, but he had that under control; it was goddamned

Francis that made him want to yell at the sky. He'd known the dead women this whole time and lied about it?

He dropped onto the edge of the bed. "You said he's in danger. What do you know?"

"I heard them talking about a priest, Father Scott, and I knew the name. They looked at you when they were talking, making sure you could not hear."

"The men with me were discussing the priest?" Then Carlos knew who Francis was. Their fairy tale in Venezuela was over.

"Yes, they said he needs to be... dealt with. They didn't think I heard, but I did, and it seemed as though you shouldn't be told, as though you know him? I thought, maybe if you knew him, you could help me? I don't want to go to England. I don't want to be here—"

"Fuck!"

She startled and whimpered again, scared he was going to beat her. She'd probably had worse done to her.

"Is that all?"

She nodded and wiped tears off her face.

"Okay, you need to go while everyone is downstairs. Just walk out of here, all right? Don't run. Act as though everything is normal. You'll be fine. Go."

She nodded and hurried from the room.

Vitari buried his face in his hands. Fucking Francis, if he'd just played at being Frankie, none of this would have happened. But no, he had to be the priest, had to be fucking Blanco Padre and help everyone, and now their little slice of paradise was over.

"No, no, please don't—" the girl whimpered.

Vitari shot to his feet and flung open the door. Two men walked down the corridor, and as Vitari emerged from the room, the man in front raised his silenced gun and put a bullet between Adelita's little sister's eyes. She rocked backwards and fell, twitching on the floor with a weeping hole in her forehead.

Vitari's heart pounded. He saw the gold nugget tumble from her fingers and lifted his gaze to stare down the barrel of a gun. "What the fuck is this?! Do you know who I am?"

The bastard smirked. "Get on your knees, Angel."

If he made a grab for the gun, the guy would probably blow half Vitari's face off. "Whose orders?"

"Just business."

"Whose fucking orders?!"

"On your knees, pretty boy."

Vitari snarled and dropped to his knees, and the gunman's partner circled behind him, probably to tie his wrists. Or execute him. Vitari had about three seconds to fix the odds or this game was over. He waited until the partner bent down and slammed his head back, smacking the man in the nose.

The gunman pistol whipped Vitari's cheek. The inside of his lip split, and blood swirled over his tongue. He spat in the gunman's face, blinding him, and charged. The gunman stumbled backwards, fell over the dead girl, and as he tumbled, Vitari grappled for the gun, caught it, cocked it, and fired, blowing the man's face away. He spun and fired again, taking his partner down with a headshot.

Three dead bodies, and none of it had been Vitari's fault.

He righted his clothes, picked up the gold nugget, wiping blood from its gold shimmer, and dropped it into his pocket. It was time to get the fuck out of Caracas, probably Venezuela too.

He hurried back down the stairs, head and body buzzing. If the men he'd traveled here with knew about

Francis, then Carlos was part of it. He'd liked Carlos, trusted him. The bastard.

He tucked the gun in his belt, against his hip, and spotted Carlos across the casino floor, still deep in conversation with his crew. Most of the other men had paired off with the girls.

"Carlos, I need a fucking word."

Carlos's easygoing smile shifted, turning wary, as he spotted a growing bruise on Vitari's cheek and the steel in his eyes. Carlos stood and reached behind him.

Vitari flicked his jacket aside, revealing the gun. "Don't do that. I don't want to have to tell your wife and kids you're not coming home."

The room fell quiet, apart from the two irritating slot machines jingling at the back.

"You want to fuck with me, Carlos? You want to fuck with the Battaglia? I can bring this whole fucking empire down." Until he knew the truth of all this, he wasn't sure whose side he could trust, including his own, but he'd play the Battaglia card he'd always relied on until it stopped working.

"Thanks for the tour, but I think we're due back, don't you?" Vitari suggested.

They filed into the cars, with Vitari keeping Carlos close.

"What's going on?" Carlos asked. "What happened back there?"

"I was attacked by two men in your casino." He figured he'd leave Francis and the dead girl out of this for now. He didn't want Carlos knowing he cared about either of them.

Carlos's eyed widened. "Not my men. They don't work for me. Why would I do that? You are everything to us, to my family, my people. You protect us, you give us what we need to hold the mines. I would never jeopardize that. You must believe me. We are like brothers, si?"

He sounded genuine, but that just meant he'd been kept in the dark too. "What about Frankie, huh? What do you know about him?"

Carlos's eyes widened. He gestured wildly. "Blanco Padre? Nothing. He's your guest, a friend, si?"

Liar.

Fuck, he had to get back to El Cristo. If they were going to pull any shit with Francis, they'd do it while Vitari was several hundred miles away.

It was going to be a long drive home.

They rolled into El Cristo at 3 a.m., with the village still draped in darkness.

He'd seen enough dead to know how to shut himself off from the brutality of it, but when the dead were innocent people and kids, people he'd danced with, people he'd eaten with, chatted with, who lay face down in the dirt, Vitari's hardened heart cracked.

The men from the convoy ran to their homes, abandoning the vehicles, and Vitari. Carlos was among them. The moaning and wailing started soon after.

Vitari climbed from the Land Cruiser, and within a few steps, came upon a trail of dark blood where a body had been dragged.

The Battaglia was supposed to protect these people—*he* was supposed to protect them.

Francis!

Vitari could see the house from the main street. All its windows were dark.

Fuck, no. He bolted up the hill, heart thudding, lungs and legs burning. "Francis!" The front door hung ajar. "Francis!" He burst in, down the corridor where Francis had kissed him.

He knew what happened, knew he was going to find Francis in a pool of blood. He steeled his heart, shut down all emotion, and freeing his gun, he swept each room. Behind one of these doors, he'd find his body, just like those people in the town. It was always going to end this way.

He swept each room, certain he was going to find him.

But there was no body. No blood. Just a broken coffee mug on the veranda.

Vitari slumped on the lounger and covered his eyes with trembling fingers. Anger was a surging, visceral heat, a storm in his head and chest. He needed to stop and breathe and think.

Francis had been taken.

If he'd just fucking played the game, if he'd just stayed in the house and stopped being so fucking nice, if he'd done as Vitari had told him, none of this would have happened.

Although, the massacre wasn't Francis's fault. That had been something else. *Someone* else.

So many dead.

But not Francis.

Not yet.

He wiped the wetness from his eyes, and as the sun rose over El Cristo's blood-soaked streets, he cocked the gun, loading a round in the chamber, and vowed to Francis's God that the Angel of Death would burn the world to save his priest.

The somber sound of whimpering drifted from almost every house, but the quiet houses were worse. Nobody had returned to those.

Vitari pushed open Carlos's front door, skipped his gaze over the sheet-covered body on the floor, and found Carlos hunched at the dining table. His wife wailed somewhere in a back room.

"I need a truck and guns."

Carlos turned his head and the agony in his soul was right there on his tear-stained face. He reached into his pocket and tossed a truck key to Vitari. "Guns are in the shack, out back."

Vitari nodded and lingered. He should say something, but what? What words could take away the man's pain? "I'll kill them all, for this." He left and headed around the back of the house, where one of the Land Cruisers was parked, to the shack behind it. Vitari began to load a collection of rifles and pistols from the store into the back seat.

He'd seen the tire tracks running through the town, heading west. Whoever had done this was holed up near the mines. He'd hunt down every fucker and execute them.

Carlos arrived, and without saying a word, joined him in loading up. Three other men pulled up in a second pickup, equally armed.

"They went west, toward the mine," Vitari said. He slung on two shoulder holsters, then checked the magazines of the twin guns.

"Toccara did this." Carlos climbed behind the wheel as Vitari rode shotgun.

"You sure?" The Toccara militia had never been a threat. They weren't more than a handful of young men with religious fervor who stuck to hijacking trucks and kidnapping thrill-seeking tourists. They had to know the

Battaglia would wipe them off the fucking map for this. Something had changed for them to attack the Vincente.

"Nobody else is stupid enough."

They'd taken Francis, not killed him, so they knew he had worth. They may have just seen his pale face and figured someone in Europe would pay a few million to have him home safe. Vitari *hoped* that was all it was.

Let him be alive.

The trucks rumbled into the jungle, along washed-out roads and through thick foliage.

The Toccara would be expecting them, but perhaps not so soon, since Vitari had cut the Caracas trip short.

"Stop here." He nodded at a widened area of track. "We walk the rest of the way, fan out, look for signs of a camp."

Fresh tracks cut up the road ahead. They weren't far from the mining operation. The Toccara or whoever was behind this had carried on up the track, toward the isolated mine, probably killing all the workers so news of their takeover didn't reach the town.

As they climbed from the vehicles, water pitter-pattered on thick leaves, either from rain or from the jungle sweating. Vitari's clothes clung to him. His grip on the gun was greasy. He hated the fucking jungle, hated everything about this.

He couldn't bring the dead back to life, but he could kill the fuckers who'd torn through his town.

A generator grumbled somewhere ahead, and as they approached, voices sailed into the undergrowth. Carlos's men wordlessly fanned out and creeped toward the outskirts of the mine.

Vitari waded into a swampy low point, then hugged a rising bank on his belly and peered over the top, and there they were. A few battered white trucks were parked around an area of cleared jungle. Tents had sprung up, canopies too, to keep the rain and heat off where the men gathered, chatting without a care, as though they hadn't just butchered over fifty people.

Francis would be in one of those tents.

A few sentries stood watch where the track entered the camp, assault rifles cradled in their arms, but they weren't paying attention to their surroundings, just the road.

Acid burned the back of Vitari's tongue. These fuckers were about to learn hurting the Battaglia was a death sentence. But more than that, this was personal. Francis was down there, and Vitari knew from experience, he wouldn't have surrendered quietly. He'd be hurt, scared, praying to his God to send an angel.

Vitari glanced left and right. Carlos and the others were concealed, ready to deliver vengeance.

He drew both guns, rested his fingers on the triggers, and nodded to Carlos. "I need the priest alive."

Carlos nodded and shouldered his rifle. The others armed up.

If they went in fast and hard, there wouldn't be a fucker left standing.

Vitari nodded, giving the signal, and they started forward.

CHAPTER TWENTY-FIVE

FRANCIS

The gag they'd stuffed in his mouth burned with salt and an oily substance that smelled a lot like diesel. His head throbbed from the fumes. But as he was tied at the wrists and ankles and dumped on the muddy ground, there wasn't much he could do except use his tongue to try to force the rag from between his lips.

Nobody was paying him much attention. They hadn't even checked on him in the tent since leaving him there.

He worked the rag free and spat threads, then swirled his tongue around his dry mouth to try to get rid of the vile taste.

Now to his wrists. He'd tried wriggling and tugging, tried to force his wrists through the cable ties one at a time, but they were too tight. He'd seen a self-defense video on YouTube, where the victim had jerked their wrists apart to snap the ties. He tried it, but only managed to cut his wrists. Maybe they were supposed to be in front of him for that snapping motion to work? He couldn't remember, but he'd give it a shot.

Curling his knees to his chin, he pushed his bound wrists down, under his ass, wriggled left and right, and yanked his arms out from under him. He struggled to get his legs through, but managed it, and now had his bound hands on his lap.

If he recalled the video correctly, he should hold his hands out—

The tent flap opened.

Francis faced the man he'd thrown hot chocolate over some months ago. Luca Esposito. Baggy camouflage gear swamped him, but there was no mistaking his thin, reedy face and bloodshot eyes.

Luca spotted the rag on the floor and snorted. "You're a slippery one, aren't you, Father," he said in English. He came forward and crouched, arms draped over his knees. His glare raked Francis from head to toe. He poked his tongue into his cheek. "You look good for a man on the run. Guess you didn't run very far from Angel, si?"

Francis stayed quiet. He'd already told them he didn't know anything, that all of this was a mistake. Nobody listened.

Luca wiped a thumb across his nose and sniffed. "What, did you think you'd found yourself a happy ever after here, Blanco Padre?"

Vitari had been right. He shouldn't have made waves, should have just stayed in the house, but he couldn't live like that.

"You did me a favor, kept Angel distracted. But I couldn't stall forever. You're a popular man, Padre. For some reason, the DeSica are offering a few million to get their hands on you. That's a lot of cash for a nobody priest."

"You working for them now?"

Luca spat to the side. "Don't insult me. I wouldn't turn you over to those fuckers if they paid ten mill. I have honor."

"Did you kill all those innocent people because of your honor?"

"What people? Oh, the locals? No, they were in the way."

Rage burned Francis's throat. "The children too, they were in your way!?" He hadn't meant to raise his voice, but the words exploded out of him.

Luca's backhand landed like the lash of a whip. Francis tasted dirt and blinked back to himself, his face ablaze. He levered himself off the ground. "You gunned them down as though they were nothing."

"Because they *are* nothing. You want me to beat you, priest? Because I will. Shut the fuck up about the people. Nobody gives a shit about them. They work for me, for the business. I'm the fucking god here."

He knew he shouldn't respond, should stay quiet, compliant, but he bared his teeth in a sneer. Vitari, for all his faults, would *never* have gunned down kids. "Vitari Angelini is a hundred times the man you are."

Luca lunged and grabbed Francis by the jaw, jerking his head back. "Vitari is fucked. He's a cock-sucking homo like you. He's never leaving this fucking jungle. But you are, you're coming back with me, Father. Some very powerful people want to get their hands on you, and they're going to be real grateful when I bring you in."

Luca panted, his breath hot against Francis's mouth. He pinched Francis's cheeks harder, crushing them against his teeth.

"Maybe you should suck my dick, huh? Is that how Angel got you to cooperate?" Luca reached down, produced a knife and cut the ties holding Francis's ankles together, freeing his legs.

Francis breathed through his nose and glared back. If Luca dared put his cock anywhere near Francis's mouth, he'd lose his dick between Francis's teeth. He tried to convey that with his glare, but Luca's satisfied smile grew.

"You like dick? You want to taste mine?"

Gunfire popped outside the tent.

Luca let him go and freed a gun from the back of his waistband. "What the fuck?"

Francis slumped on his elbow.

Rapid gunfire clattered a staccato beat. The tent's canvas punched inward, and two new holes appeared.

"Fuck!" Luca plunged his fingers into Francis's hair and yanked him to his feet. Pain speared down Francis's spine.

Luca thrust a gun under Francis's chin and sneered in his face. "Let's see how much your life is really worth."

CHAPTER TWENTY-SIX

Vitari

Luca in camo gear burst from one of the tents, with Francis clutched to his chest, a gun under his chin. Panic froze Vitari's heart. "Don't fire!"

"Lay down the guns or the priest gets to meet his God!"

"Luca, you *sonofabitch*!" Vitari eyed Luca down the sights of his gun, but Francis moved, struggling, making Luca struggle with him. If Vitari fired, he was just as likely to shoot Francis as Luca.

"Put your guns down!" Luca ordered. "All you fuckers, you work for me, you work for Don Giancarlo!"

Carlos glanced at Vitari. Vitari shook his head. There was no way the Battaglia had sanctioned this. Giancarlo wouldn't risk destabilizing the entire Venezuelan operation. This entire fuckup was Luca's doing.

"I know what you're thinking, Angel. Giancarlo wouldn't do this?" Luca laughed. "There's more at work here than your little love affair with this man of the cloth.

This is bigger than you, bigger than me, maybe even bigger than Giancarlo. Big enough he'll risk losing territory over it. You should have handed the priest over, then maybe you'd still have a chance with the family. But you're over. This fuckup is the final nail in your coffin, Angel. All these people dead under your watch? The gold mines under the control of the Toccara? Giancarlo will blame you. Everything you touch falls apart. Your only saving grace might have been bringing the priest in, but you didn't. You're a dead man. You were never worthy of the family. Some bitch-whore's son, the result of Giancarlo's fifteen-minute fuck in a whore's cunt, hidden away in England, where all the dirty secrets are buried."

His aim waivered, Luca's words finding a weakness in Vitari's armor.

"He knows." Luca's eyes shone. "He knows what you are. Knows you like to take it in the ass, Angel."

Sickness soured Vitari's gut. Luca had given the photos to Giancarlo.

It didn't matter. Giancarlo wouldn't burn him over a few pictures. He'd served the family his whole life, ever since they'd dragged him out of that godforsaken boys' home. He loved the family, loved Giancarlo. That had to count for something.

Francis's lips were moving, likely in prayer.

Some of Luca's guards had moved in, the ones who were left alive. Vitari and Carlos had killed half. Carlos's men were all armed, guns aimed, fingers on triggers, waiting for the word to blow Luca and his men away. But if Vitari gave the word, Francis would die too.

If Vitari didn't fix this, didn't regain control of the mine, he was done.

But fixing it meant Luca pulling the trigger on Francis.

Carlos and his men wanted their vengeance. Wives and children lay dead. Blood for blood.

Only Vitari and his breaking heart held them back.

He needed to end this, to order them to kill. But Francis would die.

Fuck, why did he care so much?

The whites of Francis's eyes showed, his stare fixed on Vitari. What was he thinking? Was he praying for himself, or for Vitari?

He couldn't kill Francis, even if it meant his life was over. That damn priest deserved to live more than anyone here. He was the only good thing in this place, the only good thing in Vitari's life.

"Lower your guns," Vitari ordered.

Carlos flicked a questioning glance toward him.

"Do it," Vitari snapped.

The guns clattered as Carlos and his men surrendered.

Luca's grin grew, but he kept his gun under Francis's chin.

Jesus, Vitari was going to get them all killed for one priest. "Let him go, Luca."

Luca shrugged. "Kill them!" he yelled, and jerked Francis into motion, shoving Francis ahead of him, toward one of the trucks.

Luca's men raised their guns.

Gunfire rained.

Vitari snatched up his guns and dove for cover. Rounds sprayed the generator he'd dropped behind. Paint chips and bullets flew. Vitari hunkered lower, hugged the pistols to his chest, and as bullets peppered the ground, he caught sight of Luca escaping with Francis. Luca had the gun aimed at Francis's back. Vitari couldn't hear over the roar of assault rifles, but he saw Luca's mouth move, ordering Francis into the nearby truck.

Vitari likely wasn't getting out of this mine site alive. But he would damn well take Luca down with him. Still hunkered behind the chugging generator, he cradled a pistol in his palm, lined the sights up with Luca's head as he climbed behind the truck's wheel. Francis's panicked face showed at the window.

Luca spun the truck in a U-turn and accelerated hard. The truck's rear wheels kicked up arcs of mud.

Vitari followed Luca's silhouette. In seconds, the truck would vanish down the track. He aimed, breathed out, and pulled the trigger. The passenger window shattered, and the truck veered into the trees and slammed into a rigid tree, stopping dead. Steam hissed from beneath the hood.

Vitari blinked sweat from his eyes. Now he just had to make it over there...

The generator behind him coughed and died. Thick silence fell over the mine site. He dared not look to see if Luca's men were bearing down on him. They had to be. He just needed to see Francis climb from the truck, just needed to know he was all right. Flames spluttered around the truck's grille.

"Get out, Francis," he muttered, prayed, or begged. Was God even listening?

He wasn't getting out.

Why the fuck wasn't he getting out?

Vitari poked his head around the generator. One of the incoming militia glanced toward the truck, concerned for his boss—not looking for Vitari. Vitari raised his gun, fired, then spun his aim to the man behind him, and fired, taking him out. Vitari bolted from his hiding place, and ran like the fucking wind toward the truck. He leaped a barrel, almost tripped to his knees, but regained his balance and sprinted on.

A shot rang out.

Fire buzzed up Vitari's left arm. The bicep spasmed. The gun fell from his fingers, but he still had the one gun left. He leaped over a stack of felled branches and skidded around the side of the truck. The door hung open. Francis wasn't inside. Neither was Luca.

A round plinked against the truck, narrowly missing Vitari's head.

He bolted into the brush, following a trail of trampled leaves. Francis could run like a gazelle; he'd be all right, he had to be. He'd survive, his God would see to it. Priests had to get something out of the whole devoted-for-life deal, right?

Scattered gunfire sounded behind him. Splinters exploded off the tree trunks he dashed by.

"Francis!?" Where the fuck was he?

He ran, leaped brush, slipped in the wet ground. The jungle abruptly ended, brilliant blue sky opened up, and the ground vanished. Vitari almost toppled over the edge of a jagged ravine. He skidded onto his ass, gasping, and clung to tufts of grass.

Shit, what if Francis had gone over?

A hand shot out from a nearby bush and grabbed Vitari's blood-soaked arm. Francis emerged from the thick leaves. Dirt clung to his white face. "Quick. In here."

Vitari scrabbled onto his knees, following Francis into a hidden divot that had been torn from the side of the chasm, probably from a fallen tree.

They lay side by side, listening for Luca's men. Vitari's lungs heaved. His heart thumped.

A few shouts sounded, then faded.

Vitari set the gun down and raised his left arm. His bicep throbbed. Blood soaked his shirt. He unbuttoned his top few shirt buttons and peeled the fabric back from his shoulder. The round had nicked him, but it hadn't gone through.

"Is it bad?" Francis whispered, his eyes big in the gloom.

"No. Just a scratch."

Vitari shrugged the shirt back on and lay in the damp moss and dirt. They'd wait until nightfall, then hike out of the jungle. After that? Fuck knew. He couldn't think about tomorrow. Venezuela was fucked, he was fucked. He just wanted to lay in the dirt and breathe.

What was he supposed to say to Francis? He must have been there when Luca and the Toccata stormed the town. He'd have seen at least some of the massacre. Those people were his friends too. Francis had wanted to stay, to make a life here. There was no chance of that now.

Guilt made him sick to his guts. This was all his fault.

"Why the fuck didn't you listen to me?" Vitari growled.

Francis stayed quiet, then whispered, "I'm sorry."

Vitari gritted his teeth. "Those people are dead because of your fuckin' selfishness." He said it, then wished he hadn't, but it was out there now, and grief ruined Francis's face. "My whole life is fucked because of you."

"I didn't want this!" Francis hissed. "I didn't want any of this! I don't understand why it's happening! I don't know what these people fucking want from me!"

Vitari slammed a hand over his mouth and pinned his head down. "Easy," he whispered, "Easy, they're still around. Quiet."

When the panting through Francis's nose eased, Vitari removed his hand, letting him up. Francis's glare bounced over Vitari's face, accusing, but fearful too. But under that fear, he was hurting. Just like Vitari.

"I'm sorry," Vitari said. "I didn't... What I said, I didn't mean it."

His gaze stopped twitching. "You're right though."

"You didn't do this."

"I should have listened to you."

"Well, yeah, but if you did, you wouldn't be you."

They fell quiet again, with only the noise of the wind through the trees and the water droplets dripping off fat leaves. No more sounds came from the mining camp, but nightfall was still a few hours away. They had to wait it out.

"The dead woman..." Vitari said after what had to be an hour in silence. He tried to wet his lips, but his mouth was parched from lack of water.

Francis turned his head. They were close, side by side. The fading light warmed Francis's soft brown eyes, and for a moment, fear tripped Vitari's heart. He'd almost lost him. The one good thing in his life.

Vitari coughed to clear the emotional lump in his throat. "In your churchyard. You said you didn't know her."

"I don't."

He seemed genuine, but she'd known Francis. "Does the name Adelita mean anything to you?"

Francis shuffled up onto his elbows. "Adelita, I don't..." His eyes narrowed. And there it was. He knew her. And he knew a whole lot more. He rolled his lips together, and his Adam's apple bobbed as he swallowed. "No, I don't—"

"Don't lie to me, Francis."

His gaze shifted. "I didn't recognize her. It's been years..."

Finally, he admitted he did know her. "I met her sister."

"Adelita has a sister?"

"*Had*." Vitari lost his smile at the memory of the young woman dead in the hotel corridor. "How the fuck do you know two Venezuelan girls and why did they think you could help them?"

Francis sat up and dragged his knees to his chest, holding them there. "I didn't know where she was from. I just... The place where I grew up, we met there."

Ice touched Vitari's heart. "Stanmore?"

Francis nodded. "There was a converted coach house at the back, where they kept girls sometimes. They didn't stay for long. I didn't know where they went."

"Adelita was a DeSica prostitute," Vitari confirmed. "My guess is she was smuggled to England years ago. Now her sister was supposed to join her, she decided to reach out to you for help."

Francis nodded, but his eyes had darkened. There was nothing left of his smile.

"Why you?" Vitari asked. "A priest in a nothing town in the middle of rural England. Why are you so special?"

Francis propped his chin on his knees. He couldn't have made himself any smaller if he'd tried. "I helped her before, at Stanmore. Years ago."

Of course he did. He'd help anyone, even those with rotten souls like Vitari. "Helped her with what?"

"I can't talk about this."

"Yes, you can. Because someone out there is making our lives Hell because of it."

"I can't."

"Can't or won't?"

"I found her with one of the boys," he whispered. His soft eyes darkened. "She uh... she didn't want to be with him."

Vitari sat up too and picked at the leaves around them.

He and Francis had been housed at the same children's home, and he'd assumed Francis hadn't been touched by all the fucked-up shit that went on behind the locked doors. But what if it *had* touched him? What if he just hid it better than Vitari? "You stopped it?"

"I told him to stop, he didn't like that, landed a punch. Our brawl alerted the staff."

"What happened to Adelita?"

"I don't know, I never saw her again. Or any of the girls."

"My mother was a whore," Vitari admitted. "I don't know the story, it was probably the same as Adelita's. I don't even know if she was English or Italian, or from somewhere else. She got knocked up by Don Giancarlo, my father. They shipped me off to Stanmore when I was... I don't know... five, maybe? Young enough to forget where I came from."

"You were at Stanmore?"

"Yeah."

"I didn't... I don't remember you."

Vitari smiled. "You wouldn't. They kept the broken ones out of sight."

"That's not..." Something must have occurred to him, something that choked off his words. Maybe he knew what happened to the broken ones, and he was only now realizing how broken Vitari was.

Francis probably wished he'd never touched him.

Vitari wanted to tell him about his archbishop, the man Francis had knelt to and kissed his ring. How he'd had Vitari pressed face-first against a cold wall, how he'd *touched* him, and how it had gotten worse. And how the other boys had suffered too. But if he told Francis the truth now, it would bring the boy Vitari had been back to life, the boy Vitari had been in his past, the boy he couldn't allow to exist.

"When I was twelve," Vitari continued, "Giancarlo had me taken to him. He told me I was his son, that nobody should know, and I was to do as he said. If I did, and never talked of Stanmore, he'd see to it I was safe. So that's me, tragic fucking backstory an' all. What about you? What were you doing there?"

"I don't know. It was my home."

That was bullshit. He knew, but he didn't want to say. "How did you go from that shithole to priesthood?"

Francis's cheek twitched. "It was a way out," he said tightly.

Knowing all Vitari did, about how Francis had claimed never to have a choice, and how when he'd first met Father Francis Scott, he'd had the haunted eyes of a man trapped in Hell... he wasn't sure Francis had ever gotten out of Stanmore. It was still with him, like it remained with Vitari. It waited at the back of every dream, lurked behind the everyday, waiting to ambush him.

"You think all this has something to do with Stanmore?" Francis asked, guiding the subject away from his personal life.

"If not, it's one cosmic fucking coincidence that you and me come from the same boys' home, and the dead woman met you there, and her sister corners me in a Venezuelan casino with a picture of you, begging for help."

Francis rubbed dirt from his cheek and said, "She had my picture?"

Vitari hunted through his pockets and found the picture, all crinkled and damp, but intact. He handed it over.

"Oh." Francis's eyes turned glassy. "That was my ordination. Why am I circled in red?"

"Because you're at the heart of all this."

Francis motioned to hand the picture back.

"Keep it."

"Luca said this was bigger than us," Francis said, tucking the photo into his pocket.

"My guess, someone with a lot of money and power wants you silenced. Someone else got wind of that and wants to use you against that powerful person. The question is, why now? Why not ten years ago? What changed?" Vitari watched Francis for any reaction, any clue he knew more than he was letting on, but he stared out across the jungle ravine.

"I'm a pawn in a game of power."

"Yeah."

Francis pulled his legs close again. "How do we survive all this?"

"I'll think of something." Francis looked at Vitari with real hope in his eyes, and even as Vitari's heart crumbled, he smiled. "I always do."

CHAPTER TWENTY-SEVEN

Francis

They hiked through the jungle at night, wading through long brush and batting giant, wet leaves aside. Luca was still at large. He'd kill Vitari, and Francis had no wish to get anywhere near Luca again. The vicious psychopath made Vitari look like a saint.

A horrible, choking quiet smothered El Cristo.

Vitari told Francis to wait at the tree line as he ducked low and disappeared inside the house they'd shared for months.

Francis waited, sitting on the ground, chewing his nails and listening for any rustle or revving engine. Vitari returned a little while later, speaking into a satellite phone. He huddled down in the brush next to Francis and reeled off instructions in fluent Spanish, then ended the call. "Now we wait."

"For what?"

"For Giancarlo to call back."

Giancarlo. Vitari's mob boss father. "What if Giancarlo is behind all this?"

"That's what I need to know. If Luca's working alone in a personal vendetta against me, then I've got sway. But if the *family* is backing him, then we're both fucked and we may as well take a flight to fuckin' Goa or somewhere. Giancarlo will either tell me to get fucked, or he'll smooth the way back into Italy."

"You're taking me to Italy?"

"Do you have a better idea? We keep running, they'll find us—" The phone chirped, and Vitari answered.

Francis listened to the one-way conversation, but Vitari spoke so fast, he had no hope of translating any of the Italian. He wouldn't take Francis to the Battaglia, would he? To his father? Why would he do that? They'd come out here to get him *away* from all of that.

Francis had been happy here, content, and now that was gone. He wasn't sure where he belonged, but it wasn't anywhere near the Mafia. What if he somehow reached out to the British police... Would they rescue him? Or Catalina Diaz, from the Spanish organized crime squad? Someone, some agency, must have the power to stop these people, to stop further massacres and extortion and abuse?

But if he called the police, that would put Vitari at huge risk of capture, and they'd want answers. Francis would be a key witness. They'd arrest Vitari. Everything would be splashed across the internet. All he'd done.

Francis knew too much about the mines, the drug routes, and the Battaglia were everywhere. If he spoke out against them, they'd kill him. Unless whoever wanted him alive was more powerful than the Battaglia, and Vitari's father. Who was more powerful than the Mafia? Francis's heart sank. The Church.

He hadn't wanted to think it, didn't want to open the doors and let it into his mind now. But... what if the Church had been behind this all along?

It was no coincidence he and Vitari had been raised in the same boys' home, and knowing that, the pieces of the puzzle had begun to tumble into place. Stanmore hadn't just been any boys' home. A Mafia boss had shipped his secrets there. And the Catholic Church too. Archbishop Montague had been Stanmore's patron.

Shh, don't make a noise, this will be our secret.

Vitari had asked him why now. What had changed to trigger all this.

It could have been Adelita's rush to his church, to ask for help, but it was more likely the Private & Confidential letter still in Francis's desk drawer. Someone had opened it, read it, and left it there, like a smoking gun. Or a warning.

He'd been about to sue Montague for historical sexual abuse, and there was nothing the Church despised more than one of their own breaking their vow of obedience.

"Hey, Francis?"

He blinked at Vitari's soft, half-smiling face, and the real concern he found there. Would Vitari protect him? He'd fought Luca to save him...

"I asked, are you all right?"

"Yes. Fine." But his heart thumped and his head whirled and his hands shook, and if he stood, he might fall again.

Vitari frowned and knelt in front of him. "Don't fall apart on me now. We need to get our asses to the airstrip for tomorrow morning. We're hitching a ride out of here. I know you wanted to stay, and I'm fucking sorry it's turned out like this—Francis?"

Hands were on him—hot, heavy hands. People were

dead. The Church was somehow embroiled in all of this. Was it Archbishop Montague? If that was the case, then all of this was Francis's fault. "I said I'm fine!" He shoved Vitari off. He needed to breathe. To think.

Vitari raised his hands and backed away. "All right. Okay. Fuck." He planted his hands on his hips and turned his back on Francis. "Jesus, I'm doing what I can. I know I'm not fucking perfect like you, but I'm trying to keep you alive."

"Perfect?" Francis choked on a laugh. "You think I'm perfect?" Was Vitari mad? He frowned at Francis now as though *Francis* were mad. Had Vitari not been paying attention? Francis wasn't perfect. He'd failed at every-thing. And now he was failing at this too. All of this was because of him. Adelita, the dead men in the marina, the dozens dead in the village, and those back at the mine. If he'd just done as he'd been told and been the perfect priest everyone had wanted him to be, none of this would have happened.

All he'd had to do was keep his mouth shut, and he couldn't even do that.

"This is all my fault!"

Vitari lowered his hands. "This isn't your fault."

"It is! You don't understand, I..." He stood, and wobbled. God, he felt sick, and lost, and hot all over. Every-thing hurt. He couldn't breathe.

"Francis." Vitari reached for him.

"Don't touch me. Don't fucking touch me, Vitari."

Vitari's eyes widened with shock, then his barriers came down, and even that hurt Francis inside, like a stab to the chest. Because he cared for Vitari, he'd cared for all of them. "Just... leave me alone."

"Right, because I'm soiled goods, one of the one's they

used to line up at the back and take turns to fuck while you got a one-way ticket to sainthood."

"What?" Francis met his glare.

"Politicians, rich men, celebrities, even priests, just like you. So, fuck you, Francis. I won't touch you, if that's what you want. Wouldn't want to dirty up your halo."

A sob fell out of Francis. Then another. Vitari's glare accused him of all the sins he knew to be true. He couldn't do this, couldn't hear it, couldn't see it again and relive it. He knew it had happened to others at the home, of course he did, that was why he'd tried to make a difference, why he'd been about to expose the scandal. And why they were being hunted. But it had happened to Vitari too?

Vitari stomped through the grass. "Let's get to the airfield," he grumbled.

A shudder ran through him, and slowly, with each beat of his heart, the panic subsided. Francis hugged himself and trailed after Vitari, his soul riddled with holes.

The Land Cruiser rumbled over potholes and straddled cracks in the road. Vitari's watch glinted in the sun as he clutched the wheel. A smudge of blood stained the watch face, but Vitari didn't seem to notice, or care. He'd shoved his handgun into the door pocket. The handle part stuck out, within easy reach if he needed to grab it fast.

Francis fingered a new cut on his lip, courtesy of Luca's backhand.

He assumed Luca was out there. He'd been alive after the truck had hit the tree. Francis knew that much, but he'd been focused on getting away and hadn't seen where Luca had fled to.

Vitari hadn't explained the outcome of the phone call. But a plane was coming for them, and they clearly didn't have a choice. Venezuela was no longer safe. Not that it had been all that safe to begin with.

"I'm sorry," Francis said, when he couldn't take Vitari's broiling silence any longer. He had no wish to start another argument. They were both exhausted and bruised, emotionally and physically.

"It's fine." Vitari glared at the road. His cheek twitched.

Mud clung to Vitari's neck, and a leaf poked out from his messy hair. He was always so smooth, so maintained, that seeing him frayed and anxious had Francis wishing he could do more, say more to take the pain away.

Back at the house, after the celebrations and before it had all gone so wrong, Francis had experienced one of the best nights of his life. Maybe *the* best. He'd had a few sexual misadventures during his studies. You didn't study with the same men for five years in close quarters without a few... indiscretions. At least, that was how he'd excused it. But that night with Vitari had been a whole different level of pleasure.

He'd thought they'd had something. Something good.

But now, Vitari was a stranger all over again.

Was it Francis's revelation about Stanmore that had driven a wedge between them? Or had it been inevitable that they'd end like this? Francis hadn't meant to push him away... or bring up the past.

"I'm sorry too," Vitari mumbled, then tossed one of his careless smiles at Francis. "I'm an asshole."

"True."

Vitari snorted, then side-eyed him. "You okay?"

"I think so. You?"

"Yeah. My arm hurts." He rolled his shoulder and winced anew. "Could be worse."

And just like that, with a genuine smile and a few words, the wedge between them vanished.

The truck bumped over some gnarly washed-out sections of road, but the strip of cleared land ahead indicated they were close to the airfield. The outline of a cargo plane loomed ahead, probably the same one they'd flown in on, months ago.

He'd chosen to come with Vitari to Venezuela, although he hadn't known where they'd been headed. And he had regrets, but Vitari wasn't one of them.

"I'm going to have the pilot detour to Spain. Once there, Diaz, the chief of the Spanish organized crime unit, will pick you up," Vitari said. "She's agreed to take you in, if you answer her questions about the Battaglia. After that, she'll hand you over to the British feds. Since you're such a hot target, they'll put you in witness protection."

Francis stayed silent for a few minutes, absorbing everything he'd just been told. Vitari was... saving him? "I'll have to actually be a witness?"

"Yeah," he drawled. His fingers tightened on the wheel. "I'm going to pull some strings, see if I can throw Luca under a bus."

"Figuratively?"

"If I could find a bus, I'd make it literal. He needs to die."

Francis caught his own laugh before it slipped free. "Then you're all right with the Battaglia? They didn't sanction Luca's actions?"

"Hard to tell. Giancarlo didn't say. I think I'm good. I'm in the shit, but I'm also blood. I've got some room to maneuver."

That was... a lot. He'd organized to hand Francis over to the authorities at great risk to himself. That couldn't have been easy. "Thank you."

"Yeah, well, one of us has to survive this. Better you than me." He pulled the truck onto the airstrip and slowed its approach toward the plane. The propellors weren't turning, so they had some time before takeoff.

Francis studied Vitari's face in the waning sunlight. All those sharp lines didn't seem so sharp anymore. He recalled first seeing him, on his knee, head bowed while he prayed in front of the altar. He'd known then that Vitari was different. Special. He'd turned Francis's life upside down, but he'd also shown him what it meant to *be* alive. He'd showed him true passion wasn't a noose, it was an open door. The last few months, although horrific in many ways, had also been a revelation. Francis had found himself here. He'd be sorry to leave Vitari.

"What?" Vitari laughed.

Francis danced his gaze away. His face warmed. "Nothing."

"You lookin' at me like that feels weird."

Francis laughed. "What kind of weird?"

"Like you're *looking inside me* weird."

"Maybe I am," he said smugly, looking away so Vitari didn't see his blush. "Is it a good weird, or bad weird?"

"It's—"

Something slammed into the driver's door with a world-shattering roar. The Land Cruiser tipped. Francis grabbed for the dash, but gravity had hold of his arm and flung it overhead as the SUV rolled, rattling him from side to side. His seat belt held firm, but Vitari tumbled among all the debris, raining glass, and screaming metal. Glass rained over

Francis's face. He squeezed his eyes closed, caught in the storm of noise and heat.

The tumbling stopped with a deafening silence. Francis hung sideways in the chair, trapped by the belt. Glass fell from his hair and scratched his neck, trapped in his clothes. He blinked, trying to clear the blur in his vision.

Vitari?

He wasn't in the truck. He should have been in the truck. Had he been thrown free?

Francis jabbed at the belt, but the damn thing clung on. He jabbed again and again. Finally, it gave, dumping him onto the buckled passenger door. The SUV lay on its side. The windshield had blown out, the frame buckled. He could probably crawl through it, over broken glass.

Potent fumes squeezed tears from his eyes. Was there fire? He had to escape.

"Get out here, priest!"

Luca.

Francis shrunk back, heart pounding. No, no...

"Get out here, or your charity case dies! I'm not fucking around, Padre!"

Vitari. He had Vitari.

Francis gritted his teeth, holding back a rising tide of fear and anger. He hunkered down, trying to think. Maybe if he had a weapon, something to hit him with? He scanned the mess inside the wrecked cab and there, wedged behind his seat, lay Vitari's gun.

"You've got ten seconds before I put a round in the back of Angel's head. Nine—"

CHAPTER TWENTY-EIGHT

Vitari

Fuck, it hurt.

Grit and dirt dug into his cheek. Blood dribbled down the back of his head, past his ear, and down his cheek. He lay on his chest, where his ribs burned, as though he'd swallowed gasoline and set it on fire. Luca's boot on his back wasn't helping. The heel dug into his bruised kidney.

The wreck had broken something inside, something vital, something that made his tongue taste like blood. He wasn't going anywhere.

"Get out here, priest!"

Francis. Fuck. *Run!*

He was good at running. He'd run.

Vitari clawed at the dirt.

Luca's boot landed in his ribs, and for a white-hot second, Vitari couldn't breathe or think or move. He coughed, tasting more blood, hopefully from a cut in his mouth and not the broken ribs sticking him in places they shouldn't.

"Get out here, or your charity case dies!" A gun hammer clicked. "I'm not fucking around, Padre!"

Luca had a gun on him. Of course he did... Darkness throbbed in time with his heart. Vitari turned his head, resting his chin on the grass, and saw the wrecked Land Cruiser on its side, wheels still rolling. The semi Luca had driven into them idled nearby—an old fuel tanker.

This... was not good.

"You've got ten seconds before I put a round in the back of Angel's head. Nine, eight, seven..."

Luca had known they'd come to the airstrip. Had he been told?

But Vitari couldn't think about that, just about telling Francis to run.

And there he was, crawling through the buckled windshield. He looked okay, not bloody and minced like Vitari. That was good. He'd run. "Run..." Vitari croaked. Blood dribbled down his chin. He should have worn a fucking seat belt.

"Shut up!" Luca kicked him again. Vitari groaned. He was dying here. He knew it, felt it. But Francis was all right. Francis was going to escape.

"I'm coming out!" Francis stumbled away from the Land Cruiser, hands raised, and saw Vitari. Hid face crumpled, as though he might cry. Jesus, Vitari had to be in a bad way for Francis to almost weep.

Don't do that, Vitari thought. *Don't waste tears on me.* He tried to smile, to show Francis it was going to be all right. He'd vowed to save him. All Francis had to do now was run.

Francis blinked too fast, chewing into his lip. "Let him go, and I'll come with you."

Luca's heel dug deeper. "I was supposed to, but shit happens, yah know? We're a long way from Italy. Nobody is going to cry over Angel's body."

Francis's nostrils flared and his righteous fury bled in his eyes. "You wish you were half the man he is."

What was he doing? *No, Francis, don't taunt him. Just run.* "Run!" Vitari spluttered, tasting blood again. Why was Francis coming closer? He needed to get away, not move closer to Luca. He never fucking did what he was told.

"Half the man?" Luca laughed. "Angel is a stray dog his father found at the side of the road. He's not even all Italian. He's a mongrel, and he deserves to die like one."

"Wait!"

Luca must have aimed the gun down at Vitari, for Francis to freeze like he had. Francis dropped his stance, hand pushed forward, as though he were trying to placate a wild animal. Luca was wild, all right. But he couldn't be reasoned with. Fuck, Vitari was going to die here. A bullet in the head. He knew it. He swallowed more blood. He was so fucked. "Goddamnit, Francis," he hissed.

"What did he do to you?" Francis asked. "Why do you hate him? If he's a mongrel, what does it matter what happens to him?"

Francis, fuck off! Was he trying to what, stall? What for? Nobody was coming. Francis inched forward some more, his hand still out, trying to smooth Luca's insanity.

"What did he do?" Luca snorted. "He's always been the favorite, always number-fucking-one. I'm better than he is, but Giancarlo doesn't see me. It's always about Vitari, always fuckin Vitari. Vitari's done this, Vitari protected the family, Vitari secured the deal, always him! It's my turn. I've protected the Battaglia name since I could fucking walk. The Battaglia is my family, it's in my blood, more than it is his!" Luca's kick landed in his side again, almost rolling him over. He saw the gun now, stared down its barrel. Saw death coming right for him.

"Kill me," Vitari groaned. "But let Francis go. Tell Giancarlo the priest died too. End it."

Luca narrowed his eyes. "The priest is mine."

"Don't move!" Francis yelled.

Luca jerked his head up and spat a disbelieving laugh. "Are you joking?"

Vitari twisted, gasping around the agony burning a hole in his chest. Oh God, Francis had Vitari's gun aimed at Luca. He was going to get himself killed. Luca wasn't an idiot. He knew a priest wasn't going to shoot him.

"Drop the gun, Luca!" Francis yelled. He wasn't even holding the weapon correctly. He had both hands on it, fingers slipping.

"You think you can kill me, huh?" Luca laughed. "You goin' to pull the trigger? A man of the cloth, a man of God? You're not a murderer." Luca grinned his shit-eating grin. "Stop playing, Blanco Padre. Lower *your* gun."

Francis breathed like a snorting bull. He had that gun aimed true on Luca's chest. But he wasn't going to pull the trigger. Not for Vitari. His good Catholic soul would be doomed forever. Eternal damnation. Catholics didn't fuck around with that shit. Francis helped people. He didn't kill them. He'd let the fucking Spanish would-be assassin go, he'd lost the contents of his stomach after Vitari had killed the two corrupt Spanish cops.

But then there was the Francis who Vitari knew to be in there, the man of fire and passion, the man he kept so deeply buried, few ever saw him. *That* Francis was different. That man drank beer, he threw coffee mugs at walls, and he came all over Vitari's face. That man was unpredictable, and that man was in there, staring down the gun's sights, with his finger on the trigger.

Oh fuck, he was going to shoot Luca.

"Francis, don't," Vitari gasped.

He'd damn himself, in his own mind. He'd never come back from that. You couldn't confess away murder. He was going to shoot, and he'd despise Vitari for it forever.

"Francis, put the gun down," Vitari begged. He got an arm under himself and lifted his head, trying to make him see it was going to be all right. He didn't need to do this, not for Vitari.

Luca snorted. "A fucking priest is not going to shoot me."

"Yes, he is."

Luca looked again at Francis and bared his teeth in a snarl. "I'll kill your fuck-buddy here. Is that what you want, Father?"

"Put. The gun. Down," Francis said, eerily calm. He dropped one arm and held the gun steady in his right hand.

Luca's laugh spluttered and trailed off, and there in Francis's eyes, Luca saw the truth.

Francis *would* shoot him.

Luca swung the gun from Vitari to aim at Francis. "You don't have the balls, priest."

Fuck, Francis wasn't even breathing hard now. He stared back at a man holding a gun on him, as cold as any killer Vitari had known.

"Don't, not for me, please..." Vitari begged. He tasted blood on his lips. "Francis, not for me."

If Francis did this, it would ruin him, and Vitari couldn't stand it. He'd rather die than drag Francis to Hell. Cool tears touched Vitari's hot, grazed cheeks. "Please."

"You'll go to Hell," Luca said.

"Then I'll see you there," Francis replied. And pulled the trigger.

The gun bucked. Luca stumbled, reached for his chest. But it was the exit wound in his back he should be more concerned with, where the round had blown his heart out through his ribs.

Luca dropped to his knees, then slumped forward and smacked face-first into the ground.

A sob fell from Vitari. No, no... Not for him. Not for the boy he'd been, who'd cried alone in the dark, waiting for the sound of the dead bolt to slam down. He was dying, and his final act on this Earth had been to ruin the most beautiful thing he'd ever known.

This wasn't real. It couldn't be. He didn't want to go.

Francis called his name, but he was far away, somewhere in the darkness, and that was okay, because it meant he was far from Vitari. He had to stay away. He was safer there, far from Vitari's darkness.

Francis had pulled the trigger.

He'd killed a man. To save Vitari.

He'd never be forgiven.

CHAPTER TWENTY-NINE

Francis
    Two Weeks Later
    England

Westminster Cathedral was not the more famous Westminster Abbey, but it was one of the largest, most beautiful, and awe-inspiring Catholic cathedrals in all of Europe. Francis's black, soft-soled shoes made only a whisper as he walked down the nave between the pews. He wore plain clothes and the white collar, as expected of him. He was supposed to wear the cassock, but when he'd tried, he'd almost emptied his stomach.

It was a process, Father Hawker had said, when Francis had been politely encouraged to take confession. He hadn't told Father Hawker half of what he'd seen and been a part of, and never would. Some secrets had to be buried.

Then the summons had come while he'd still been in London, answering endless police interviews in which he'd lied—and found himself convincing, when it mattered. No, he didn't know why the Mafia continued to kidnap him. No, he couldn't identify any of them. No, he hadn't seen much of the enforcer known as Angelo della Morte, real name Vitari Angelini, just that there had been some kind of gang battle in Venezuela, in which Vitari had almost died.

He wasn't sure yet if he'd lived, but he'd been stable in the Caracas hospital where Francis had been forced to leave him. The British police had sent someone from the National Crime Agency to collect Francis, and they would have arrested him if he'd told them he wanted to stay by Vitari's bedside.

He'd been in protective custody for two weeks, until now.

The Cathedral was empty, probably because of the man dressed in an all-white robe, waiting at the altar. Archbishop Montague lifted his head and smiled as Francis approached. He'd shaved off his beard, and the transformation was severe. He'd gone from kindly old man to imposing, handsome patriarch.

Francis swallowed the acrid taste in his mouth and smiled back.

"Ah, Father Scott," Montague said, then extended his right hand, his ring glinting.

Francis went down to one knee, took the man's fingers in his, and kissed the ring. Acrid nausea burned the back of his tongue.

"A terrible ordeal, my friend. Terrible."

Francis rose and looked Montague in his cold, flinty eyes. "Yes, it was."

"But it's all over now."

"There's no indication the Mafia will cease to try and—"

"Oh, they've ceased," Montague said, with absolute confidence. "You will not be bothered any longer."

How could he know that? Francis swallowed the question, afraid of the answer.

"I want to talk about you and your bright future with us, Father Scott. Let's put all this behind us, shall we?" His arm landed on Francis's shoulders, and as he guided Francis back down the aisle, not even the thick cloth of Montague's robes between them could mask the memory of Montague's touch on his bare skin.

"I'm not going to be of much use to the Church," Francis said, keeping his voice calm. "The police have suggested I should be placed in witness protection."

"Oh, that's not necessary." Montague chuckled. "You'll simply come here, to Westminster, and work alongside me. Someone of your caliber should never have been placed in St. Mary's. You're wasted there."

The floor fell out from under Francis, and he almost dropped with it. Only Montague's arm held him up. "I'm to work here?"

"Yes, under me," he smirked, eyes so kindly, they couldn't possibly hide a thousand sins. "As it always should have been." His arm slid free, and the archbishop glided toward the main doors. "I've already made the arrangements. Your life is here now, Francis. Safe, at my side. Come along, and I'll show you to your accommodations. They're not far from mine."

Francis clutched the back of the nearest pew. Of course this was his punishment, for what he'd done. For killing a man. Taking a life. He deserved this.

He'd endure. He had no choice.

He was Father Francis Scott, youngest ordained priest

in England, prodigy of Archbishop Montague, and wasn't he just fucking perfect.

He loosened the choking white collar, lifted his chin, and followed the archbishop from the Cathedral.

CHAPTER THIRTY

Vitari

He dreamed of Francis holding a gun to Luca's head, then blowing him away. In some of those dreams, Francis turned the gun on Vitari and Vitari went to his knees. Sometimes Francis fired, and Vitari woke with a jolt. Other times, in those dreams, Vitari sucked him off while Francis held the gun to Vitari's head. He liked those dreams the most.

When he woke, Francis wasn't in the chair by the hospital bed, where he'd expected him to be. But Sal was. And when he woke again, nobody was there, which was worse.

He lasted two weeks in the Venezuelan hospital, healing from a punctured lung, with armed guards at the doors, either to keep him in or others out. When Sal returned, he told him to get him out of the country, and the next day, he was on a private plane, touching down on a landing strip in Calabria.

Home was a small apartment near the waterfront. He

hadn't spent much time in it for a few years, but he needed it now, needed to rest and regain his strength before he faced Giancarlo. Unfortunately, Giancarlo wasn't known for his patience.

On the third day since Vitari's return, Giancarlo came to visit.

"Sit," Giancarlo said, as though the apartment were his.

Vitari sat on the couch. The balcony doorway was open, and a swift sea breeze kept the apartment cool.

Giancarlo nodded for his entourage to leave, and the armed men filed out, leaving Vitari alone with his father. Giancarlo sat in silence. Waiting for an explanation.

Vitari cleared his throat. "Venezuela was—"

"Venezuela was an unacceptable disaster," Don Giancarlo said.

Venezuela had been a fucking mess. "Luca fucked it up—"

Giancarlo raised his hand. "No excuses."

Vitari clenched his jaw and bowed his head. "I accept full responsibility," he ground out, loathing every word.

"The business lost a great deal of investment in those mines and on the Vincente operation. Before your arrival, the region had been running smoothly."

Vitari knew that. They'd lost good people too. Luca's intervention had been a deliberate disaster, and he hadn't done it alone. Luca hadn't had the balls to sweep in like he had and start a territory war. He'd said he had Giancarlo's permission, and maybe he had. Vitari wasn't sure. But why sabotage your own operation and millions of euros? Unless there had been something—or someone—there that was so devastating, it could ruin Giancarlo. Unless there were a lot more secrets in Stanmore Boys' Home than the shit Vitari had been through. Secrets that could bring down the Battaglia boss?

A whole lot hadn't added up since he'd been ordered to watch a priest in a nowhere English town.

He didn't know where Francis was. But he *did* know he'd been at Vitari's bedside. He'd been the one who'd saved Vitari. Nobody else would have.

Vitari owed Francis his life.

He didn't know what it all meant, just that Francis was still in danger, wherever he was. And maybe so was Vitari. He met his father's gaze. He loved Giancarlo, but he also kept a gun taped under the coffee table between them.

"The priest is no longer a concern of yours," Giancarlo said, rising. He moved to the balcony and stood there like some fucking Italian work of art, overlooking his empire.

"Is he safe?"

Giancarlo returned to the couch but stopped behind Vitari. Vitari shrank under his father's glare, feeling like a small child again. Lost in the dark.

"He is protected," Giancarlo said, glaring down his nose, making Vitari feel smeller with every passing second. "You are not to go near him. You do not contact him. If I discover you've had contact with the priest, you will be cast out. Excommunicado. Dead to me. Do you understand, my son?"

This was about the photos.

Vitari wet his lips and nodded. At least Francis was alive. But Giancarlo had the photos, which meant he had some leverage over Francis too. He'd keep the images and use them when he believed it would be the most effective. The photos burned Giancarlo too, as Vitari was his son, and sucking a priest's cock didn't reflect well on the family.

Giancarlo nodded, turned away, but quickly turned

back, and stabbed a finger at the air. "If you suck a man's dick again, I will personally cut out your tongue."

He left the apartment, his words heavy in the air. Vitari stared toward the open balcony door. All things considered, he'd gotten off lightly. He still had all his fingers, and his tongue, for now. And he knew Francis was alive. Considering the monumental fucking disaster everything had been from the beginning, they were both lucky to be breathing.

Maybe it wasn't luck.

He moved onto the balcony and stared at the turquoise waters.

Maybe it was Francis and his prayers, because there was no other explanation for how the Angelo della Morte had survived when the odds had been so stacked against him.

Maybe God did exist. But if that were true, He'd surely abandon Francis now.

Wherever Francis was, he'd be hurting, and Vitari couldn't get to him. Ever.

He was on his own.

Just like Vitari.

CHAPTER THIRTY-ONE

Francis

The days passed in a whirlwind of introductions, acclimatizing to the bustling City of Westminster life. It was easier to throw himself into every possible task and fill the hours from dawn to dusk, than to stop, rest, and think. Thinking led to remembering, and remembering led to regret and grief. And guilt.

He had an office in an old converted chancery building on the grounds of Westminster Cathedral, a few doors down from the archbishop's room. The floorboards creaked outside his office door whenever anyone passed by. He hadn't yet stopped flinching when someone did. Thankfully, the archbishop was also too busy with his duties to pay much mind to Francis.

Francis kept his head down and did all that was expected of him, and more, but in many ways he missed the people of St. Mary's, even Mrs. Roe and her frequent visits to complain about her husband or the buses. That part of his life, although brief, had been the most normal. He wished he'd appreciated it more.

He sat back in the office chair and rubbed the bridge of his nose. The words on his planner blurred. His back burned, between his shoulder blades. He needed rest. It had been weeks since he'd joined Westminster, and he hadn't yet had a moment to himself. He couldn't continue like this, but if he stopped, he feared the demons waiting in the dark.

A rap on his door startled him from his drifting thoughts.

Archbishop Montague entered, his appearance shockingly normal in civilian clothing, but of course, he still wore the necessary collar and ring. His smile reached his slate-grey eyes.

Ten years ago he'd been dark-haired and full of flashy smiles. He'd visit the boys' home to lead them in prayer, and Francis would sit at the window and watch for Father Charles Montague's little red sports car, thinking the priest —not yet an archbishop—must be a very important person to own such a car. He'd been handsome, charming, and kind.

Francis had wanted to be just like him.

Montague propped himself on the side of the desk and folded his hands over his knee. "I hear you're settling in well. I had no doubts, of course. You were always an exemplary student."

"Thank you."

"But it's important to rest. Wounded healers are often the first to fall."

Francis swallowed the sour taste on his tongue. *Wounded.* Did he mean by recent events, or from years ago, when he'd been the one to inflict those wounds? "Yes, I will." He forced a smile.

Montague reached over and placed his hand on Francis's shoulder, giving it a gentle squeeze. Francis sighed through his nose, fighting the instinct to shake him off. "Why don't you take Saturday off? Come to dinner with me. We're both so busy, I doubt we'll have much time to see each other over the next few weeks."

"I'm... Thank you, but I have much to do." He gestured at the planner on his desk, and the plethora of colored swirls and scribbled dates. "I really must catch up with all —"

"That can wait. I must insist." He leaned closer. "Your well-being is very important, especially after your ordeal. I will see to your care personally, Francis."

He was close, so close Francis could smell the coffee on his breath and the cologne he wore, the same woody, rich cologne he'd worn for years. The smell of it turned his stomach.

He'd knelt to Montague, kissed his ring, and vowed to obey and serve. When he'd been ordained, he'd also signed a contract that ensured his silence when it came to internal matters of the Church. He couldn't legally or spiritually refuse him.

Shh, don't make a noise, this will be our secret.

But it was just dinner.

"Thank you," Francis said, forcing out the words. "I'd like that."

"Good boy." Montague patted his shoulder and stood. "Around eight o'clock?"

He left without waiting to hear Francis's answer. Because Francis had no choice.

He stared at the closed office door, his heart and head strangely silent, as though both had been emptied.

The phone on his desk trilled. He blinked at it, then

mechanically scooped up the receiver. "Father Francis Scott."

The caller remained quiet. But Francis heard his soft breathing, like sultry whispers in a dark room. His heart lurched to life. It couldn't be...

He leaned back in the chair, holding the receiver close. The caller moved too, his clothes rustling. Francis closed his eyes, and he could feel those fluttering breaths on his neck, feel the soft touch of his lips. *Ruin me.*

"Angel?" he asked, using the alias. It seemed safer, and more befitting in this moment. Somehow, across the miles, with barriers between them, Vitari knew Francis needed him.

"Hello, Father."

Francis opened his eyes and leaned forward. Vitari shouldn't be calling. Whatever they'd had, all the things they'd done, it was over, in the past. A different life. But Francis's heart thumped, beating hot blood back into icy veins, thawing his body, bringing him back to life around the tiny, damaged spark of his soul.

Vitari lived.

"Will you take my confession?" Vitari asked, in his sly, mocking tone.

Francis sighed, as though he were the one unburdening his soul. "You know I will."

To be continued in *Ruin Me, Forgive Me #2*.
It's not over yet for Francis & Vitari. Join them as they are thrust together once again in a world of violent crime and vicious murder.
Ruin Me, Forgive Me #2 ∼ out now.

ALSO BY ARIANA NASH

Sign up to Ariana's newsletter so you don't miss all the news.

www.ariananashbooks.com

***

Shadows of London

(Five book urban fantasy series)

A sexy assassin, a billionaire boss with secrets, and magic bubbling up through the streets of London. All in a days work for artifact agent, John "Dom" Domenici.

Start the Shadows of London series with Twisted Pretty Things